# Lucky

# Penny

Happy reading!

By Elinor Battersby

# Chapter 1

The first day of summer.

Not only that, but the first day of the last summer.

This time next year we'll be done with school, and summer won't mean the same thing any more. No more bike rides and sleepovers. We won't be spending our days trying to soak up every last drop of freedom before school resumes, instead we'll be desperately job hunting or getting ready to move away for university. This is our last summer inhabiting the lives we've grown up in.

I pull the covers back up over my head, sinking down into the musty warmth that's accumulated overnight.

"Penny!"

I can hear mum calling me. I fumble for my phone

on my bedside table, turning it to face me and peering blearily at the screen. It's only eight am! On a Saturday!

"Penny!" she calls again, her voice closer now.

She's tracking me down to drag me forcefully from my slumber.

"Penny, you're not still sleeping are you?! I'd have thought you'd want to make the most of the day!"

This isn't a statement that deserves a response but I grumble incoherently back at her from the relative safety of the duvet.

I listen out but-

Nothing.

I pull back the covers a touch and risk a glance. She's standing looking down at me expectantly, hands on hips.

Mum pose.

I struggle up to a more dignified seated position and push my hair out of my face.

"What's up mum?" I ask with the assumption of poise and hopefully very little detectable resentment.

“Coop's at work and I'm about to head out to the shops. I need you to come down and keep an eye on Oliver.”

There's no point complaining, a lifetime's experience has taught me that it won't help. She's only just got back to the point where she can enter a shop at all. Early on a Saturday morning is a calculated choice, a time when Sainsbury's is going to be at its most quiet and its least threatening.

“Course mum, I'll be right down.”

I see the flicker of relief in her face as she gives a brief nod before sweeping back out of the room in a whirlwind of chocolate brown curls and forced determination. I pull a brush through my mess of copper locks, binding them up into a bun on top of my head and then pad downstairs in my pyjamas.

As expected, mum's hovering in the hallway, her bag over her shoulder, waiting for me to appear so that she can get going. She may as well be tapping her wrist-watch.

"Alright, I've got him!" I tell her with a smile.

"You'll be alright here?" she asks, her tone light but brittle.

"We'll be fine. I have him. We'll be fine."

These are the words she needs to hear and she gives me a small apologetic smile before unlocking the door and heading out.

"Olly Wally!" I shout in a sing song voice, making my way towards the lounge with large, loud steps. I hear a muffled giggle and make my steps as loud and exaggerated as I can. I am a giant approaching my prey. Another giggle leads me around the sofa to a small figure, crouched down in a ball, hugging his knees. His whole body is shaking with excitement and he looks up in panic and delight as I descend upon him with a roar.

"Peeennny!" he squeals as I lift him into the air and toss him onto the sofa before covering his little face in kisses and tickling him ruthlessly.

"You alright Olly Wally?" I ask when he nestles into me, cuddling up to halt my attack. It's well known to be the only tried and trusted defence to a tickle assault.

He nods cheerfully before returning his attention to the Pokemon episode on the television.

"Have you had breakfast?" I ask.

That recalls his focus.

"Can I have pop-tarts?!" he asks immediately, his imploring eyes fixing on my face. Olly mastered the starving puppy expression at birth.

I only hesitate for a moment, building suspense, just long enough that he's utterly elated when I agree.

"Strawberry or chocolate?"

"Chocolate!" he cries happily, punching the air in triumph like a cartoon character.

I heat them on the lowest setting of the toaster and let them cool a little before bringing them in to him on a plastic plate. Oliver has a tendency to break things. I slide a couple into the toaster for myself and put the kettle on for tea. I join Oliver on the sofa and try to pick up the thread of the episode he's watching. It looks like Ash and the gang are working to help an injured

Pokemon and Olly's bouncing up and down in his seat, practically rending his clothes in his anxiety. He's seven years old and he lives and dies with every TV show. Watching anything at all with him is an emotional roller-coaster.

"Is it going to be alright?! The Charmander?!" he demands, his voice pitched with alarm.

"I'm sure it will be Olly Wally," I tell him soothingly.

"Have you seen this one?" he asks quickly.

"Nope."

"Then you don't *know.*" His eyes are wide, his tone plaintive.

"But I'm sure," I tell him, stroking his soft blonde hair with one hand.

"*How*?" he asks me, imploring.

I could go into a lengthy explanation about the generally cheery disposition of children's television writers, or perhaps point out that not a single Pokemon has perished in the entire show so far, but it wouldn't help. He's going to remain in a state of panic until the

Pokemon is saved. Luckily the episodes aren't long and within a few minutes he's whirling around the room whooping with glee that everything turned out alright.

"He's fine! Do you see that Penny, he's fine!" he cries before launching into a long and involved account of everything that happened during the first part of the episode, that I'd missed. It was probably only about five minutes of the show but somehow the description takes twenty and he has to start again twice.

"It sounds great Olly Wally. What are you going to watch now?" I ask him, keen to distract him before he can decide to treat me to a description of any other episodes he watched this morning.

It works. In seconds he has the Disney channel open and is scrolling through the options, debating the rival merits of Big Hero 6 and Minions.

When mum gets back I help her unload the shopping from the car and put it away. She bought more pop-tarts. They're an unnecessary apology for the past few weeks but I appreciate the gesture-and the sugar content.

"Do you have plans today?" she asks me casually despite already knowing the answer.

"I'm supposed to go to that end of the year party and Charlie's sleeping over afterwards," I tell her slowly. I let each word stand for a moment before following it with the next one. I know it's hard for her, parties are still relatively uncharted territory for us.

She pauses, her expression wary.

"Whose house is it?" she asks, her brow furrowing.

"Luke Burrows from school."

"And you won't be going anywhere else? The party and then home? Charlie will be with you?" Her questions chase one another out, not giving me time to answer. Is she going to say that I can't go? Would I be disappointed if she did? Unbidden, a pair of bright blue eyes flashes into my mind briefly and I have my answer.

"I'll stay at the party and then come straight here with Charlie," I tell her.

"Luke Burrows." She says the name slowly, testing it

out.

"Richard and Mary's son," I remind her.

She nods and finally makes eye contact with me.

"Yes, yes I know them, they're very nice. Have a lovely time sweetheart!"

She gives me a kiss on the cheek and I let my breath out. Charlie would have killed me if I backed out now. She's been talking about this party for weeks. Apparently this is the start of our 'perfect summer', our last golden days before the drab grey of the real world settles on our shoulders.

I spend the rest of the morning giving my inner introvert free reign. I binge watch a new Netflix series in my room and eat an entire bag of Cool Original Doritos that I had stashed under my bed. I'm just starting to contemplate a nap when I hear the doorbell. I assume that it's just Coop getting home from work but thundering footsteps on the stairs tell me I'm wrong.

"What are you doing?!" Charlie shrieks at me, taking

in the delightful scene of slobbish indolence before her.

"Watching TV," I offer feebly.

"It's the first day of summer! Have you been here all morning?! What is that smell?! How many Doritos did you eat?!"

"I haven't been here *all* morning. I watched Pokemon downstairs with Olly for a while too," I tell her defiantly.

"You're hopeless!"

"Why? What was I meant to be doing?" I ask exasperated.

"Having an adventure! We're seventeen Penny! We are young and gorgeous! Now is the time to take risks and make mistakes! Fall completely in love with a handsome barista! Sleep with a married man! Run naked through town!"

I stare at her blankly.

"I think we may have very different plans for this summer."

She flops down on the bed beside me with a gusty

sigh of frustration.

"If you plan to spend the whole time pigging out in front of Netflix then we definitely do!"

To be quite honest, a summer spent with Netflix and snacks sounds pretty wonderful to me, but Charlie has been changing lately. She seems restless and she's less patient with me than she used to be. I know that her mum's been working a lot and since it's just the two of them this leaves Charlie pretty much alone and it causes some tension, but I'm worried that part of the problem is me. Worried enough that I don't want to ask.

"Not the *whole* summer! One morning! We have the party later, don't we?" I ask her, trying to match the excitement that I know she feels.

"You're definitely still allowed?!" she asks immediately, flipping over onto her front and pushing herself up on her elbows to look at me.

"Yep, I checked with my mum earlier today. You know, when I *wasn't* watching Netflix?" I add, giving her a playful dig in the ribs.

"Amazing! It's going to be so much fun! Sarah says *everyone's* going to be there!"

"Who's everyone?" I ask uneasily. Charlie's world seems to have expanded lately, while my own has stayed comfortably the same size.

"Marcus for one," she tells me, waggling her eyebrows suggestively.

Marcus Kain is by far my least favourite addition to Charlie's new social circle but I give what I hope is a cheery smile and move on.

"Kate and Sophie are going, right? And what about Josh and Abed?"

These four and Charlie make up pretty much the entirety of my friend pool. I've known them all since nursery and I've just never felt the need to socialise further.

Charlie sighs faintly.

"Yeah, they're all going. You could talk to some other people too though ya'know."

"It's not my fault that I have such great taste in

friends! The ones I already have provide everything I need!" I tell her with a grin that she doesn't return.

"Don't you wish that your life was bigger?" she asks me seriously.

"Running around naked bigger?"

"Just bigger," she repeats, searching for something in my expression.

"I'm happy. I'm safe."

"Those aren't your words," she snaps, suddenly annoyed with me.

"They are!" I counter half heartedly. She's right though, I'm parroting my mother and we both know it. I just don't know what else to say. I'm happy with my life as it is but more and more often Charlie's getting these little bursts of anger at me, like I'm holding her back.

"It's just- I've been talking to someone recently, and they've made me realise how *huge* the world is. We live in this tiny little town but there's so much more out there Pen!"

"Who have you been talking to?!" I demand quickly.

A slight blush and downcast eyes are the only response I get.

"Is this *Marcus*?" I ask her, my tone dripping disdain.

"Marcus is fun!" she fires back, immediately annoyed again.

"Marcus is awful! He makes me feel like a freak," I grumble.

The words hang in the air and we both take a moment to mull over the obvious retort.

It's not Marcus' fault that I feel like a freak. I am one.

Neither of us says it but we both know the words are there, plastered in the air between us. Charlie's the one who cracks first, her face breaking into a sly grin.

"Besides, Marcus is friends with Alex!" she crows.

She knows she's scored a point with that one. Alex and his blue eyes have been a weakness of growing concern for years. He didn't go to the same primary school as us, but he goes to the same secondary school so we've known him since we were eleven. Six years. Six years and I don't think I've ever managed to have a real conversation with him about something other than schoolwork. Imaginary conversations? Sure- thousands! It's just real ones that I seem to struggle with.

"Is he going this evening?" I ask in a small voice, too high pitched to be casual.

In response Charlie grabs me round the waist in a mock tackle, tickling me, her unrestrained laughter wrapping around us.

She pulls back, breaking the spell.

"We need to make sure you look *great* tonight!"

I've actually already picked out an outfit. I show it to Charlie but she is beyond unimpressed. I'd selected my warmest jeans, thick socks, a blue t-shirt that I like and a sweatshirt.

"It's an outdoor party! I don't want to get cold!" I tell her, clinging to my sweatshirt as though its a life preserver.

"If you get cold, just get a little nearer to the fire! Or

find someone to keep you warm," she tells me, raising one eyebrow and dancing her hips Shakira style.

"Or I could just take a jumper!" I counter.

She holds up one of my summer dresses like she's assessing its potential viability and I baulk. I'd be frozen in that! Besides, it's not a dress I tend to wear even in the heat of the day. It has thin straps and barely approaches my knees. It's not the sort of thing I feel comfortable in. I ease it out of her hands and place it firmly back on the rack.

Charlie selects another, even shorter dress.

"Charlie if you seriously suggest that one I'm wearing my fleece!" I warn her.

"Argh! Not the gross fleece!" she cries, covering her eyes theatrically.

"*And* a coat!"

In the end we manage to find a compromise that's acceptable to both of us. I get to wear jeans, though not my warmest ones, and a sweatshirt, though I have to wear a skimpy top underneath and I have to promise to take off the sweatshirt for at least an hour.

With my wardrobe crisis averted, Charlie turns her attention to hair and make-up. To my horror she's actually set aside the entire afternoon to get ready. I've never spent more than fifteen minutes on my appearance, but it's fascinating to watch Charlie work. She starts with foundation in a neutral beige. It's like she's stripping her face back to nothing, blocking it out into a blank canvas. Then, she paints on a new face. It looks a little like hers, but hardly more than a passing resemblance. She brushes on new cheek bones, new shadows along her jaw. She darkens her eyes and lengthens her lashes. She colours in her eyebrows and gels them up, broadening them.

Charlie's always been pretty, though not in a striking way. She has a nice face. Her nose is a little wide and her jaw is a little strong, and her tangled mass of blonde curls has been the bane of her life, but she's always looked nice. She is the quintessential English country girl. Sturdy, smiling and kind.

But now, with her face painted like this she looks... different.

"You look amazing," I tell her in response to her enquiring glance, "But, isn't it a bit much for just a garden party? And it doesn't really match your clothes."

Charlie looks down at her denim shorts and pretty green top and laughs dismissively.

"Well then it's just as well that I'm not wearing this," she tells me with a wink.

"What? What are you going to wear?"

"You'll see! I bought something new! My mum would hate it," she laughs.

"When did you get it? You went shopping?"

I can't quite keep the hurt out of my voice and Charlie blushes a little but brushes my words aside.

"I needed to get a few things," she tells me loftily.

"I would have come with you. Did you go with someone else?" I know that I shouldn't ask, that my questions are pinching at her patience, but I can't help it, I just can't let it go.

"I'm allowed to have secrets!" she hisses at me, pressing one thumb to her temple as though I'm giving her a headache. It's a move my mum favours too.

Penny Cooper- inciting headaches everywhere.

"I'm sorry- I-" I begin, but Charlie cuts me off, plastering a smile back on her face.

"No problem! Let's do your make-up!"

I thought that she was angry at me, but if anything she sounds a little guilty. Maybe she does feel bad about leaving me out after all. The thought should make me feel better but it doesn't.

"I don't want to wear too much make-up, just some mascara like normal really," I tell her with a shrug.

"You have to wear more than that! This is a party!"

I'm really not keen but I don't want to rock our sinking boat any more than I already have so I acquiesce. Thankfully, Charlie decides that my freckles rule out the use of foundation so she just dabs a little concealer under my eyes and blends it in with her finger. She does insist on eyeliner however, and even a little sparkly eyeshadow.

With mascara and some red lip tint, I feel completely overdone but I do have to admit that it looks nice.

"Now take your hair down," Charlie tells me, holding up a brush.

"I was going to wear it up," I hastily inform her.

"I know you were. You always wear it up. You have beautiful hair, you should wear it down so that people can actually see it!"

I stare at my reflection in the mirror as I pull out my hair tie and settle my hair around my shoulders. I pull a brush through it and try to observe the overall effect. It's a bright copper colour, just like a fresh penny in fact. It's been years since I've worn it down. With the eyeliner and the red lips, I look older. The resemblance isn't nearly so strong. I don't look like Rose.

"Alright, but I'll keep it tied up until we go. Mum-"

My words fail. I don't know how to explain mum's almost desperate desire to see my sister in my face, or the fear that grips her when she does. Every year that I've aged and Rose hasn't, the resemblance between us has lessened and I know that mum has mixed emotions about that.

I do too.

"I get it, we'll take it down on the way there," Charlie agrees, squeezing my hand.

That's the great thing about Charlie, I don't need to explain everything to her, she's known me all my life and she knows all my secrets- Even if I'm starting to realise that I don't know all of hers.

# Chapter 2

Coop's insisting on feeding us before we go. Apparently we need to line our stomachs with something that'll soak up all the alcohol. Charlie's all for it but, seeing as I don't intend to drink, I think the mountain of pasta and bread he presents us with might be a bit excessive.

"We're going to a party, not running a marathon!"

"Ah Penny, little do ye suspect it but a teen party can feel a lot like a marathon!" Coop counters cheerfully.

"You're not making it sound very appealing," I grumble back.

"There's the drinking, the dancing, the shouting, the impromptu games of drunken skill..."

"Less and less appealing."

"It's going to be fun!" Charlie tacks on the end,

throwing Coop a warning look.

"Oodles of it!" Coop agrees with a wide grin.

"Besides, who says no to spaghetti and meatballs?!" Charlie demands, happily spooning huge servings onto both of our plates.

With a sigh of defeat I hop up onto a kitchen stool and begin diligently spooling pasta tendrils around my fork. We're eating in the kitchen, a location usually only allowed for breakfast, since mum isn't here to enforce the dining room policy. She's decided to have dinner with a friend, in a poorly disguised attempt to pretend that I'm not actually going out. This way she doesn't have to worry about me, she can just tell herself that I'm safely ensconced in my room.  It's not a particularly difficult illusion to maintain, after all, it's usually true.

"Olly!" Coop calls, not for the first time. Oliver however is totally engrossed in his Lego construction and Coop's voice just doesn't seem to have enough authority to drag him away.

"NOW, Olly Wally!" I shout.

After a moment we hear the scrambling run of little legs, accompanied by the thuds of Olly bouncing off the walls.

"Is dinner ready?!" He bursts into the kitchen like an excited puppy, his eyes wide with elation at the sight of the pasta already doled onto his plate.

"It's been ready for five minutes!" his Dad tells him, rolling his eyes as he lifts Olly up onto a kitchen stool.

Coop and Olly are practically doubles. I've seen a few photos of Coop when he was a child and it's like looking straight at little Oliver now. They're both short, round and blonde. They're a little baby faced and have the same blue-grey eyes. Coop's hair is thinning a little on top but apart from that Oliver is his absolute mini-me. Mum must have almost entirely recessive genes because honestly, none of her children have looked much like her with her dark eyes, olive skin and dark curly hair. I am average height, average weight with brown eyes, freckles and bright copper hair. It's undeniably a striking combination.

The eyes I did get from my mum, the one feature she managed to pass on, but the hair and everything else I get from my dad. He and mum got a divorce after what happened and then he pretty much dropped off the map. He resurfaces every once in a while to spend the day with me but mum thinks it isn't healthy for me to spend too much time with him and he isn't exactly fighting her on that supposition.

And so, James Cooper, Coop, stepped into the father role.

My class-mates always giggled embarrassingly over my real dad's good looks, their mothers simpered and smiled whenever they spoke to him, but personally I agree with my mum. Coop is by far the better choice. I love my dad, I really do, but mum was a mess after Rose and I was only eight years old. The delights of childhood trauma mean that I've blocked a lot out, but I remember a lot of shouting and crying and then one day dad was just gone. Mum was a wreck. Coop arrived on the scene and he may as well have been wearing a cape.

He got things back on track and made sure there was always food in the house. I always had a ride to school. I was tucked in every night.

He went from mum's awkwardly smitten work-friend to her fiancée and then her husband in the blink of an eye. He was a sweet, unimposing anchor of normality and we clung to him like emotionally damaged limpets to a rock. By the time Olly came along, we were already a family.

"What have you got on your face?" Olly asks curiously, head tipped speculatively to one side.

"I'm wearing make-up," I explain simply.

"Why though?"

"To make her look beautiful!" Charlie interjects before I can form my own, undoubtedly humorous response.

Olly blinks at this, clearly puzzled by the notion and mulling it over in his little head.

"I have make-up on too, see?" Charlie points out,

totally unnecessarily turning her head from side to side to display her handiwork.

"You have *lots* of make-up on! Like face-paint!" Olly agrees, nodding solemnly.

Coop and I both snort into our food while Charlie fights to keep her composure.

"Make-up makes people look nicer," Charlie tells him slowly.

"Is there something wrong with your face underneath?" Olly queries, his face screwed up in confusion.

"Of course not, it doesn't mean there's anything wrong with my face! Make-up just helps make the good things about your face look even better!" Charlie tells him in slight desperation.

Olly thinks this idea through and apparently it finds favour because after a minute or two his face breaks into a wide grin and he turns excitedly to his dad.

"I really like my nose! My nose is a good thing! Can I wear make-up?!"

"Course you can bud, but not until you're older. When you're Penny's age you can accentuate your nose all you like," Coop agrees cheerily.

"Accentuate my nose. Acc-en-tuate my noooose."

Olly rolls these words around his mouth for the rest of the meal, to the detriment of the pasta eating process. I think he might be my favourite person.

The consumption of our monolith meal means that we both have to vigorously brush our teeth and then I have to reapply my lip tint. I got off light though, Charlie has to carefully remove any pasta sauce from her face and then touch up and blend her foundation and then start again with her lip liner, lipstick, lip gloss combo. This process takes a ridiculously long time but at last she's happy with the effect.

"Are we ready to go then?" I ask hopefully from my seat on the bed.

"One minute! I have an outfit change to do first, remember!"

I like what she's wearing now, but I know it's useless to say. She pulls off the green top, shimmies out of her denim shorts and commences struggling her way into a tangle of black fabric and sequins. When she's done she looks like a different person.

"So? What do you think?" she asks me, giving a twirl.

"Are you sure that's right for a garden party like this? It looks more like clubbing clothes," I suggest awkwardly.

This isn't what she wanted to hear. Her face loses it's expression and her tone is waspish.

"How would you know? It's not like *you're* ever going to go to a club!"

It's clear that she feels this is an insult and I'm appropriately stung by the venom in her voice, though I agree with her words completely. We both got fake IDs six months ago, hers is in the name of Genie and mine is Glenda. They're not particularly good quality and the idea of trying to actually use them fills me with dread. I only got one because I couldn't bear for Charlie to do it without me. The thought that she would literally have a pass to a whole world I couldn't enter had made me feel pathetically panicky, so I was now the proud owner of my own flimsy piece of plastic with my picture beside a ridiculous name and a date of birth a decade too early.

"Those clothes just don't look like you," I try to explain.

"Maybe there are better people to be!" she cries in frustration.

"But I like *you*," I tell her feebly.

She looks down at me intensely and I can see the anger in her eyes. The love and the frustration. I can see she feels trapped. I know that feeling.

"Let's just go," she snaps, pulling on her coat and zipping it up to her chin.

"You're wearing your coat?" I ask, surprised.

"I can't risk Your Step-Dad telling my mum what I'm wearing," she explains shortly.

Coop's always been 'Your Step-Dad' to Charlie.

She's still loyal to my real dad.

She's not looking at me. I can see the obligation of our friendship weighing heavy on her shoulders. I fumble for her hand and give it a squeeze.

"You look amazing! I'm just jealous," I tell her quietly.

Maybe it's true.

Charlie takes my hair down for me after we leave my house. She runs her fingers through it and smiles and the weight of panic falls from my chest. We're OK.

Luke Burrows lives a fifteen minute walk away though it turns out to be more than twenty in Charlie's ridiculous shoes. It would have been seven or eight if we cut through the woods, but we don't do that. Attending this party definitely fulfils any imagined facing-my-fears quota for the day.

We can hear the music long before we reach our destination. It's a pounding drum'n'bass that makes me wonder whether Charlie might be more appropriately dressed than me after all. I should have known. I seem to have some kind of jinx when it comes to selecting clothes. No matter what social event I attend, it always seems as though all the other guests have conferred together, so that they're all dressed in variations of the same theme, while I'm the only outlier.

"This is Luke's party?" I ask uncertainly as we approach and I hear the sounds of laughing and shrieking getting louder. I have only a vague idea of who Luke Burrows is, but I'd supposed him to be quiet and not particularly sociable.

"Barely. He has the best garden for it, that's all. It's big and because of their farm it's not too near other houses so there wont be complaints from neighbours. So the party is at his, but really Marcus did most of the organising."

Her voice is brimming with pride but I feel a small swoop of sympathy for Luke. I don't really know him that well, but it sounds like none of his other guests will either.

"Are his parents going to be there?"

"That's the best part! They're not!"

Charlie is gleeful but my stomach is sinking swiftly to settle somewhere around my knees. We've reached the garden gate and Charlie has already shrugged out of her coat and is hoicking her top up in a valiant effort to keep her breasts contained.

"Ready?" she asks me with a grin.

I paste a smile on my face and nervously touch my hair. She pushes open the gate and bursts into the garden, tossing her coat down onto a mound of outer-ware and striding confidently forward. I'm too slow to keep up with her: by the time I'm over the threshold and have struggled out of my jacket and sweatshirt, she's gone. I edge forward slowly, desperately scanning the garden for one of my small selection of friends. It looks like our whole school year is here, gathered around the fire pit, sprawled on the garden furniture or just clustered around in groups, shouting to one another over the all-pervasive beat of the music. There's even a table tennis table that's been commandeered for beer pong and at least twenty people are gathered around it cheering on the players.

Everyone looks at ease, evidently enjoying an evening of frivolity, and I wonder briefly how they do it. They all seem so calm together, unphased by the music and the crowd.

My heart is starting to race as I slowly tread forward, my head swivelling round like a top, frantically searching for safe haven.

There!

I can see Kate talking to her drama friends and I make a beeline for her, following a small path of stepping stones as far as it'll take me before eventually darting across the grass.

"Hey Penny!" Kate chirps happily.

She can't see the panic in my eyes. She thinks nothing of my hand gripping her arm.

I wish Charlie hadn't left me.

"When did you get here?" she asks me.

“Just arrived,” I murmur, too quietly for her to hear me over the din. She gets the gist though and smiles in response.

“Your hair looks lovely!” she shouts, gesturing to my bright, flowing locks in admiration. I can see a few of her group looking at me too and I have to fight the urge to immediately pull it up into a bun.

I smile uncertainly and try to think of something to say but Kate's attention is reclaimed by a girl called Jenny who she was talking to when I arrived. I stay there, on the periphery, trying to look as though I belong. Eventually someone will realise that I don't take drama and Kate is my only friend here. I'd like to have moved on before that happens.

I wish I could find Charlie.

After a few minutes I spy Josh and Abed out of the corner of my eye. They're both part of the group at the beer pong table and there's no way I'm going to approach them, I might be made to join in the game.

There! I can see Sophie! She's just walking across

the grass towards the house! I slip away from Kate and her friends and dash across to Sophie, slipping my arm through hers.

"Penny! Look at you! You look gorgeous!" Sophie tells me, pulling me in to a hug.

"You too," I tell her, nodding at her long, blonde hair. Like me she usually ties her hair up, but tonight she's clearly relishing having it down, swirling around her shoulders.

"Are you headed for the bathroom as well?" she asks me.

"Yep," I agree, relieved to have a destination away from the chaos and noise of the garden.

She links arms with me again and we head into the house. A series of printouts depicting the 'bathroom' symbols from around the world have been stuck on the walls with blue-tack, leading us along a hallway and round a corner to a queue of other people already waiting in line. All girls.

"Urgh! It is always the way, isn't it?" Sophie

complains good-naturedly. She's very hard to genuinely ruffle, it's one of the things I like about her.

"Always a queue for the ladies room!" Anna Choi chimes in from further up the line.

"Why is that?" Sophie wonders aloud with a laugh, "Are girls really so much slower at peeing?"

"We're just slowed down by the desire to do inconsequential things like hand washing."

Sophie gives a burst of delighted laughter and the other girls closest chuckle too. I can feel myself blushing but it's nice. I smile and allow myself to feel like a part of the gentle ebb and flow of conversation as we stand in line, awaiting our turn. When we reach the front I let Sophie go before me since I don't actually need to pee, and then I use my turn to check my hair and face and then wash my hands quickly- I don't want to lose Sophie too, but she's waiting in the hallway for me and smiles when she sees me.

"Let's find a drink."

The kitchen has been totally taken over with bottles

of spirits, a huge array of mixers and seemingly endless bottles and cans of beer. A couple of weeks ago Marcus collected ten pounds from everyone who intended to come to the party, and then his older cousin took him to buy 'refreshments'.

I've never had more than a tentative and wholly regretted sip of any kind of spirit since they all seem to burn and coat my tongue, leaving my eyes watering and my stomach churning. I'm considering getting myself a plastic cup of lemonade and just saying it has alcohol in it, but it would be too embarrassing to be caught lying. Instead I go for a beer. A single bottle of beer that I can sip slowly and hopefully make it last until Charlie's ready to leave. Gosh, I'm a party animal aren't I.

Sophie pours herself a Jack Daniels and coke and then leads me back into the garden. If anything it actually seems louder then it did before, but the music has changed to the current hits and a few people are attempting to dance. We move forward, staying close together, laughing when Sophie points out some particularly elaborate dance moves from Nick, a boy I used to sit next to in Geography.

It's the flash and glisten of sequins that leads me over towards the fire pit. Most of the people gathered here are just shifting silhouettes but I can see spots of light being thrown back at me off of a spangly top.

"Penny! Sophie!"

I don't know how she's managed it, but Charlie's already drunk. She lurches over to us, unsteady on her wedge sandals, and flings her arms around us.

"Isn't this fantastic?!" she hisses at us, her breath hot and sickly sweet on my skin.

"Yeah, great!" Sophie agrees with a laugh before rolling her eyes at me.

"And doesn't Penny look *hot*! Pretty Penny!" she shrieks the words and cackles, pulling me forward toward the group around the fire. My heart sinks when I see Marcus, sat in a garden chair as though he's in a throne. He looks me up and down slowly, making my skin crawl. I wish I'd kept my sweatshirt on. He smirks slightly and his eyes linger over my chest and my bare shoulders.

"Alex! Look! Penny's here!" Charlie cries in an elaborate stage whisper that floods my face with heat.

There he is. He's right there. His blue eyes are dancing in the firelight and he's looking right at me. Oh God, I could kill Charlie!

"Hi Penny."

I'm frozen in place. I manage to make an incoherent sound that I desperately hope sounds like a greeting but then I falter, not sure what to do. I have an almost irresistible urge to run.

"Would you like a seat?" Alex asks me with a kind smile.

He's sat on a low wall that borders the fire area, and after a gentle nudge the silhouette next to him peels away and fades into the surrounding darkness of the garden.

I move forward and sit awkwardly beside him, not sure what to say. I'm glad that I have the beer to occupy my hands. I take a few swigs in quick succession and choke as the bubbles fill my throat and sting my nose.

"Are you alright?" he asks, his tone concerned.

"Yeah, yeah, just not used to drinking beer," I tell him, relieved that I've actually managed to talk.

"Well, here, I'll make you a different drink!" he offers happily, pulling out a bottle from beside the wall. They've clearly got their own little refreshment setup here and he makes me a drink in a plastic cup, handing it over triumphantly.

"I'm sure you'll like that better," he tells me confidently.

He's probably right. I'd like anything he gave me. This is *Alex Hall.*

I take a tentative sip. It's almost just Coca-Cola but then there's a warmth and a spice to it that isn't unpleasant. Still, I think I prefer plain soda.

"It's great, thank you!" I tell him with a smile that hurts my cheeks.

"I don't think I've ever seen your hair down before,

it looks really nice," he tells me, gently touching a small section of my hair where it falls forward over my shoulder.

I can't breathe.

I can see Charlie behind him, draped in Marcus' lap, dancing her eyebrows at me in victory.

"Thank you," I manage after a moment, wishing I could bring myself to make a more substantial response. I want to be witty and charismatic- to blow him away with my charm, but the wide smile is still stretched across my face and I'm sure that I must look like an idiot or maybe a crazy person.

Alex doesn't seem to mind, he puts an arm around my shoulders and I take another sip of my drink to keep myself from fainting.

There's about ten of us sat around the fire now, all on low walls or garden chairs. Sophie has vanished and I feel a pang of regret but swiftly push it down. I'm here, beside The Alex Hall and his arm is around my shoulders as though it's the most natural thing in the world. Everyone is discussing their summer plans, talking about holidays they're going on or events they have booked. I wish I had something to add but I don't have a single thing arranged for the coming weeks. Maybe Charlie's right, maybe I'm living too small.

I try desperately to think of something witty or interesting to contribute but my mind is a complete blank. Tumble weed is rolling by, unhindered by any thoughts at all. This is the problem with keeping most conversations contained securely within my own imagination- No real-world practice! When Alex turns slightly and addresses me directly in a low voice I almost jump out of my skin.

“It's a great party, huh? Great way to start the summer. I've got a busy few weeks ahead of me so it's really good to blow off some steam.”

I smile at him blankly before realising with a start that I should ask him why he's going to be so busy, but luckily he comes to my rescue, carrying on regardless of my ineptitude.

“I'm going to be doing a football camp this summer, there's been a few scouts looking at me already. I play well enough to go pro, everyone says so. Now it's all just the politics, ya know?”

He smiles at me and rolls his eyes as though I of course understand about the politics of professional football. I beam back at him and try to think of something to say but in the absence of any burst of inspiration I settle on a vague, undefined noise. I go to take a sip of my drink but somehow I've already finished it. Alex immediately makes me another and when he replaces his arm around my shoulder he shifts a little closer to me and I can feel the heat of his body beside mine. His blue eyes are so close.

“I'm a great player, but coach says there are a lot of great players out there. It's all about getting people's attention.”

I don't understand how anyone could not pay attention to him. My blood is humming and fizzing with heat and excitement and alcohol and I think that I might actually tell him how attention-worthy I think he is, but when I open my mouth to speak, his lips are on mine.

Alex Hall is kissing me.

I wasn't ready for it. This seems to have come from nowhere! From fantasy to reality in 0.3 seconds. I didn't see it coming and I'm worried that my teeth bumped into his on initial impact, but still, he's kissing me and the whole world is melting away. He's kissing me and there's nothing else in existence that matters right now. My drink is clutched awkwardly in my grasp and one of his hands is moving over my front in an alarming manner, but he's kissing me. When he pulls back he smiles down at me and says,

"Very nice."

I'm not really sure what that means. The kiss was nice? Or was he referring to his exploration of my chest area? I wish that I could ask Charlie about it but she's engaged in a vigorous make-out session with Marcus and I wouldn't know what to say anyway.

I have dreamed about this moment for years. I've

played out hundreds of scenarios in my head. I've practised theoretical conversations until I could almost believe that they were possible, but somehow none of them ever went like this. To cover my confusion I take another long sip from my drink and Alex swiftly tops it up. It seems to be getting stronger but that might be my imagination. It certainly seems to be getting easier to drink at any rate.

"I've been playing since I was three. Dad's a big fan and he's always wanted me to go pro," he tells me and it takes me a moment to realise that he's still talking about football. My first kiss has been and gone, lost to a conversation about a game that I have zero interest in. The heat of the fire is starting to pull at my focus, making me feel tired and slow.

"It requires real commitment to be this good at something. Work ethic! That's what it is! But then, it can all be for nothing if you don't get some lucky break. It's crazy! I could work as hard as I want and I could be the absolute best, but I still might not make it big, even though I deserve to! I just have to find a way to get my name out there. It's mad right?" he asks me, looking for confirmation.

"Mad," I agree, nodding my head vigorously. I'm feeling increasingly warm and my head is foggier than ever. The nodding seems to set off a series of befuddled shock-waves.

He opens his mouth again but he just takes a sip from his own drink and I almost sigh with relief. I'm doing my best to keep up with everything he's saying but his words are starting to get a little fuzzy around the edges and he seems to be going so fast. His arm is still around my shoulders, keeping me locked into a small, warm world of our own. The feeling of it, the weight and closeness is nice but I'd love a bit of fresh air. I'm just starting to think that I might nip to the bathroom, just to get a little space, when he turns towards me and his eyes widen almost comically in a carefully crafted eureka moment.

"Hey! I just had an idea! Do you ever do

interviews?"

I think for a moment that I must have misheard him. The words just don't make sense.

"About football?" I ask, uselessly.

"No, of course not," he responds with a small laugh.

"I don't understand," I admit, wishing it wasn't quite so hot here.

"Well, like we were saying, it's crazy that I could be so good and work so hard and still not get my chance," he tells me slowly, nodding slightly with each word, willing me to follow his train of thought.

"Yeah," I agree nodding, still not sure where on earth I can come in to this.

"So I need to get my name out there. If I could get some visibility, maybe I'd get a contract to play for a pro team," he tells me, as though this should explain everything.

"I don't get it, how am I supposed to help? I don't know anyone who does football," I explain, worried that he's been misled somehow. I don't *think* I've said anything to give him the impression that I have an 'in' in the pro-football world, but to be honest the whole conversation so far has already become a bit of a haze.

He's looking exasperated now and a little frustrated by my uselessness.

“You don't need to know anyone in football,” he tells me in uneven tones before taking a breath and smoothing his voice back out into its usual charming timbre.

“People have heard of you, people know your name, that's what I need for myself,” he explains, reaching up and playing with a lock of my hair again.

“What?”

The fire doesn't feel so warm any more and my drunken haze is starting to recede but my mind is still sluggish and reluctant.

“I just need to get my name out there. You agreed with me that it's not fair for me to miss out on my chance when I deserve it... but you could help me. Have you ever been asked to do an interview? About what happened when you were a kid?"

He's gazing at me with an expression of polite enquiry, his hand now stroking my bare arm.

My thoughts seems to have stalled, iced over. I want desperately to believe that I've misunderstood. My brain seems to be rebelling, refusing to accept this person beside me as the real Alex Hall- my Adonis- the star of all my daydreams.

"No," I manage, pushing the small word out with a monolith effort.

"But you could, right? I mean, it was big news all over, wasn't it? You *must* get the occasional reporter asking about it. If you did one and it went well you might even get asked to go on TV!"

His tone implies that he thinks this would be some kind of treat. Can he really think that I would want to go on television and talk about this? Can he really suppose that I want to give interviews and make a spectacle of myself over this? I lost my sister.

"No."

The word comes easier this time but he barely seems to hear it. He tightens his arm around my shoulders and gives me a small smile that an hour ago would have made me melt. He's treating this conversation like a seduction, I realise.

"You'd be great! You could tell them what happened and they'd ask you questions and stuff and you could be like a spokes-person. You could make a difference. And I'd come with you of course, I could come on camera with you and everything," he tells me, like he's offering to do me a favour.

"I could make a difference? Like, bring Rose home?" my voice is level, my face expressionless but I'm gratified to see him flinch.

He squirms slightly but does his best to shrug it off and resume the narrative that he's mapped out, but I've turned to ice and I'm sure that he can feel it. The heat of the fire and his arm around me is nothing now.

"You could start with just a small interview with the local paper or something," he suggests, valiantly soldiering on as though he has any hope of convincing me. Maybe he really thinks he does.

"To be a spokesperson? For what exactly?" I ask, looking him square in the face, a challenge in my eyes.

"Well, you know-"

"No, I don't. For Rose? She doesn't need a spokesperson Alex, she's gone. She's been gone for ten years and all the interviews in the world won't get her back. And tying your name to a lost ten year old isn't going to get you a football career." I try to stay calm but I spit the final words and he recoils, pulling his arm back as though I've struck him.

"I'm just trying to be helpful!" he retorts, "Charlie said you like me and I felt sorry for you! Everyone knows the sob story, I just thought I might actually help!"

He's transformed in an instant. His voice is raised and he's the very image of wounded honour.

Everyone around the fire is watching us now, all eyes fixed on the scene unfolding before them. Even Charlie and Marcus have stopped kissing to see what's happening. Her eyes meet mine and she has the good grace to blush. Alex Hall. He's puffed up, painting himself into the role of hero but it doesn't suit his current expression, his face twisted into a sneer.

"You didn't want to help me! You wanted *me* to help *you*!" I counter, shaking with rage.

He scoffs, chuckling into his hand.

"How could *you* help anyone? You couldn't even-"

He stops, toeing the line, but it's too late. The words are there, I can see them.

You couldn't even help your sister.

# Chapter 3

I push up from my seat and run. I go towards the house, wanting to put walls between myself and Alex and the words that scrawled themselves between us. I stop at the door, looking round for Charlie but she's not there. She didn't follow me.

I feel a hot, sharp stone in my throat that tells me I'm about to cry and the bathroom queue is, inconveniently, at least twice as long as it was before. In the spirit of emotionally distressed exploration I turn left instead of right, seeking an alternative escape route. Where else can I go? There's a staircase. Maybe there's another bathroom upstairs. There are no lights on and I get the distinct impression that I'm not meant to be up here but I'm unsteady on my feet and more than anything I want to sit down behind a locked door and cry in peace. I stumble on until I see a light flickering through a half open doorway. I make for it, pushing the door with more force than I intend. It bangs open making my head spin.

"Bloody hell!"

A boy with floppy dark hair is sat on a bed watching something on his laptop. He jumped at my arrival and isn't looking too pleased to see me.

"Sorry. Just wanted to... make an entrance," I tell him, wavering slightly on legs that don't seem inclined to hold me up and extending my arms with a flourish.

"You're not supposed to be up here," he tells me, confirming my suspicions.

"Says who?" I demand.

"Me. It's my house."

"Ah! Luke Burrows! The resident and homeowner!" I cry, pleased to have worked out his identity.

"Enjoying the party I see," he notes with a slight smile.

"It's wonderful! Just a shame about all the people."

"I thought much the same thing myself," he agrees sympathetically.

"People do have a tendency to ruin even the nicest of social gatherings, don't they?" I comment sadly.

"People can ruin anything they put their minds to," he tells me with a shrug.

"Is that why you're up here?"

"I was at the party for a bit, but I don't like the music and I'm no good at beer-pong." he explains.

"Bloody nightmare then. You're better off out of it."

He laughs before looking at me speculatively.

"Why are *you* up here Penny?"

"Same, I'm *rubbish* at beer-pong." I look around the room for a moment, trying to remember what I was doing, then I turn back to him, "You know who I am."

"Yes I do," he agrees uncertainly.

"That is because I am a celebrity!" I tell him solemnly, punctuating each word with a clumsily pointed finger.

"A celebrity?"

I look at him blankly. He knows what I mean. Everyone knows.

His walls are covered in posters and bookshelves. There's lots of sci-fi and fantasy, the Percy Jackson books are in evidence, though The Lord Of The Rings looks the most well read. I spot some slightly dusty Harry Potter books and out of nowhere a thought fills my head and I crumple over laughing.

"What?" he asks, bewildered.

Eventually I calm down enough to get the words out, still choking them between laughs.

"I'm the girl who lived!"

He almost smiles. The laughter dies in my throat. It isn't funny at all really.

I turn around without a word and head back the way I came. The desire to cry has subsided and I just want to go home. I'm going to grab Charlie and head back to mine. I want my own bed and my own house and enough solitude to start the process of forgetting that this nightmare of a party ever happened. The stairs are tricky but I manage to navigate them without serious mishap and I stumble back outside, enjoying the feeling of the cold night air on my face. I can still see Charlie twinkling by the fire. She's draped across Marcus' lap and her face seems to be attached to his. As I get closer however, he pulls away and raises a hand in greeting.

"Oi! Rose!"

I stop so fast I almost trip over myself.

"If you're looking for Alex, he's moved on Rose, to someone who isn't so stuck up!" he shouts it loudly, smiling at the friends gathered around him as though he's displaying spectacular wit. Alex isn't there but everyone else in the group is chuckling softly, watching me for a reaction. All except Charlie. Her face is turned away.

"Charlie? I want to go." I say the words as loudly as I can but they still only just reach her.

For a moment I'm terrified that she's not going to come with me but then she disentangles herself from

Marcus like an earring snagged on a jumper. She uncoils, stumbling slightly and steps towards me.

"Let's stay a bit longer," she says, looking back to where Marcus is watching us with evident amusement.

"What?"

I don't know how she can suggest that we stay here, like it's no big deal.

"He just called me *Rose*!" I hiss.

"He's just joking! He's kidding around! Alex is his friend and you totally just shouted at him in front of everyone!" she counters defensively.

I don't know what to say. I don't see how she can not be on my side of this. I can't see any side but mine to be on!

"Please," I utter feebly.

"You go if you want to but I'm going to stay."

"But... you're sleeping at mine," I remind her.

"I'll come later. I won't be long, just- I don't want to go yet."

Her jaw juts determinedly and her eyes are bright,

sparks catching in the firelight.

I could stay, but Marcus and his friends are still chuckling just behind Charlie and I've spotted where Alex disappeared off to. He and Anna Choi are entwined in an all-absorbing embrace up against the garden fence to my left. I sway on my feet and my stomach heaves. I want to go home.

I dig through the pocket of my jeans until I feel the sharp crenelations of my key. I pull it out and press it into Charlie's hand.

"Let yourself in when you get to mine. Don't walk on your own."

My words are low and urgent but there's a lull in the music and Marcus and his cronies are able to make them out. They break into a fresh bout of laughter at my fearful intensity, the sound bouncing and ricochetting around inside my head. Charlie turns away from me, her face flushed with embarrassment. But she takes the key.

My feet feel unbelievably heavy as I walk away. They

catch on every tussock of grass and every paving stone. Rose's name follows me as far as the gate, the crowd behind me keeps lobbing it my way, waiting for a direct hit, but then I'm outside and the shouting stops. Their target removed, their attention has immediately wandered. After all, it's just a game.

"Why do they do that?"

"WHAT THE BLOODY FU-" I spin round, losing my balance and topple towards the ground but hands catch me, righting me before I hit the earth. I blink in the dark, my heart pounding, and Luke Burrows comes into focus.

"Sorry," he tells me sheepishly, "I didn't mean to scare you."

"Suddenly speaking out of the pitch black was probably a mistake then," I snap, clutching my chest to better appreciate the racing of my heart. After a moment it slows and I look up at Luke again, realising that he must have followed me out.

"Why do they do what?" I ask at what I feel to be a

much more reasonable volume.

“Why do they call you that? I remember people used to do that when we first started secondary school. I never understood why.”

“My step-dad, Coop, says they just want to see if it upsets me.”

“Are they hoping that it does?” he asks.

“I don't know.”

Neither of us really knows what to say and I just desperately want to get back to mine. I give a vague shrug that I hope says 'goodbye, thank you for hosting this party though I had a terrible time', but as I start to walk he falls into step beside me.

“You know that's your house, right?” I ask him, gesturing to the din and chaos behind us.

“That one?! Are you sure?! Who the heck are all those people then?!” he demands, his brow furrowed in confusion.

I snort but don't respond. It's taking a lot of focus just to keep my feet moving, one foot in front of the other.

“I didn't have you pegged as being much of a drinker,” he tells me after another minute of walking.

“Well I guess you can have your peg back then. I am *un*peggable. Though, this is actually my first time drinking I suppose,” I admit.

“What did you have?” he asks curiously.

“I don't know. Something... spicy tasting, in coke,” I offer, my hands flapping and gesturing ineffectively.

“You don't even know what you were drinking?” he asks, clearly a little horrified.

“*Alex Hall* made it for me,” I tell him as though this explains everything.

“Ah, of course. Mr Blue Eyes And Dimples.”

Oh God! The dimples! I'd forgotten the dimples!

“Yep.”

“Are you two together? I didn't realise,” he comments with just a slight edge to his voice.

“No. No we are not. Despite the blue eyes. And the dimples. Unfortunately it turns out that Alex Hall is a self-serving egostactical neanthedal!" I declare, my volume mounting with each word.

"An egostactical neanthedal huh? That is a shame."

"An ego-tisss-tical..." I trail off, my focus back on my feet.

I'm almost home now and my bed is calling me.

"I didn't know that you were funny."

"What?" for some reason his statement bugs me and I spin about to face him.

"You. I never knew you were funny," he reiterates.

"I'm not funny, I'm drunk."

"I'm pretty sure alcohol doesn't make unfunny people funny, you don't suddenly develop wit. It just makes funny people louder," he tells me reasonably.

"I try not to be loud," I tell him vaguely.

"I'm realising that. Why?" he asks curiously.

I don't know how to explain and with an unspecified amount of alcohol coursing through my bloodstream it probably isn't the time to attempt it.

I give a long sigh instead and try to look up at the

stars but everything is shifting unnervingly.

"What were you watching?" I ask him suddenly.

"What?"

"In your room," I add, though I feel an explanation should be superfluous.

"Oh, Star Trek."

"The new one?" I ask with interest. I'm always on the lookout for a new show to binge.

"No, Captain Piccard."

"I don't know what that means."

It's his turn to sigh, like I've just gone down in his estimations. To my surprise I find myself wishing that I'd had a better answer. No matter, I'm finally home.

"Didn't you give your friend your key?" he asks as I make my way up the drive.

"Coop hid one outside just in case." I tell him, picking my way across the small patch of grass to the flowerbed under the widow. I lift up a rock there and taped underneath is the spare key- only left outside for very specific events such as this one.

"Et voila!" I whisper triumphantly.

"Well I guess I'll head home then," Luke says almost reluctantly.

"Thanks for walking me."

"No worries."

There's a subtle hum of expectation or tension in the air that I don't know how to understand. I turn to go, my face flushed for no reason.

"Bye then," he offers, already starting to walk away.

"Enjoy your party," I call after him in a low voice, hesitant to disrupt the calm of the dark street.

He leaves with a wry smile on his face and I suspect he's going straight back up to his room and the next episode of Star Trek when he gets back.

I let myself in and make my way up to my room as quietly as I can. My mind is a fog and the air feels thick and stale, warmed by central heating into a soupy mass. I have never been so grateful to have my own bathroom before. I shut both my bedroom and my bathroom doors and then sink down onto the cold tiles as my stomach rolls. I heave and retch, emptying the entire contents of my body into the toilet. When I'm just an outer shell, porcelain thin and trembling, I wash my face and rinse my mouth, climbing beneath the covers of my bed to wait for Charlie.

# Chapter 4

Morning is an onslaught of sounds and smells. Olly is shouting something to his dad and I can hear the television playing one of his more obnoxious shows. There's the smell of bacon frying and the floral air freshener that my mum cranks up to full power whenever Coop makes breakfast. My head is pounding and my mouth is dry, my tongue cleaving to the sides and feeling ten sizes too big. I stumble to the bathroom, rinsing my mouth out with water again and again before cupping some in my hands and gulping it down. I splash my face with the cold water until I start to feel a little more human, though my reflection in the mirror still looks pretty ghastly. I pull the bathroom door open, planning to go straight back to bed, but-

The bed is empty. I walk all round it, checking the floor. Nothing.

I find the tangled pile of clothes that I wore the previous night and extricate my phone from my jeans pocket. Nothing. No missed calls, no texts.

Where's Charlie?

This question swells to fill the room, pressing out into every crack and crevice, leaving no room for me. My phone battery is low so I plug it in before selecting Charlie's name and putting through a call. It goes straight to voicemail.

I send her a quick message and then try to organise my thoughts. Maybe she stayed with someone else. Maybe after our argument she didn't want to come back to mine or maybe she was too drunk to get here- given my own less than sea-worthy state I could understand that. I dial Kate who answers after the tenth ring, her voice thick.

"Is Charlie with you?" I ask quickly, trying to keep my voice calm.

"No, I thought she was sleeping at yours," she mumbles, her words heavy with sleep.

"She was meant to, but I left early," I admit.

"Oh," she responds, still barely awake.

"You didn't see where she went? Who she left with?" I ask insistently.

"Nope, I barely saw her at all."

I hang up without saying goodbye and immediately dial Sophie. She picks up after a much more reasonable two rings and sounds alert and fresh- almost painfully so. Again I get straight to the point, not wanting to waste any time before I descend into full blown panic. I'm trying to tell myself that no one else would be worried right now, it's only my personal history skewing my response. Chances are Charlie is fine and I'm just overreacting.

"Charlie isn't with you is she?" I ask hopefully.

"Charlie? No, she's not. I thought she was going to sleep at yours."

My heart sinks.

"That was the plan but I left early and she never showed up at mine," I tell her, trying to keep my voice calm.

"Oh yeah, I heard about you leaving, are you alright? Those guys are jerks."

"It's fine, it doesn't matter," I tell her honestly. Marcus, Alex, all of it seems small this morning, just a hard knot of anger and disappointment in my chest. Uncomfortable but easy enough to ignore.

"Did you see Charlie much after I left? Do you know where she might be?"

"She probably just crashed at someone else's," Sophie tells me lightly.

"She's not answering her phone," I counter.

"Well she had a lot to drink," she reminds me. I can hear the smile in her voice but the pool of dread in the pit of my stomach is still simmering away.

"That's true, but it doesn't help me find her. How am I supposed to figure out where she is?!"

My panic is rising now and Sophie can hear it

thrumming in my voice.

"Maybe she's with Marcus," she suggests.

Marcus! I can't believe I didn't think of him! The dread stills, though it doesn't drain away.

"I don't have his number."

"I have it, I can send it over to you. She's probably with him," Sophie tells me in her most soothing tones.

I dial his number and no one answers. For a moment I breathe a sigh of relief. If neither of them is picking up, maybe they are together after all. A few seconds later though, a text comes though from Marcus' number.

"Who is this?"

I'm not sure what to do. If I say it's me I doubt he'll answer the phone. Instead I decide to just message him back.

"Is Charlie with you?"

Three little dots appear, telling me that he's typing a reply. I hold my breath as I wait. He seems to be typing for an inordinately long time and then-

“no.”

“She's not there? Do you know where she is?”

I fire back my message, my hands starting to sweat.

Again those three dots keep me waiting, my eyes fixed on them as they cycle round.

“Who is this? Charlie and her dramas not my problem.”

What does that mean?! Did something happen between the two of them? He definitely seemed involved with her at the party before I left! I try calling him again but he doesn't answer. I message,

“It's Penny Cooper”, but he doesn't reply and still doesn't answer when I call again. He says she's not with him and I don't know who to try next. I call Josh and Abed, redialling until they answer, but neither of them has seen Charlie and they both profess to having no idea who else she could be with. I call Charlie's phone half a dozen more times and send her a string of increasingly panicked messages but - nothing. My messages aren't even sending properly, the first little tick appears, showing my phone has sent it, but the second tick isn't there. What does that mean?! I google it quickly and the Samsung website callously informs me that this means the receiving phone has not received the message. It may be switched off, damaged, or out of service.

Charlie switched her phone off?!

It doesn't sound like her. She never turns her phone off! Even in the cinema she won't go further than silencing it and stashing it deep in her bag. But she can't be out of service, it's a rural town but not *that* rural! I can't think of anywhere local that doesn't have phone service. I scroll through my phone with its measly collection of saved numbers. I have half a dozen more class mates in there, their details mostly stored during the course of school projects. I call them all. One after another. To my surprise they all answer and no one sounds prohibitively horrified or annoyed to hear from me, though none of them are able to help either. Lisa from Science class remembers Charlie and Marcus having an argument and she thinks it was about another girl, but she wasn't really paying attention and she's not sure. A couple of the others confirm that they saw Charlie around the party but they didn't notice anything unusual except that she had definitely been drinking. A lot.

Fear has my stomach gripped in a tight fist and my breath is coming in short bursts.

I can't believe I left her there.

"Are you alright girls? I brought you some tea and ibuprofen," Coop announces cheerfully, pushing my door open, a mug in each hand and a small box poking out of his shirt pocket.

Something in my face must tell him that something's happened because he puts the tea down on my bedside table and strides forward quickly, dropping down to a crouch to look into my eyes.

"What is it?" he demands, the usual bounce and cheer absent from his voice.

"Charlie's not here," I whisper, afraid to say it aloud.

He doesn't answer. He doesn't ask me if she's

already left, he doesn't ask if she went to someone else's. He doesn't offer me hopeful platitudes. This isn't a hopeful platitudes household.

"What happened?" he asks eventually, when I haven't managed to force any more words out.

"I-I-I was drinking. We both were. But then- I got upset and I wanted to come home. She wouldn't come with me! She told me to go! She said she'd meet me here! I gave her my key!"

I'm firing out these short, frantic sentences, desperately hoping that he can catch them and piece them together to make sense of what happened. Maybe he can find her. With all his adult wisdom, maybe he can fix this for me.

"You've called her?" he asks quickly.

"I've called and messaged but she isn't answering! I've called our friends and every other number I have!"

"Her house phone?"

My heart stutters. I haven't called her house phone. Maybe she's just at home, in bed. Maybe everything is fine. Maybe she was angry at me because of everything with Alex Hall and she just didn't want to sleep over. My heart swells with hope but then deflates. I think about that absent second tick on my phone screen. Somehow, I don't think she's at home.

I lift my phone hesitantly but Coop reaches out a hand to stop me.

"Lets just nip round there, eh?"

He doesn't think she's at home either.

This isn't a hopeful household.

I pull on jeans and a sweatshirt before dashing downstairs to where Coop's waiting in the hall. Mum's out, watching Olly try to nerve himself up to participate in some under-tens football, so we don't need to sneak or hide but we both stay quiet anyway. We grab our shoes from the shoe bin in the porch, Coop opting for his usual loafers and me digging out some flip flops since I forgot to put on socks.

Charlie's house is only a few minutes away, around

the other side of the woods. Hers, mine and Luke's would make a triangle with the woods in the middle but Coop and I don't cut through the trees to get to hers, instead we traipse around the winding streets and I can't help but feel that we might be wasting precious minutes doing so.

Charlie's mum, Wendy, opens the door to us with a bright smile.

"Are you dropping Charlie home?"

And there it is. That's our answer. She isn't here.

Wendy's looking behind us to where her daughter should be standing on the narrow path. That patch of air disturbed by her absence.

I try to say something but the words won't form in my mind. It's so quiet inside my head that I almost fancy I can hear the crashing of waves.

Coop steps up to the plate.

"The girls got separated at the party and Charlie never came back to ours Wendy," he tells her simply, no sugar coating or dancing around the issue.

"What do you mean? Where is she?" Wendy asks, an edge to her voice now. One that I recognise.

"Are you sure she didn't come back here? She's not just asleep in her room?" Coop asks, his usually jovial voice gentle.

"No, she's not here, I was just in her room to get her washing," Wendy explains, her pitch rising.

She's not looking at Coop. He's the one talking but her eyes are on me. I'm the one she trusted her daughter to last night. I'm the one who came back without her.

"I don't understand, what's going on? Where is she?" Wendy asks me, her eyes pleading for an explanation that I don't have to give.

I swallow and try to moisten my dry throat, willing myself to say the right thing.

"She didn't want to leave the party. She wanted to stay. I gave her my house key and I told her not to walk alone..."

I'm making excuses. I should never have left the

party without Charlie, but I did. I wait for anger and reproach to swell behind Wendy's eyes but she pulls me into a hug, just a little too tight, like she's trying to feel Charlie hidden beneath my skin.

"Wendy, love, she's probably fine, just sleeping at a friend's house, but we can't find her. Just to be safe, I think we should call the police."

Wendy has a whole list of numbers. She's part of a school phone-tree system for snow days. She has five designated numbers that she calls in the event of the school being closed, and they've each been allocated five more, and on and on. We decide to implement the phone-tree now, to check with everyone in our year group all at once. We offer one another smiles and nods and brittle, high-pitched laughter as we repeat to ourselves that she's probably with a friend. But we call the police first.

It takes thirteen and a half minutes for the cavalry to arrive, by which time we've called the five numbers in the phone-tree and we've started hearing back from the next layer of branches. Coop takes the phone into the kitchen to carry on noting down names and numbers as more and more parents call. I stay in the lounge with Wendy while she speaks to the three officers who've come to investigate.

I can see it in their eyes, hear it in the slight hesitation before speaking - They're not sure that there's really something wrong. They think that Charlie's going to walk through the door at any moment and roll her eyes at all the fuss.

God, I hope they're right.

Somehow though, I don't think she will. It's not just my drizzly disposition or my personal history, I keep thinking about that single tick beside my messages. I keep checking but they're still not delivered. Not received.

All eyes keep flicking towards me.

"Alright Ms Hople, we'll start making some calls now and get some officers straight out to search."

They're not going to tell her to wait. They won't

advise her not to panic. They can't muster the words with the worst case scenario perched on the edge of the sofa. I stay put like a living, breathing, warning poster throughout the morning. My every fibre is itching to get out there and beat the bushes but the frantic look in Wendy's face keeps me in place.

"What time did she leave the house yesterday?" one officer asks.

"Just after lunch, it must have been about two," Wendy tells them.

"And where did she go? Straight to this party you mentioned?"

"No, she went to Penny's house. They're best friends."

All heads swivel to face me. I give a small nod.

"Penny, you agree with that sequence of events? Charlie arrived shortly after two?" the same officer asks me.

"Yes, we just hung out at mine, in my room and got ready for the party."

"Was anyone else there?" the officer asks.

"Yes, my family. Then mum went out and Charlie and I ate with Coop and my brother," I tell them, gesturing towards the kitchen where I can hear Coop answering yet another phone-tree call.

"And then?"

"Then we went to the party."

"What was Charlie wearing?" one of the other officers asks Wendy.

"She was wearing denim shorts and a green top, sort of floaty. And she had her coat with her. It's one of those dark green, waxed ones." Wendy tells them confidently.

I cough and splutter a little and everyone turns back to me. I can feel my face, burning the kind of vibrant red that only someone with ginger hair can achieve.

"She wasn't wearing that," I mumble in my smallest voice.

"What?!" Wendy demands, her body physically recoiling.

"She got changed at mine."

"No, I helped her pick out that outfit!" she tells me, her gaze roving my face as though she's hoping I'm lying.

"She got changed."

I don't know what else to say. Wendy seems to sag inwards and I wish I could say something to comfort her but I don't even know what those words would look like.

"What did Charlie wear to the party?" the officer asks me.

I try not to look at Wendy as I answer. I know she isn't going to be happy about it.

"She was wearing a short black skirt, a back strapless top with sequins and wedge high heels. I have a picture."

The room moves towards me as one when I unlock my phone. I took a couple of pictures in my room, before we set off and one on the walk to Luke's house. The two in my room are selfies of me and Charlie, fully made up. I think again that she barely looks like herself, but still the image of the two of us, faces side by side smiling at the camera makes my heart falter. The photo I took en route is a full-length shot of Charlie struggling to walk on country roads in her heels. Her expression is light, her face upturned with laughter. I hear the sharp intake of breath from Wendy as she leans over to see the pictures.

"I don't even know where she *got* those clothes!" she whispers in a stricken voice.

"She said they were new but I don't know where she got them either," I add.

"Money's a bit tight at the moment, we don't have the cash to get anything new right now! I don't understand how..." Wendy trails off, her hand covering her mouth like she's worried she might be sick. The rug has been pulled out from under her nice stable life and things are starting to topple to the ground.

"Does Charlie have a job or any other source of income?" the officer asks, looking from Wendy to me and back again.

We both shake our heads.

"Is there anyone who might give her money? Family members perhaps?"

Again, we shake our heads.

"It's just us. I never really knew Charlie's dad, he's never even met her. My parents have both passed away and I'm an only child. Charlie's all I have."

She chokes out the last words on a sob and buries her face in her hands. The officer waits a couple of beats for Wendy to pull herself together and then presses on.

"So Wendy, you last saw Charlie at around two in the afternoon when she left to go to Penny's. Penny, what about you? What time did you last see Charlie?"

A pebble rises in my throat, choking off my voice.

"I-I-"

"Penny?"

"I-I'm not sure. I'm not sure what time I left the party- I'd um- I'd been drinking a bit," I tell them, my face flushing a deep burgundy.

"Was there much drinking going on at the party?" the officer asks lightly, as though it's of no concern, which I suppose given the current situation, it isn't.

"Yes, I think most people were drinking really," I

admit in my small voice.

"Was Charlie drinking?"

The silence is so loud it's practically ringing, bouncing off the walls and back towards us.

I nod. The smallest movement I can manage but the officer notes it down confidently.

"Would you say that she was drunk? When you left?" she asks me in that same matter of fact voice.

I nod again.

Wendy sighs and reaches out, squeezing my hand.

"Did you make any calls when you left the party? Send any text messages? Anything that might give us a specific time," the officer asks, moving smoothly back to the timeline.

"No, sorry."

"Would your parents know what time you got home?"

"My mum takes something to help her sleep, she won't know, but Coop might," I suggest, gesturing again towards the kitchen where Coop's still on phone duty.

One of the other officers peels off and disappears into the kitchen returning a minute later.

"Apparently she got back just after ten thirty," he tells his colleague. She notes it down.

"That seems quite early. Why did you leave the party at that time?" she asks me, her notebook held at the ready.

"Some of the boys were teasing me, so I just wanted to go home," I tell them, my eyes fixed firmly on the floor.

"But Charlie didn't want to leave?" the officer asks.

"No, her boyfriend-"

"Boyfriend?!" Wendy cuts in and I flinch.

I suspected that Charlie hadn't told her mum about Marcus. Wendy wasn't keen on the idea of her daughter dating and I can't imagine any parent being pleased with a creep like Marcus Kain being in the picture. If I wasn't so worried about Charlie I wouldn't mention him, but now isn't the time for half truths and omissions.

"Marcus. Marcus Kain. He's the one who organised

the party.

“Marcus Kain organised the party? I thought it was at the house of a Luke Burrows?”

“It was, but that was just because Luke had the best garden apparently. Marcus arranged it all and bought all the drink and everything.”

A small kernel of bitterness in the back of my mind hopes that Marcus gets in trouble for the alcohol but he probably won't. He's not the sort of person who has to face consequences.

“So, you left some time around ten thirty and Charlie was with Marcus. Have you spoken to him? Checked she's not with him now?” she asks.

Wendy sits up, her eyes bright with hope but I swiftly stamp it down.

“I called him this morning. He hasn't seen her, he made it sound like they had a fight or broke up maybe,” I explain.

The officer asks for Marcus's number and I give it to her.

"But she was definitely still at the party when you left," she repeats, underlining something she's written down.

"I thought she'd be fine! I told her not to walk alone! I gave her my key!" I say desperately, my eyes so wide they sting.

"Of course, no one is saying that-"

"It's just a few streets away!" I cut her off, my tone still frantic.

"Even quicker through the woods."

At these words all eyes turn to the other officer who spoke them, horror on every face.

He looks round, confused and his colleagues strive valiantly to calm this new wave of alarm.

"You think she went into the woods?!" Wendy cries, looking at each of the officers in quick succession, her eyes determinedly not straying to me.

"She wouldn't! We never go into the woods!" I declare fiercely.

"You have to search! You have to go and look for

her!" Wendy wails, her thin form trembling.

In a second Coop is there, his hands under her elbows, holding her up.

"We'll be searching the woods shortly. We'll be searching the surrounding streets and the woods," the officer tells Wendy trying to calm her, but it seems as though Wendy can't hear her. Her eyes have the look of a startled rabbit and her gaze is roving wildly around the room until at last she settles on me, studying my face, my eyes, my freckles, my red hair.

But she's not looking at me.

# Chapter 5

The police organise a search to begin within the hour. People are already on alert because of the phone-tree so word spreads quickly and there are almost two hundred assembled when it's time to start. The hum of such a large group, all talking and muttering is almost deafening. I message Wendy to tell her how good the turnout is. She's not here, she's at home posted by the phone with a sympathetic police officer and a nervous friend, but I want her to know how many people are here, helping.

They divide us into two groups, one to search the woods and one to search the surrounding streets. My heart is pounding as the officers make their way though the crowd allocating us our areas, but I'm assigned to the streets team. I breathe a sigh of relief and shuffle closer to the rest of the group, awaiting further instructions. We're broken down into a series of smaller teams, each to be allocated a different street. My group gets Lowe's Way. This is the long, somewhat winding road between Luke's house and the more built up residential network of streets around mine.

The town of Upper Chalfont isn't big, we're just a small, frank, grey patch on the map surrounded by green. A search party of two hundred people can thoroughly cover half the town in under an hour, and we do. We knock on doors and search streets, calling Charlie's name and looking for any sign of her. The police took copies of the photos on my phone and printed up some flyers with astonishing speed. They give Charlie's name, age and description and there are three pictures. They used one picture that Wendy provided of Charlie on a normal day, but they also needed to clearly show how Charlie had looked last night. They used the one of her in full length walking along the road and one of the two of us together, cropped down so that I'm just a hank of copper hair and a sliver of freckled cheek.

Doors are being knocked on all over the search area and people are being asked if they've seen Charlie since ten thirty yesterday.

To me this feels ridiculous but I suppose I understand why we're doing it. We need to cover every base. We need to speak to everyone and try everything, but I feel like I'm just playing a part. I'm going through the instructed motions but what I really want to do is talk to every single person who was at that party and find out what happened. Someone must know what time Charlie left. Someone must know what happened to her. The police are doing this of course, they sent an officer to talk to Marcus almost as soon as I mentioned him. They made a list of Charlie's friends and anyone else I could remember being close by when I left. and they're questioning them all. They're probably talking to Luke Burrows too, since the party was at his house.

I have to keep reminding myself that they *are*

investigating. *We* might be walking the streets pretending that Charlie just got lost or wandered off somewhere, but the police are still investigating. They're trying to find out what happened to Charlie and they will.

They have to.

This can't happen again.

Two of the members of my search team are older women that I recognise but don't really know. They've formed a clique of two and they chat together on the walk from one house to another.

"I can't believe we're here doing another search party! Most people go their whole lives without being part of something like this, and this is my second time in a dozen years!" one tells the other in a low, excited voice.

"You've done this before?!"

"Oh yes! A little girl went missing here a few years ago!"

"Aw! Never! How awful!"

"So sad," the first agrees, her eyes flicking towards

me. I keep my face passive so that she doesn't know I can hear them but beneath the membrane of my skin my blood is boiling.

"How long ago? Did you find her?" the second woman asks excitedly.

"Must have been about ten years ago now, but no, we never did find the poor little thing."

Tears sting my eyes. Hot, bitter tears that I can't afford to indulge in right now. I don't need the reminder. I of all people know that search parties don't always work and people aren't always found. I don't need to be reminded of Rose. She's already present in every moment, every second, her skeleton moves within my limbs with every step. But right now I need to focus on Charlie.

"Such a tragedy. Do you think it's connected?"

I stop dead, the woman's words pounding in my ears.

*Do you think it's connected? Do you think it's connected? Do you think it's connected?*

The search team meanders on unconcerned and I turn on my heel, running back the way we came, my flip flops slapping against the tarmac.

I can just make out their final words, drifting to me on the breeze.

"Poor lamb, it was her sister that disappeared all those years ago, her name was Rose -"

And then I'm gone, they can say what they like, it doesn't matter.

*Do you think it's connected? Do you think it's connected? Do you think it's connected?*

The words are a drum beat, carrying me along.

*Do you think it's connected? Do you think it's connected? Do you think it's connected?*

They are the blood in my veins, the beat of my heart.

*Do you think it's connected? Do you think it's connected? Do you think it's connected?*

I can't believe I didn't see it before. I can't believe that it wasn't my very first thought. Upper Chalfont is tiny! We only have one primary school and one secondary school a bus ride away! We don't even have a McDonalds! We have houses with thatched roofs for Pete's sake! We are famous for exactly one thing. Rose.

Ten years ago, a little girl vanished while playing with her sister in the woods. That little girl was never found. My family's tragedy is our town's one claim to fame. What are the odds that ten years later another girl would go missing? Not only that, but right by or even *in* those same woods?! And those girls *knew* each other! Charlie and I were already best friends by that summer, she played with me and Rose all the time!

This can't be a coincidence.

Instinctively my feet are carrying me home but that isn't where I need to go. I keep on, past the house and on towards Charlie's. Flip-flops aren't made for running in and I can already feel a blister forming between my toes but I can't slow down. The command post for the search teams is set up on the edge of the woods, a street away from Charlie's house. I can see a police car, a fold-out table and a couple of officers including the one from Charlie's house this morning. She sees me coming and her eyes widen in surprise. I don't stop running until I'm right in front of her, panting and clutching my side.

"Penny Cooper? Are you alright, has something happened?" she asks me quickly.

"Do you think it's the same person?" I gasp without preamble.

"I'm sorry?" she asks, but her expression closes off somehow and I know that she understands.

"Is it the same person who took Rose?!" I demand.

"Is there any reason to suppose it might be?" she asks me.

I can't believe this! Is she being intentionally dense?! How could there *not* be?!

"Two girls in the same small town?! They even knew each other! What are the odds?!" I cry, surprised by how loud my voice is. My volume is usually capped at a demure low/medium.

"Penny, I understand that this must be hard for you,

but statistically it's very unlikely for one offender to abduct a ten year old and a seventeen year old. There's also been no similar instances in the intervening years."

Her voice is gentle but firm and I realise that she's been expecting this question - maybe not from me, but from someone. It was inevitable that at some point the connection would be made, but surely that's because the links are so obviously there!

"I understand that preferential offenders have a 'type' and don't often deviate from it, but they can if an easy target presents itself! Or maybe she was taken *because* she knew Rose! Like a- like a trophy! A reminder of Rose to help him relive the crime!" I suggest, my voice frenzied and my mind racing.

She looks at me blankly.

"I listen to a lot of true crime," I explain, my voice dropping back down to its usual register.

"That's... surprising," she mutters.

I wince.

"Penny, the chances are your friend is safe and

unharmed somewhere, sleeping after a night of drinking," she tells me brusquely.

"Then why haven't we found her? Why does no one know where she is? Why are we searching the woods?" I ask, firing off questions before she can form a reply.

"If something *has* happened then statistically it's most likely an accident. Charlie may have fallen or hurt herself. You said yourself that she was intoxicated. We're doing everything we can to find her, but at this time there's no reason to suspect that this is anything like what happened to your sister."

"We don't know what happened to my sister."

She doesn't have a response to that and I sag, my panic all burned away. I'm left with just my dread, hard, heavy and sharp edged now, resting deep in my gut. I can't explain how, even to myself, but I *know* that Rose and Charlie are connected. Unfortunately I also know that this police officer isn't going to agree with me.

I turn to go but she calls me back.

"Penny! If there's anything that you think of,

anything that could help, you can call me any time."

Her voice is unexpectedly kind and she's holding out a card to me so I step back to take it. I register fleetingly that I've never been given a business card before. It reads 'Detective Sergeant B. Walters' and has a couple of different contact numbers, a land-line and mobile. I wonder what the B stands for. Beryl? Belinda? Betsy maybe? I offer a small smile in thanks and keep the card clutched in my hand as I walk away, hoping against hope that I'll be able to use it.

"Penny!"

My mother's chalk white face greets me in the doorway when I arrive home. She flings herself down the front path and into my arms.

"I'm sorry mum," I murmur into her dark curls, stroking her back.

"See Paula, Penny's fine," Coop says in his calm, upbeat voice as he follows her out the front door and leads her gently back into the house. He headed straight home from Wendy's knowing that mum would be in panic as soon as she heard what had happened but he was too late - one of the other mums at football had broken the news after getting their call from the phone tree. Mum had run onto the pitch and dragged a very confused Oliver away with her. Olly explains all of this to me while I make him a distressingly sweet and milky tea and fetch him some biscuits. His matter of fact tone breaks my heart.

Coop puts mum to bed for a rest and then comes down to join us in the kitchen.

"Any news from the search groups?" he asks with a swift, cautious glance at Olly.

"Nothing," I tell him, before squishing my brother in a tight hug and sending him to the lounge with his drink and snacks.

"Good turn out though?" Coop asks once we hear the television switch on.

"A couple of hundred people," I tell him.

"I'm sure they'll find something soon then."

"I don't know. I mean, they didn't last time, did they?" I point out, trailing a design in the sugar crystals spilt across the counter.

"There's no reason to think this will be like last time."

The words grate on me, opening up tiny wounds that smart and sting.

Why would anyone assume that it won't be like last time? It feels just the same to me.

"You think it's connected?" Coop asks, reading my mind.

I half shrug and half nod, not sure how to explain my feeling of total conviction that the two disappearances are linked.

"I think it's probably natural to be afraid of that possibility, but the chances are, Charlie's just at a friend's house or something."

He's trying to be reassuring but he's feeding me the same lines as DS Walters and it's just making me feel more alone.

"Maybe," I mutter, taking my tea and leaving him in the kitchen with an anxious look on his face.

I retreat up to my room and immediately open my laptop and pull out my phone. I silenced it while I was at Wendy's but I can see I have more than a dozen missed calls and messages. Word has spread throughout our year-group that Charlie is missing and there's been a resulting flurry of contact. Sophie, Kate, Josh and Abed have all messaged me asking if I'm alright and a couple of similar messages have come though from numbers that I haven't got saved. A message from Marcus has a different feel to it. He's sent,

'Thanks for sicking the police on me.'

I feel a small stab of victory but it's short lived. I desperately want to be *doing* something. I can't just sit here waiting for some kind of development.

After a moments thought I respond to all of the messages I've received, including Marcus' saying the exact same thing.

'Do you know what time Charlie left the party?'

The last time I saw Charlie was at approximately ten thirty. It's just about two thirty now. That means that Charlie has been missing for sixteen hours. Sixteen hours gone. I need to start whittling down that time.

After another minute I send the message to the other numbers I have saved too.

I stare at my phone, willing it to chirp but it stares resolutely back at me. I open up a new document on my computer and title it 'timeline,' but I still have barely anything to add to it. I hear a chime and leap for my phone but it's just the doorbell downstairs. I turn my attention back to my laptop, typing in my ten thirty party-departure, but then there are footsteps on the stairs.

“Visitor for you Pen,” Coop tells me, pushing the door open to reveal Luke Burrows standing behind him.

“Luke,” I state unnecessarily, with more wariness than delight.

Undaunted, he smiles and steps into the room.

"Mind if I come in?" he asks, settling himself on the foot of my bed.

"Tea Luke?" Coop asks, ever the gracious host.

"He's not stayi-" I begin before Luke cheerfully cuts me off.

"Milk and two sugars please!"

I give Coop a slightly panicked look and Luke immediately adds,

"Food too if there is any, I plan to be here a while."

"I can probably rustle something up!" Coop tells him with a grin.

"But- but-" I stutter ineffectually.

"Make sure this door stays open though please," Coop tells us brightly, almost as though he has to deal with me having boys in my room all the time.

"Not an issue." I assure him grimly.

"Insulting," Luke claims with a wounded expression, his hand clutching his heart.

I stare darkly back at him, waiting for an explanation that doesn't appear to be forthcoming.

"What?" he asks me blankly.

"Why are you here?!" I demand.

He scratches his elbow, nervous suddenly, and directs his gaze at the floor.

"I heard about Charlie. The police have been searching my garden all morning."

"Did they find anything?!" I ask eagerly, leaning forward in my seat.

"Her coat was still there."

I lean back suddenly as my stomach drops.

"What does that mean?" I ask the ceiling.

"What does that mean?" I repeat the words and turn to my laptop, typing in the new detail though it brings me no closer to a solution.

"What's that?" Luke asks, shifting over slightly to get a better look at the screen.

I don't answer him. He wouldn't understand.

"You don't think she's just lost, do you."

It's not a question but I shake my head in response anyway. I don't think Charlie is just lost. I think she's taken.

"I saw her after that," Luke tells me, gesturing towards my sad, single entry timeline.

"You did?" I ask, my excitement mounting again.

"Only briefly, but when I got back from walking you home I went inside and she was in the hallway with Marcus Kain. They're like a couple, right? Or as much of a couple as anyone like Marcus ever is," he ends with a disdainful shrug and I feel a small thrill that I'm not the only one who declined to join the unofficial Marcus Kain fan-club.

"They were inside the house? What time was that?" I ask, swivelling back to face my computer.

"I'm not sure. It was right when I got back."

"Apparently I got home at ten thirty, so if we put your sighting at... ten forty to ten fifty five? To be safe?"

"That sounds about right, yeah," he confirms.

"Did it look like they were going somewhere? Or were they talking? Could you hear what they were saying?" I ask intently.

“I don't know, sorry. Really, I just noticed that she was drunk and hoped she wasn't going to throw up on the carpet.”

I give a sigh of frustration. I need more information! I need to go back and see exactly where Charlie was, what she did, who she spoke to! If only there was some way to-

I grab my phone and start typing, then throw a look at Luke.

“How many numbers do you have for people in our year? Or email addresses?”

“What? Why?”

“I have an idea.”

Between us we have twenty five numbers and email addresses, mostly from Luke. We contact every one, giving them my number and email address and asking to be sent every single photo taken the night of the party. I promise not to share any of them with the police which I hope will make people more inclined to cooperate. I want to message Marcus again but if he didn't respond earlier, he's definitely not going to reply when I ask him why he was in the house with Charlie at ten forty-five and ask him what happened next.

The brief burst of activity over, my excitement recedes and I'm left with just the dread and the pounding in my head.

*Do you think it's connected? Do you think it's connected? Do you think it's connected?*

Luke's phone buzzes.

"Sam says he just sent you some pictures. He says he didn't take many but he's sent what he has."

I check my emails and there it is, an email from Sam Turner, quickly followed by one from Jay Desai.

I open Sam's first. There are just seven images and I can't see Charlie in any of them but I save them to a new folder on my desktop just in case. Tim has a lot more pictures and Charlie is in the back of one of them, dancing by the fire. The time-stamp shows that it was nine thirty, it doesn't tell us anything new, but it's so strange to see her there, safe and real and present, her arms held aloft and a smile on her face. How can she be missing?

I save all the photos as I receive them but so far nothing jumps out as being helpful. Sophie, Kate, Josh and Abed all reply with vague and non-committal ideas of when they might last have seen Charlie, but no one has anything concrete. Kate thinks that there might have been a fight or argument at some point, but she's not entirely sure because she was taking part in some impromptu karaoke at the time. She can't even be completely sure that Charlie was involved in the fight, but she *thinks* that it was her.

"People will keep sending pictures. We'll see something soon," Luke tells me consolingly.

"That's assuming that something happened at the party. What if she left the party? What if she left alone because I wasn't there and something happened when there weren't any cameras around?"

He doesn't have an answer for that. I didn't expect him to really. I don't know why I even asked it, except that the panic was building up so high inside me that if I didn't siphon some off I thought I might choke on it.

Luke is spared from trying to respond by the sound of knocking on my open bedroom door.

"Alright! I have two teas and some bacon sandwiches!"

Coop is holding the food and drink triumphantly aloft and Luke hurries to help him, carefully taking the two mugs clutched in Coops hand and placing them on the desk before setting the plate piled with sandwiches tantalisingly within my reach.

"Have you eaten today?" Luke asks me pointedly.

"I'm not hungry."

I need to stay focused. I need to keep checking the pictures and find out what time Charlie left the party. I need to know the last time she was seen.

"Food is fuel Pen, you need to eat," Coop declares.

"Shall I take these cups down? You haven't even-"

He stops short and I turn to look. He's staring down at the two full cups of tea that he made for Charlie and me this morning, abandoned on my bedside table to go cold.

He takes them and leaves without another word.

I need to stay focused.

Luke, it turns out, has no such concerns. He consumes his first bacon sandwich with gusto before immediately starting on a second with a much more analytical air.

"This is really good you know. You should try one. Just the right amount of butter, good fluffy white bread, perfectly cooked bacon. It probably won't make Charlie any more missing than she already is."

His words are glib but his tone is so tender and his eyes are sad.

I roll my stinging eyes but I take a sandwich. It feels too present in my mouth, the act of chewing seeming to slow laboriously, but I do feel better for eating something.

I keep checking pictures but there's still nothing useful. It seems that most people took a lot of pictures at the start of the night and then fewer and fewer as the festivities wore on. The seventh set of pictures is when I finally hit gold.

Charlie.

She's in the background, just stepping through the back door from the house onto the patio. She looks pale, her made-up face and bare arms and legs are bright and ghostly in the darkness. The time-stamp of the picture is eleven fifteen. *Eleven fifteen!* Finally I have a new final sighting for the timeline! Charlie was still at the party at eleven fifteen and she was heading back outside from the house. Where had she been in that missing window of time with Marcus? Where was she after the eleven fifteen photo? Where did she go? There were so many questions, but still, I'd chipped away a little of that time-frame. Forty five more minutes accounted for, but it had taken forty five minutes to do. Charlie had still been missing sixteen hours. I feel like I'm fighting against a rip-tide. It's three fifteen now. Still light out.

"I want to go and help with the search," I say, gazing

out of my window.

“Yeah?”

“Yeah, I want to search the woods.”

# Chapter 6

I stand on the pavement staring into the trees. I'm teetering on the edge, between worlds, allowing myself this brief interlude to feel absolutely terrified before I do what needs to be done. I can feel Luke's curious gaze on me, waiting to see what happens next. He accepted it without question when I walked three streets away despite the woods being literally outside my window, pressed up against the house like a shadow.

"I haven't set foot in there in ten years," I tell him with a wry smile.

"Seriously?"

"Seriously."

"Not since the day your sister...?" he trails off, fearful to say the words in case they cause me to shatter.

He's still looking at me curiously and I give him a bright smile before stepping forward.

I've only told him part of the story. I've left out the nightmares that woke me screaming, drenched in sweat, calling my sister's name. I'm not going to tell him about the dreams that plagued me for years, of shadowed branches reaching down and snatching Rose from beside me. These woods have been the monster of my nightmares since I was eight years old. The funny thing is, now I'm here, they just look like trees.

I make my way swiftly, with Luke Burrows at my side the entire time. I'm still not really sure why he's here but I'm glad I'm not alone, so I don't ask.

"Are you alright?" he asks me after a few minutes.

"Yeah, I'm OK," I reassure him, still picking my way through the under-brush.

"Maybe that means you're stronger than you think."

"I think it just means that I'm not eight years old any more."

We carry on in silence, listening to the search team

calling Charlie's name through the trees.

I don't know what I was hoping to find. I suppose I never quite rid myself of the notion that the answers to everything were amongst these trees, but there's nothing here. I'm not going to stumble across some sign of Charlie, some clue left behind. The search for Rose went on for days in this small patch of trees. They went over the same area again and again and found nothing at all, no sign. I still think that Charlie might have been in here last night, but there's nothing here for me now.

"So, what are we doing here?" Luke asks politely as the light starts to fade.

I stop moving and slump against the nearest tree, turning to face it and press my forehead to the bark.

"I have no idea," I mutter, the confession burning my tongue.

"Is the tree hugging helping?" Luke asks me.

"Yes. Yes it is. I hear all the good investigators do it."

"No offence or anything, but can you cite your sources on that one?"

I give a snort of laughter before pushing myself back to an upright position.

"Probably Crime Junkie. They're very big on investigatory tactics."

"Crime Junkie?" he queries.

Damn.

"It's a true crime podcast," I admit.

"Wow. How very, unexpectedly morbid of you," he comments conversationally.

"I just - want to know what's out there," I tell him, deciding not to add that 'Morbid' is in fact the name of another fantastic Podcast.

"I stand by my commentary on that one. Bit dark."

"Yeah, probably best not to mention it to my mum."

"Ah no! Now what will we chat about?!" he cries in dismay.

I don't know how he's managing to make me laugh when my whole body is thrumming with panic but I'm grateful for it.

"I need to get home. I should check if more pictures

have been sent over."

"Alright, sounds like a plan, let's go," he agrees cheerfully.

"You're coming?" I ask in surprise.

"Of course!" he tells me with a wide grin.

I don't know what to make of him. I've never really even talked to Luke properly before. I've always done my best not to talk to anyone! So why is he suddenly here, helping me look for Charlie? He's smiling and cracking jokes so presumably he doesn't think something terrible has happened to her, but if that's true why is he here at all?

"Do you know Charlie? Are you friends?" I ask him, watching his face closely for a reaction.

"Not really, no. We've had some classes together over the years, chatted a bit, but I wouldn't really say we're friends," he tells me.

I narrow my eyes in suspicion and he raises his hands defensively.

"I'm sure she's very nice! I just don't really know

her!" he explains hastily.

He didn't understand my glare and I decide not to enlighten him.

I can't quite get my bearings so it's Luke that points the way back towards my house. We exit the trees out of sight of any of the windows and have to loop round to get to the front door.

"You don't have a key for the back?" Luke asks me.

"The back door is locked. It's been locked for years," I tell him.

"What?"

"It used to always be open, Rose and I were in and out of that door all day through the summers, but after she was gone my mum locked it up. The whole back porch is closed now. We had a new door put in off the dining room so we can get to the garden, and a huge great seven foot fence around that to 'keep us safe'."

I don't know why I'm using air quotes here. My mum *was* just trying to keep me safe with the fence. I was so relieved at the time to be cut off from the woods, and Olly has never known any different. Sealing off the porch felt like the right thing to do too. When I came back that day alone, I walked through that door without my sister and everything was different. The whole world had changed and none of us understood it yet. I couldn't set foot in there and neither could mum. We closed it off and sealed away that part of our lives.

It's funny, I only ever think about me and mum when I look back like this. Dad was still around then, but I guess he'd already started to disappear. Coop was the one who came round to help us put the fence up. He was soft and kind and made me laugh when the world had become a terrifying place. A little like Luke I guess, though that's where the resemblance ends.

No panicked cries greet my return which means that mum must still be lying down upstairs. I feel a small pinch of anxiety that this is going to cause another 'phase', but beside my fear for Charlie it barely even registers.

"Hello Pen, I'm afraid Olly and I have eaten but I did manage to save you some," Coop tells me as I enter.

"There's enough for you too, if you're staying," he adds when he sees Luke behind me.

"I am, thanks," Luke tells him confidently.

I roll my eyes but I don't argue. If I'm being totally honest I don't want to be alone. I lead the way to the kitchen and heat up the risotto on the stove-top, spooning it onto two plates. We carry them upstairs to my room and I go to my desk leaving Luke to sit on the bed again. I set my plate down beside my laptop and immediately turn my attention to the screen, waking it up with a click of the mouse.

"Eat something first," Luke instructs me through a mouthful of arborio rice.

I dutifully bolt down a couple of mouthfuls while my emails load. A dozen more people have sent across pictures and from the attached comments I suspect that I have Sophie to thank for that. Most people seem to be pretty certain that Charlie is crashing at a friend's house and revelling in the drama. I cast an eye at the window. The sky between the trees is getting darker every minute. Night is falling and as far as I've heard, Charlie still isn't home.

Wendy promised that she'd call me but I can't resist. I pull out my phone and dial their land-line.

"Hello?! Charlie?!"

Wendy's desperate, pleading voice cuts through me.

"No, sorry Wendy, it's just me. I just wanted to check in. She's not home yet?" I ask unnecessarily.

"Sorry Penny sweetheart, no. No she - they've been searching but -" she can't get the words out and I don't know what to say to help her.

"Have the police said anything?" I ask.

"No, they're looking though. I'm sure they'll find her."

"I'm sure they will."

We fall silent, our platitudes hanging weightless and insubstantial before I hang up.

"Nothing?" Luke asks me.

"Nothing."

There's something in his face that I can't identify.

"What?" I ask anxiously.

"I just - I kind of thought that maybe she was just fine, y'know? Maybe she was just at someone's house. But -"

He trails off, he too looking out the widow at the fading day.

Seven pm. Charlie has been missing for nineteen hours and forty-five minutes.

"I'm going to keep checking photos."

I stare intently at the screen, searching everywhere for some trace of my friend. I find her in a few more pictures, in the background, her face glued to Marcus' for the most part. Again, they're all from earlier in the evening, but then finally, I strike gold.

"She's here!"

Luke scoots over to peer at the screen over my shoulder.

"She bloody is!"

Charlie isn't just in the background here, she's centre stage and it's clear why. Someone took a photo of Charlie and Marcus mid-argument, her face contorted with misery and anger, his aloof and disdainful. I long to reach through the screen and smack that look off of his face. I scroll back to the previous image and the one before that and my blood starts to boil. I'd mentally discarded them without considering. I couldn't find any trace of curly blonde hair or black sequins, so I hadn't really looked at what was happening, but right there in the middle of the garden Marcus Kain was kissing Claire Netherhall. He had arms wrapped around her, one hand on her bum and his face pressed so firmly against hers that I bet she could taste Charlie on his tongue.

"That bastard!" I shout, standing up.

I want to run, to move, to track down Marcus Kain and give him a good kicking.

Luke gives a low whistle, still surveying the picture.

I click back to the photo of Marcus and Charlie

fighting. It's timestamped just two minutes after the previous shot. She must have witnessed the kiss. I look again and my heart stutters. Eleven forty.

Eleven forty!

I hastily open my timeline document and add in the new entry, my fingers barely able to keep up with my thoughts.

Charlie was clearly upset and this must have been the 'drama' that Marcus was referring to this morning. But what did it mean? I go back to the pictures and scroll to the next one. This shows Marcus turning to his friends, a laugh breaking out across his face. I scan the darkness around him. I can just make out Charlie walking away, her back to the camera, the light of the fire picking out the closest edge of her arm and leg. She's walking towards the back of the garden.

"What's back there?" I ask Luke, pointing at the screen.

"Not much. Shrubbery, walls around some raised flower-beds. Some people were sat around there talking at the party I think."

"Can we go there now?" I ask quickly, getting back to my feet.

"It's getting dark. We should wait until tomorrow when you can actually see the garden. Besides, the police already searched the whole place for clues," he reminds me.

I know he's right but I also can't bear the thought of waiting hours longer before making another move. He must be able to read this in my face because he gently but firmly guides me back into my seat.

"Eat your cold risotto and keep checking pictures. You can look at my garden tomorrow," he tells me.

"And talk to Marcus Kain," I add in a voice that surprises me with its sharpness.

"You want to talk to Marcus?" he asks me uncertainly.

"I definitely do."

"You're not going to hurt him are you?"

"That depends very much on what he says."

I'm not even sure whether I'm kidding. I've spent a decade trying to be as small and quiet and invisible as possible but right now I want to be loud and fierce and screaming. I don't know where Charlie is but I know that Marcus hurt her and I want to make him feel a little of that hurt.

"You're a very surprising person," Luke tells me with a small smile.

I can't exactly disagree, I'm surprised myself.

"Who sent those pictures?" he asks.

It's a good question. I navigate back to the original email and check.

"Louise Chambers."

"Of course. She's such a gossip!" he comments, rolling his eyes.

"I need to talk to her."

I reply to her email, asking for her number, and I'm gratified when she responds almost immediately.

"She says she'll talk to me!" I exclaim, already typing the number into my phone.

"Louise Chambers?!"

"Hiya Penny!"

"Louise, thank you for the pictures you sent, I was wondering if you could talk to me about them," I gabble in a rush.

"Yeah sure! It's crazy, right?!" she asks, her tone more excited than concerned.

"You've heard about Charlie?" I check.

"Of course! So crazy! Do you think she's run off because of Marcus?" Louise asks me eagerly.

I hesitate for a moment. I don't think that Charlie's run off at all, but Louise's tone reminds me of the reporters who used to haunt our street and it awakens a deep instinct not to share.

"Did you hear much of their argument?" I ask instead.

"Oh tons!"

"It was about Claire Netherhall?" I probe.

"About *the kiss*!"

She lends the words the sort of emphasis that I'd

imagine giving a natural disaster or similar landmark event.

"What did they say?" I ask, trying not to let the frustration creep into my voice.

"Well, she was livid, obviously. She was shouting about him *betraying* her and he was all 'we're not a couple' and she was crying a lot then," Louise recounts happily.

"What else?"

"Well, she said something about, 'what about what just happened?' and he was like, '*nothing* happened!' in a really significant way," she tells me.

"What did that mean?" I ask her, confused.

"No idea. Apart from that there was just a lot of the same really. You know the usual stuff. She was saying how awful and unfair he was and he was saying that she was being dramatic and she wasn't worth the effort. Typical girl being a drama queen and guy being an ass."

"Then what happened?" I ask quickly.

"Nothing, he laughed at her and she walked away."

"He laughed? About what?" I ask.

Marcus doesn't seem to take anything seriously but I still don't see what he could find to laugh about mid-argument.

"Ummm... gosh, it's hard to remember. I think... I think she said something about not needing him anyway. Maybe she said something about having someone else who cares about her. And Marcus just laughed his ass off and she ran off."

"She said she had someone else? Did she say who?"

"I don't think she gave a name, but if she did I didn't hear it. Isn't she your best friend? Shouldn't you know?" Louise asks in surprise.

It's a good question.

"Where did she go?" I press on.

"Just away. Further into the garden I guess." Louise tells me, but I can tell that she's losing interest now that I've proven to be so woefully short on new information.

"Did you see her again at all?" I ask desperately.

"Nope, sorry. That was it. I didn't see Charlie or

Marcus again really. I was inside a lot after that, it was getting cold."

I hang up and sit with my phone clutched in my hand.

"So, what did she tell you?" Luke asks me, his eyes bright with interest.

I relay the conversation as accurately as I can and then while it's still fresh I write it all down in yet another document on my PC.

"Do you think she was telling the truth?" he asks when I'm done.

"Louise?"

"No, Charlie. Do you think she really has someone else she's dating or was she just saying that because of Marcus getting with Claire? It's the sort of bluster that someone would say."

I take my time thinking it through. He has a point but -

"No. No, I think there really was someone. For a while I've been feeling like Charlie's keeping something from me, and then there's the clothes," I tell him.

"Clothes?"

"Yeah, the clothes that Charlie was wearing to the party. Her mum didn't buy them for her, they couldn't afford to get anything new right now. Her mum didn't know where they came from and Charlie was weird about it when I asked too, like it was a secret. Someone must have bought her the clothes or at least given her the money for them," I explain.

"Clothes like that... if someone bought them for her that's pretty... intimate. It must have been a boyfriend, right?"

"Unless they just gave her the money and she bought the clothes herself," I point out.

"But who would be giving Charlie money and why?"

I chew my lip nervously. I have a churning feeling in my gut that rests uneasily against all the existing fears settled there. Charlie's struggled with hers and her mum's financial situation for basically as long as she's been aware of it. As a single parent Wendy's done her best but she's a shop assistant at the garden centre. It isn't very well paid and they've struggled a lot over the years. More and more recently, Charlie has seemed frustrated by the limitations of her life. I was so worried about being one of those limitations that maybe I didn't pay enough attention to the others.

What trouble might Charlie get into with a financial incentive involved?

"I'm starting to think that Charlie had a lot of secrets."

Luke doesn't leave until Coop stands on the landing coughing significantly and even then he seems reluctant. We'll see how keen he is to be involved when I show up at his house at the crack of dawn tomorrow morning to search his garden.

I change into my pyjamas but aside from that not much changes for me. I remain at my desk going though every single photo that I'm sent, scouring them for any sign of Charlie. I need more pictures but I don't know how to get them. It feels like most people agree with Louise and think that if Charlie really is missing, it's by choice. I know there must be more photos out there but -

I'm an idiot. I open up a new tab and go to Facebook.

Jackpot.

Well, maybe not jackpot precisely, but there are definitely photos here that I haven't seen. Our first year in secondary school, all the parents were hauled in for a seminar on 'Online safety,' which essentially served to stunt everyone's online development. Not for us the TikTok accounts and Instagram profiles. Our entire school is stuck in the early two-thousands, with Facebook pages, Facebook groups and little else. As far as I can tell it's just us and people in their sixties complaining about each other and swapping gardening tips but for now it serves my purpose. It looks like half the people from the party have uploaded photos of that night. I scan through them and find three more sightings of Charlie. One is a smiling shot of her and Marcus, cuddled up together on the same garden chair. To my eyes he looks smug and conceited but Charlie is smiling broadly, her eyes sparkling and happiness written all over her face. I think back to the photos of the argument. They came so far so fast. The next sighting is just the flash of Charlie dancing in the background. I don't know what time it was taken so I message the person who posted it, asking to be sent the original. The last picture I find takes my breath away. It must have been from near the beginning because I'm in it too. Alex Hall is beside me pouring a drink into a plastic cup and Charlie is on my other side, her face turned towards the camera as she speaks to someone behind it. The flames are reflecting in our eyes and casting an orange light over our skin. The firelight is blanketing us in a warm glow, turning my copper hair to dark red. I know it's mad, I really do, but just for a moment when I first see it,

I think it's Rose.

# Chapter 7

I keep scrolling through pictures, navigating from one person's Facebook page to another. Some of them are starting to mention Charlie directly. A couple of her friends from netball have posted on their timelines, 'Charlie Hople, you're in my thoughts', followed by a variety of heart emojis. I'm not sure why but it makes me feel a little like I can't breathe.

It does however, give me an idea.

I have always been, at best, a passive Facebook user. I basically never post anything and I'm rarely ever tagged. I have a page but mainly to stop Charlie complaining about my social deficiency. Despite this, I am aware that other people do use Facebook in a more active way and in fact for some people it's their primary means of communication. Perhaps I can use that to my advantage. It takes me an embarrassingly long time and a staggering number of Youtube tutorial videos, but eventually I manage to make a new Facebook page titled 'Have you seen Charlie Hople?'

I'm not sure if this is really something that I'm allowed to do, but I figure that if the police have a problem with it I can just take it down. Maybe. I might need some help.

I send invites to everyone I can think of and hope that it balloons from there, but I'm still waiting, staring at the blank page when I finally fall asleep, slumped over onto my desk.

"Penny?"

I start awake, my eyes instantly wide and my heart racing. I look around wildly but it's just Olly, hovering uncertainly in my doorway. At some point someone, probably Coop, seems to have draped my duvet over me but I'm still sat at my desk. I sit upright and shuffle slightly to try and return some feeling to my bum.

"Olly?" I ask, looking at him through a lingering fog of sleep.

"I brought you some pop-tarts," he tells me, holding a plate aloft with a small, shy smile.

I beam at him and hold my arms out wide, the corners of the duvet clutched in my hands. He grins, puts the plate on the bed and rushes forwards into my embrace. I wrap him up completely in the hug, practically lifting his small form off he floor.

"Thank you Olly Wally," I murmur into his hair.

"Are you alright?" he asks me when I let him go.

He sounds anxious and I wish that I could tell him everything's fine. He wasn't alive when Rose disappeared but it's been an ever present shadow over his whole life. Sometimes longer, sometimes shorter, but always there.

"I'm worried about Charlie," I tell him honestly.

"Why?" he asks me, his eyes wide.

"We don't know where she is."

He's scared and I almost wish that I hadn't said

anything, though it's not like we could keep it from him indefinitely. I reach up and cup his chubby face in my hands, tilting it up to look at me.

"But we're looking for her. And we're going to find her," I tell him firmly.

"Not like Rose," he whispers so quietly that I can barely hear him even though I'm just inches away.

"No, not like Rose."

I fold him in another hug and tickle him until he squeals with glee.

"Well that's a lovely sound to start the day to!"

I look up in surprise as mum enters with a mug of tea and sets it down on the desk for me.

"Mum!"

I'd expected her to be staying in bed again today. Or for the next month possibly.

"Morning, love. I'm going to go round and sit with Wendy for a bit this morning. Do you want to come with me?"

"I- Uh-"

I'm so shocked I can barely get any words out at all. I can't believe that mum is in one piece, let alone ready to go and help hold Wendy together. I can't go with her though.

"I was going to meet with Sophie actually. We're both really worried and we thought it would help to be together," I tell her, feeling an uncomfortable pinch at the lie.

It can't be helped. If I told mum that I was going to go and search Luke's garden and then start accosting classmates and trying to track down Charlie, she would put a stop to it instantly.

"That's a good idea. It's good to rally together. Make sure you have your phone with you at all times though and please check in with me regularly."

There's a sudden flash of expression across her face, like an image just played behind her eyes that I couldn't see. She gets a glazed look and I reach out for her hand giving it a quick squeeze.

"I'll check in every hour."

I eat my pop-tarts while they're still warm and drink my tea while I go though my emails looking for new pictures. Next I check the Facebook page and I'm pleased to see that it's getting good traction. There are already three hundred followers which means that it's gone way beyond the numbers of our school year. A few people have posted pictures here from the party. It's mostly posed pictures of Charlie with friends, selfies of her with other girls from netball or guys from Marcus' group of friends. They look like they're from quite early in the evening and none of them have timestamps attached anyway, they just show the time they were posted. The interesting thing is the comments. It seems like half our year group has something to say about Charlie being missing, ranging from 'this must be awful for her mum, I hope she's home soon' to 'so much drama, this is just like her'.

A few of the girls have posted heartfelt pleas to Charlie to come home but mostly it's turned into a forum of speculation. The fight with Marcus is discussed in detail though no one seems to be able to add much more than Tina already told me. I'm about to leave it when something catches my eye. There's a post from an anonymous account.

There's no picture and the only name is NoMatter. I click on the profile but it's blank, with no pictures and no posts. I go back to the comment and read it again.

'Maybe she got what she deserves.'

I get dressed and ready for the day quickly before heading out. I feel as though I should be packing a torch and compass or maybe some sort of survival gear, but all I have is my phone. Same thing I suppose. It's already nine twenty, later than I had planned to set out, but if I'd left earlier than this mum would have been suspicious.

Charlie has been missing for thirty three hours and forty minutes. By the time I reach Luke's house it's thirty three hours fifty-two and that's only because I hurried.

Time isn't on my side.

The absence of loud, pounding music makes the air feel cool and still. I'm unusually aware of being able to hear birds singing and someone's dog barking a few streets away. I detest walking up to people's houses and knocking on the door or ringing the bell. It feels like a horrifying intrusion that must surely open me up to all sorts of anger and abuse. Even at Charlie's house, if she isn't absolutely completely aware that I am about to arrive, I prefer to call her and stand outside on the pavement waiting for her to come and collect me. No doubt I'd be calling Luke now if I hadn't neglected to get his number yesterday. Maybe I should make another document, detailing all the contact numbers and email addresses I get hold of while I'm reaching out to people about Charlie. That way I'd have his and any others that he has that I don't.

For the party we entered through the garden but the gate is locked from the inside now. I don't think I could have gone in that way anyway though. Ringing doorbells might be awkward but I suspect it's not a patch on being found creeping around someone's garden without permission. Instead I approach the door, a beautiful big wooden construction with stained glass panels. In lieu of a doorbell I knock and wait.

After a minute a wobbly, distorted figure approaches, becoming taller and clearer the closer they get. The door opens and my heart sinks when I see that it isn't Luke, it's his dad Richard.

"Penny! How nice to see you! Has there been any word on your friend yet?"

He smiles kindly at me but the question still sets me on edge.

"No, not yet. Is Luke here?" I ask in my smallest, most Pennyish voice.

"He is, one moment. LUKE!" he turns and calls back into the house before returning his attention to me.

"The police were here yesterday of course. It makes me wish that we'd been around for that party, but we thought that you'd all prefer it if we made ourselves scarce and we had plans anyway so..."

He trails off and I wonder if he wants me to tell him that it isn't his fault Charlie is missing. It seems unlikely that he's looking for reassurance from a seventeen year old, but I'm still half-heartedly considering it when Luke comes down the stairs, increasing his pace when he sees me.

"Penny!" he almost smiles.

"You said I could see your garden."

I shoot the words out in my usual semi-whisper and keep my eyes lowered.

"Of course, yeah, come in."

I slip past Luke's dad and his puzzled expression as unobtrusively as I can and follow Luke through the house. It doesn't seem particularly worse for wear after the party, or the visit from the police yesterday.

"Did the police search your house yesterday?" I ask Luke.

"They looked around a bit and asked if there was anything left from the party. There was a whole bunch of stuff. There were coats and jackets and even some trainers. They found Charlie's coat and took that away with them," he explains.

"So they didn't do a *proper* search?" I press.

"What do you want them to be looking for?" he asks me, raising his eyebrows.

It's a good question.

The garden looks like a whole different world in the light of day. I stop as soon as we step outside and try to get my bearings. I can see where the firepit was positioned and after a minute I recognise where the table tennis table was set up. From there it's not too hard, I just bring up the pictures on my phone and move around, mapping out the events in my head.

"This is where Charlie and Marcus were standing when they argued, and then she walked this way."

It's a bit vague, at least a third of the garden is 'this way' but at least it's a start. Just as Luke said, there are raised beds with low walls around them where I vaguely recall people sitting and talking. I wish now that I'd been paying more attention but my focus had been on Alex Hall. He'd seemed so important at the time. Charlie had walked towards those raised beds and low walls- had she been heading to someone in particular? She was upset, had she been going to talk to a friend? Or just looking to get a minute alone? When I'd argued with Alex I'd basically run straight out of there, but Charlie wasn't like me, she doesn't run from confrontation.

Luke watches my wanderings with a look of interest.

"Any more pictures?" he asks.

"Nothing from after eleven forty still."

"I saw the Facebook page, that was a good idea," he comments.

I nod slightly.

"What happened?" he asks.

"That's the whole question isn't it," I murmur.

"No, I mean what happened to you?"

I look up quickly. What on earth does that mean?!

He flushes slightly.

"I don't mean - I mean, what happened to you since

yesterday," he explains, running his hand through his hair and blushing furiously.

"Nothing," I tell him, still not sure how to take his words.

"You've changed again. You're not talking, and when you do it's like you don't actually want anyone to hear you,"

I sigh but I don't say anything. I'm a quiet person, there's nothing wrong with that.

"There's nothing here," I say eventually, looking round at the garden in disappointment.

"Sorry."

"I need to get going," I tell him, tucking my phone back into my pocket.

"You going home? Do you want me to walk you?" he asks.

"No, I need to figure out where Marcus lives."

"What?"

"Marcus Kain, I need to go and see him," I repeat.

"You're going to just show up at his house?" he asks

me, his expression inscrutable.

"He stopped responding to my messages or answering the phone." I tell him by way of explanation.

Luke just stares at me like he's not sure whether or not I'm going mad, but then -

"I know where he lives."

It turns out that Marcus and Luke used to be friends, back when they were in primary school. It was years ago but still, I'm surprised.

Marcus doesn't live in Upper Chalfont, he's actually one tiny, inconsequential town to the West, so I'm relieved when Luke offers to drive me. We borrow his dad's car, a big mud-stained Landrover that practically screams 'country vehicle'.

"So what do you plan to talk to Marcus Kain about?" Luke asks me.

"Where he and Charlie went inside your house, what they said in the argument and where Charlie went after that," I tell him promptly.

"Huh."

"What?"

"I guess maybe you haven't changed so much after all."

I don't know why this bothers me. Luke Burrows doesn't know the first thing about me, he has no right to be analysing my behaviour and commenting on me from one day to the next. Yesterday was a high pressure situation. So is today for that matter! I could do without the critique.

"I don't *change*," I grumble, instantly annoyed by how sulky my voice sounds.

"You absolutely do. One day you're calling people up out the blue and hunting through the woods and cracking jokes, and then the next you're this mouse, barely talking. But now, we're heading to Marcus Kain's house so that you can ask him a whole bunch of questions that he absolutely is *not* going to want to answer."

"Look, I'm a quiet person. I'm shy. After everything I've been though it's perfectly understandable." I'm repeating almost word for word exactly what my mum has told every teacher about me since I was eight years old.

"Yeah, except, I'm pretty sure that you're not."

I turn to face out the window, not deigning to respond. Luke Burrows is an idiot.

Marcus Kain's house isn't what I would have expected at all. If I'd given it much thought, I would have been anticipating a tacky mansion with faux columns. His ego and sense of entitlement had me looking for a pool or, at the very least, a water feature. Instead, we pull up outside of a semi detached two story brick house that looks just like all the others in the street.

"Here?!" I ask in surprise.

"I know, it looks so normal doesn't it?" Luke comments with a grin.

"You'd certainly never know that an egomaniacal budding sociopath lives here."

To my relief, Luke rings the doorbell and after just a

few seconds a sweetly smiling blonde woman answers the door. She looks between us and I fix a polite smile on my face but her gaze settles on Luke.

"Luke Burrows! It is so lovely to see you! I had no idea that you and Marcus were spending time together again! That is *such* lovely news!" she enthuses, ushering us inside.

Luke smiles a little nervously back at her and I'm worried that he might say something stupid and get us sent straight back out so I intervene.

"Is Marcus in?" I ask quickly.

"Yes, yes, he is..." Mrs Kain tells me, her words trailing off and her face paling as she recognises me. It's a phenomenon that I've grown used to over the years but right now I don't have time for it. Charlie doesn't have time.

"Yes, I'm Penny. Penny Cooper, formerly Penny Owens. Is Marcus' room this way?"

My tone is brusque and business-like and I see Luke grinning out of the corner of my eye.

All she can do is nod and gesture helplessly as I pass her by. I'm up the stairs and on the landing before she can muster another word but that's alright, the element of surprise might work in my favour. I try a couple of doors, finding a very flowery master bedroom and a bathroom before I discover Marcus.

Now it makes sense. This room, this is Marcus Kain. There's a flat screen TV taking up half of one wall and every kind of gadget I can think of. I see at least two different games consoles, their controllers littered around the room.

Marcus is sprawled on his bed, his face fixed on the TV screen, controller in hand and a headset allowing him to verbally abuse whoever he's currently playing Fifa with over the Wifi. He looks up as we enter and it might be my imagination but he doesn't exactly look thrilled to see us.

"Morning Marcus," I chirp happily, "You stopped responding to my messages."

"Yeah, there was a reason for that," he grunts,

pausing the game and swivelling to face us.

"Well this doesn't look how I remember it," Luke mutters, gazing around the room in awe.

"Yeah, this stuff is all from my dad," Marcus explains with a broad smile.

"From your dad?" Luke asks, confused.

"Yeah. He and mum split a few years ago but he's minted and he makes sure I get all the best stuff."

His tone is totally blasé and I can't help but wonder what it would be like to feel so unemotional about my parents' divorce. He really seems to feel that he's got a great deal here. Maybe because his father is still there, involved, buying him presents whereas mine is... absent.

"Good for you. Have you heard from Charlie at all?" I fire out in clipped tones.

He sighs and slumps back onto his pillows again.

"I told you, I'm not getting involved in her drama."

"Drama?! She's missing!" I cry, my anger bubbling to the surface with alarming speed.

"Psht! Sure."

He picks up his controller again as though the conversation is over and I stalk towards him and snatch it out of his hands.

He sits back up, irate, but Luke cuts in.

“Maybe just answer Penny's questions and then we can get out of your hair, yeah?” he suggests calmly.

As though reminded of it's existence, Marcus runs his hand through his dirty blonde hair, pushing it back off of his face as though he's in a shampoo commercial. I grip the controller so tight that I'm surprised it doesn't break.

“What are you then? Her bodyguard?” he asks, looking Luke up and down. Luke is fairly tall and he's grown out of his skinny phase but his lean form looks insubstantial next to Marcus Kain's bulk.

“I'm her beautiful assistant,” Luke tells him, deadpan.

Marcus snorts but I see the calculations going on behind the eyes. He knows it's the easiest way to get rid of us.

"Sure, whatever," he agrees, rolling his eyes.

"You and Charlie went into the house for almost half an hour during the party. Where did you go?" I ask, keen to make the most of his sudden compliance.

"We just wanted a bit of privacy," he tells me with a smirk.

"What?"

The look on his face makes me feel sick.

Charlie, what on earth were you thinking?!

"You know, we wanted some time alone," he presses on, seeing my face flood with colour.

"No," I say, more in repulsion than because I actually don't believe him, but I see a flicker of annoyance in his eyes and I jump on it.

"No."

I say it louder and more clearly this time.

"Well, maybe we didn't actually *do* anything, but only because your friend is a tease! Getting all dressed up, and she's all over me, but then I find us a quiet little spot downstairs with the coats and suddenly she's a prude."

He practically spits the words and I feel an itch running though my limbs. I want to hit him. I want to really, really hurt him. I didn't know that I could feel angry like this! Charlie always wants me to socialise more, but *this* is what I'm missing?!

"In with the coats?" Luke asks blankly, "You mean the utility room with the washer and drier and stuff?"

"Romantic," I say, my lip curled into a sneer.

Marcus brushes this off like it's nothing, but I can imagine Charlie there with Marcus Kain, in the utility room with the coats, deciding not to give up her first time to this entitled creep and I feel immeasurably proud of her and unutterably sad.

"So is that why you made out with Claire Netherhall?" I ask, every word dripping with disdain.

"Claire's hot," Marcus tells us with a shrug.

I clench my hands, my blood temperature increasing another degree.

"But you were with Charlie!"

"I never said she was my girlfriend or anything, we weren't exclusive, we were just having fun," he tells me, like he's explaining something very obvious to someone very simple.

I breathe deeply, desperately trying to stay calm.

"But Charlie was upset?" I ask shortly.

"Yeah I guess. She shouted and stuff, but that doesn't make it my fault that she's run off. She just wants the attention."

I start to move forward. I'm not even sure what I'm going to do but Luke's hand on my arm stops me.

"Tell me more about the argument," I hiss, my voice low.

Totally oblivious to my rage, Marcus laughs.

"She was going mental! All this stuff about betrayal and heartbreak, like we weren't just drunk and making out! And then she starts telling me how she doesn't need me anyway! How she has someone else! Yeah right! If she had someone else she wouldn't be standing there crying at me, would she!"

"Did she say anything about who he was?" I ask, almost pleading.

Marcus gives me a surprised look.

"She's actually seeing someone else?! What are you doing talking to me then?! She must be with him!"

I press my hands to my forehead, trying to smooth out my tangled thoughts.

"I don't *know* that she's seeing someone. There's just some things that she said that made me think that she might be... but I don't know."

"That slut," Marcus declares, shaking his head dismissively.

"*You* made out with *Claire*!" I'm not sure if I'm calling Marcus a slut here, or Claire, but to be honest I'm happy to cover all bases.

"So?" Marcus asks, nonplussed.

"Bit of a double standard there, mate," Luke explains, earning himself another look of incomprehension from Marcus.

"Did Charlie say anything else relevant?" I ask,

returning to the task at hand.

"Nope."

I can see he's getting bored now. Soon we're going to lose him entirely.

"Where did she go afterwards then?" I try.

"I told you! I don't know where she's run off to!" he barks in annoyance.

"No, after the fight, where did she go straight after that? What time did she leave the party?" I press.

"No idea. I barely saw her after that. I guess maybe I saw her get another drink a bit later, but - I – don't – know – what – she – did."

He spits the words out and sits back.

"Any idea what time you saw her get a drink?" I ask hopefully.

He stares back at me, unmoving.

"Was she with anyone?" I ask.

"Yeah. Yeah I think she was. Sarah H maybe," he tells me with a small shrug.

Sarah H. or Sarah Hargreaves, is a friend of

Charlie's but unfortunately she and I have never gotten along. Charlie and Sarah have sat together in classes for years since their last names fall next to each other in alphabetical order, but Sarah thinks I'm 'weird'. She's never done anything to hide this belief and I've never done anything to change it. We're not close.

"Thanks," I tell Marcus vaguely, heading for the door.

"When they find her, you can tell that attention seeking bitch to stay away from me," he states, incapable of letting someone else have the last word.

"When we find her I'll remind her that you're bottom-feeding scum and she'd be better off without you."

I didn't mean to say it. I'm not usually prone to outbursts of temper, I'm more of a 'keep your head down and try not to get noticed' person, but hearing Marcus Kain with his IQ of twelve and even less empathy talk trash about Charlie... well. I guess it pushed me over the edge. I barely take another step however, before Marcus pushes back.

In a split second he slams into me, his arm across my throat and my head bouncing off the wall behind me as he pushes me up against it. Hard.

I've thought a lot about how weak I am. How vulnerable. I've considered at length how easy it would be for someone to overpower me, to hold my arms, to pin me down. That might sound crazy, but it's been drilled into me for the last decade. This, however is my first ever practical experience of it. I freeze. Just for a moment, but I do. I have no idea where to go from here and my body just stops. But then Luke is in the fray, forcing his way between us, his face millimetres from Marcus' and his grey eyes flashing black. He drives Marcus backwards until he hits the bed and topples onto it. Then he leans forward, looking intently into Marcus' face.

"Not ever. You don't touch her."

He hisses the words with an intensity that makes me shiver even from across the room.

Without Marcus' arm pressed against me, I've slid down to a crouch, slumped against the wall, but Luke turns from Marcus without a second glance and strides over to me, lifting me gently to my feet and leading me from the room. We don't speak until we're back in the car and I've managed to take a few breaths without trembling. It all happened so quickly that I can't wrap my head around it but one thing is certain-

"You're one heck of a beautiful assistant."

"Why thank you." he replies, raising one eyebrow suggestively.

I blush furiously but I manage to choke out a shaky laugh.

"Are you alright?" he asks me, suddenly serious.

"I'm fine, I just - I froze up."

I drop my gaze, feeling my eyes sting.

"That's not an unreasonable reaction," he points out.

"Not exactly heroic though."

"Well how about I do the heroic bits while you do all the thinking and planning and talking and figuring stuff out?" he suggests brightly.

"Alright, you be the hero, I'll be the thinker," I agree.

"Brains and brawn!" he declares, dramatically flexing an arm that I can't help but notice is actually more impressive than I'd assumed.

He follows my rather intense gaze and a small smile curves his mouth. My face darkens to a deep russet but before he can comment a yellow beetle pulls up in front of us.

I know that car.

I leap out, almost tripping over my own feet in my haste.

"Claire! Claire!" I call out, flagging her down before she's even finished the careful adjustment of her outfit.

She looks up at me slowly, her eyes cold.

"Penny Cooper. Why are you talking to me?"

Her words drip venom but I don't care.

"Did you see Charlie at the party?" I ask quickly.

Claire rolls her eyes and sculpts her face into a perfect expression of disgust.

"*Everyone* saw her. Making a *fool* of herself."

"What do you mean?"

"I mean that girls like that don't get with guys like Marcus," she says in frustration, as though she's tired of having to explain this to people.

"But she was though," I point out.

"Only because he's so competitive! Marcus is ambitious! He's going to make something of himself!"

I'm not sure we're talking about the same person now and I don't really see how competitiveness explains his relationship with Charlie.

"Marcus is a moron with a temper," I tell her flatly.

"Marcus was with me, all night. And your friend is a skank and an attention seeker."

She turns on the spot and strides away, practically skipping up Marcus' driveway.

"Well isn't she an absolute delight?" Luke remarks when I climb back into the passenger seat, stunned.

I don't respond, I just watch her ring the doorbell,

checking her reflection in a small compact mirror.

"Penny? What now?" Luke asks me.

"What if Marcus hurt Charlie?" I ask in a small voice.

Luke follows my gaze and we both watch as the door opens and Claire Netherhall steps inside.

# Chapter 8

There's nothing I can do right now, short of bursting into the house and dragging an unwilling Claire out with me, and I doubt that would go down well. Instead I pull out my phone and write down every detail of my conversations with both Marcus and Claire, as close to word-for-word as I can remember.

"Did you find out something useful?" Luke asks curiously.

"I don't know yet. I don't think so, but it's best to have all the details just in case," I tell him.

In all honesty, it seems like they told me a whole bunch of nothing but I really don't want to admit that. The one promising detail seems to be that Charlie was with Sarah H after her fight with Marcus. He might have been talking at random, just trying to get rid of me, but Charlie and Sarah *are* friends so its definitely worth following up on.

"Can you drive me to Sarah H.'s house please?" I ask.

I'm not sure how long he's going to hang around today, but I'll definitely make the most of his chauffeur services while I have them.

He's about to start the car when my phone rings and, seeing who it is, I reach out a hand to stop him. It feels as though my heart is clawing its way out of my chest and my breath can barely wheeze past it but I answer the call.

"Hello, Penny? This is DS Walters. Could you come in to the station and have a word please?"

The police station doesn't look how I remember. It's more like a doctor's surgery, with its soothing pale blue walls and generic art prints. The overall effect is clinical, non-threatening and utterly terrifying. Is there news?

Have they found something?

I'm guided along a corridor, my heart in my throat, until we reach a room that resembles a small dentist waiting room, with low, cushioned chairs with metal frames. There's a small coffee and drinks setup in one corner and I wonder vaguely if this is some sort of staff room, but then my eyes fall on Coop and my thin veneer of strength cracks. I fall into his arms and I'm eight years old again, tears streaming down my face, so much like my sister's.

"Coop! What's happened?! Have they found her?" I choke out between sobs.

"No, no, nothing yet, they just have some questions. I asked your mother if I could be the one to come with you," he tells me soothingly, pretending as though mum could have set foot in this place.

"Is she still with Wendy?" I ask, comfortably perpetuating the charade.

"No, she's home with Olly now that I'm here with you."

Makes sense.

DS Walters knocks lightly on the open door and enters as I hastily dry my face.

"Sorry Penny, I didn't mean to worry you," she tells me sympathetically.

"That's alright, I was already worried," I tell her with a faint, wry smile.

"I take it you haven't heard from Charlie then?" she asks me lightly, gesturing for us to sit down.

"No, nothing. My messages still aren't reaching her. That means her phone is switched off, right?" I ask her. Switched off or destroyed, but I don't want to go there.

She just gives a half nod and smiles encouragingly at me.

"I've been hearing a lot about how close you and Charlie are," she tells me.

"She's my best friend," I agree.

"That's what everyone says. You and Charlie have been best friends for years, yes?"

"Pretty much since nursery," I tell her.

"If anyone would know where she is, what she's thinking, it's you?" she asks me searchingly.

What? I don't understand. They can't think that *I* have Charlie.

"What?"

"Has she ever talked to you about running away?" DS Walters asks gently.

DS Walters. Detective Sergeant B. Walters.

She's an idiot.

"No. Charlie hasn't run away, she's in trouble."

I say the words clearly, needing her to hear me and understand.

"Don't worry Penny, Charlie is a minor, whatever happened we are still taking this very seriously," she assures me, as though that helps at all.

"But she didn't run away!" I repeat.

"What makes you think that?" she asks me.

It sounds like a reasonable question but it's like trying to prove a negative, or asking someone to tell you how they know that air exists.

"Because I know her!" I try, but I know it's not enough, it's a child's argument.

"My understanding is that Charlie had been acting unusually lately?"

"Who told you that?" I ask quickly, relieved that someone else had noticed this besides me.

"Her mother mentioned it, and some teachers. Even some other friends that we've spoken to. Do you agree? Was Charlie's behaviour unusual at all?"

I nod, reluctant to commit my voice to any argument that could help them to decide that she voluntarily absconded from her life.

"And I understand that Charlie argued with you and also with her boyfriend at the party on Saturday?" she asks me.

"We didn't argue, she just didn't want to leave and I did," I insist.

DS Walters just looks at me, giving me time to follow her reasoning.

"She wouldn't run away," I repeat.

"If she did, do you have any idea where she would go?" she asks me.

"She wouldn't run away."

"But if she did. Are there any friends that she might go to? Anyone that her mother doesn't know about?"

"No!"

"Do you have any idea where the money was coming from?" she asks me, suddenly changing track.

"What money?"

"Charlie has received between fifty and one hundred pounds three times over the past two months from the same account. Her mother didn't know anything about it," she explains.

"Whose account is it?" I ask quickly.

"We are sourcing that information but it takes time."

"Well can't you put a rush on it or something?! Anything could be happening to her!"

I'm practically shrieking now but DS Walters just stares back at me, maddeningly calm. I can feel Coop's eyes on me, anxious and concerned but I don't care.

"She didn't run away! She wouldn't do that to her mum, or to *me*! She didn't walk off in a mini skirt and sequin top, leaving her coat behind and switching off her phone and go off to some stranger! She would have packed a bag, she would have taken clothes, she would have told me where she was going!" I insist, my tone almost pleading.

"Would she?"

Simple words but they hit me like a punch to the gut.

Would she?

I've felt for a while now that Charlie was keeping secrets. I've sensed that there was something going on that she didn't want to tell me about. I bury my face in my hands, trying to press my certainty back into shape.

"The Saturday afternoon before the party, how did Charlie seem?" DS Walters asks, pressing her advantage.

"She seemed... like Charlie," I tell her with a shrug.

"She wanted us to take our time getting ready; she wanted to impress Marcus. She teased me about spending the summer watching Netflix. She said that now was the time to live, to be young and stupid," I elaborate.

"Young and stupid?"

"Yeah, she said we should be running through town naked and having affairs with married men," I explain.

DS Walters face freezes slightly and Coop starts beside me.

"She talked about having an affair?" she asks in a carefully calm voice.

"She wasn't being serious!" I exclaim.

"Are you sure?"

I'm about to vehemently state that I am, but then I pause.

Am I sure? Charlie has always liked older men, she's always had crushes on teachers. Her first great passion was for my dad, much to my horror. She's joked time and time again about her 'daddy issues' ruling her romantic inclinations. How far would she go? Would she really have an affair with a married man? Could that be where the money is coming from? Would that mean that she's safe?

I look back at DS Walters and I can see that she reads the uncertainty and anguish in my face.

“I don't know,” I mutter.

“Has she ever seemed close with anyone?” she asks me slowly, wording the question with care.

“No,” I respond, shaking my head.

Surely I would have noticed?! I've been on the lookout, every moment for ten years, I've been keeping my eyes peeled for anyone who seems to pay just a bit too much attention. Anyone who seems just a bit too interested. I've been actively looking for a threat in every face I see. How could someone slip past me and get to Charlie without me seeing it?

“You're going to keep looking for her?”

My words are a question but my tone doesn't brook any argument.

“We will keep looking,” she agrees.

“Have you checked her phone records?” I ask

quickly.

"We've applied for them and we should have them soon," she tells me a little reluctantly.

"What about her email account? And social media? Charlie used Facebook a lot -" I say in a rush, but DS Walters raises a hand to stop me.

"We're pursuing every avenue open to us."

"So you've looked at her emails?" I ask again.

"We have someone going through them."

I nod to myself, relieved.

"There doesn't appear to be anything out of the ordinary so far, except for some emails to someone named Genie Turns. genieturns95@gmail.com, does that sound familiar at all?" she asks me.

"No - I mean... the name rings a bell, but no."

"Alright, it may not be relevant anyway, it seems that she only ever sent them copies of her schoolwork."

"There's no one at your school with that name?" Coop asks me.

"No, not that I'm aware of," I tell him.

"As I said, it may be nothing," DS Walters repeats.

"What about Facebook? Have you looked at her messages?" I press on.

"We're looking, but again there's nothing out of the ordinary,"

I nod but I'm already trying to think of anything else I can ask about. DS Walters pre-empts me though.

"We *are* looking for her Penny," she tells me sincerely, reaching out a hand for mine.

I just wish that I could shake the feeling that they're not looking in the right places.

Coop takes me home and the whole way my thoughts are a deep, baritone hum, so loud that I can't focus enough to tease them apart. It's only as we pull into the driveway that my head clears enough for me to worry what kind of mother I'll find inside, but when I open the door I'm greeted by the sound of county music and the overwhelming scent of vanilla.

The scene in the kitchen is one of utter domestic

chaos. There are broken egg shells, smears of butter, pools of milk and clouds of flour seem to still hang in the air, but Olly is beaming at me, standing on a chair, mum's arms around him to keep him steady and guide his hands.

"We're making you something!" he roars, at the only volume available to an excited eight year old boy. Loud.

"Making me something?" I ask him, my voice bright with an interest I desperately want to feel.

Mum sees the lie in my face and gives me a sympathetic smile.

"Olly understands that you're worried and he wanted to do something to help you," she explains.

Unexpectedly, tears prick my eyes.

"Well that is just so nice of you, Olly Wally!" I tell him, planting a kiss on his cheek that makes him squirm.

As an afterthought I kiss my mother's cheek too. It smells of flour and sugar and feels surprisingly substantial.

"How was it?" she asks anxiously, looking between

Coop and me.

Coop shrugs and I try to think of an appropriate answer.

"I wasn't really able to help at all. I don't know anything. They want to know if she was seeing someone and I..." I trail off, feeling useless.

"She didn't tell you?" my mother asks, surprised.

I see Coop give her a warning look and she raises a hand quickly to her mouth as though to take back the words.

"Charlie was keeping secrets," I tell her quietly, glancing at Olly to see how much he's listening. He seems engrossed in cupcake icing but I don't want to start talking about affairs when he's in the room. The world should be a trustworthy place when you're eight.

My mother sighs.

"I'm sure she'll come home soon," she says, but she can't look me in the eye. She can't look into my face, just like Rose's, and tell me everything will be alright.

The cupcakes are pretty good. There's the odd lump or two of flour, but the icing is nice and the sponge around the lumps is fluffy. I consume two cakes while I type up everything new I have. Most of it can't be neatly sorted onto my timeline document so it ends up as a disconcerting stream of consciousness. I print it off and start highlighting parts that feel important but really, that just makes it all look more deranged. I find myself wishing that Luke were still here to bounce ideas off, but he dropped me off at the police station and then, very likely, fled. I can't blame him, he doesn't even know Charlie, this really isn't his problem, but still... it would be nice to have the company.

I toy with my phone, contemplating messaging Luke's newly saved number but ultimately I throw it down onto my bed and turn back to my laptop.

Charlie has been missing for almost thirty-seven and a half hours.

I'm not going to think about the statistics. They are not my friend right now.

Instead I go back over my conversation with DS Walters. She clearly thinks that Charlie left under her own steam, but that doesn't mean that she's wrong about everything. If there's one thing that my mother drilled in to me, it's that anyone can be a threat. Anyone can be a predator. Who more so than a married man who's sleeping with a teenager? If Charlie really is having an affair, doesn't the man involved have a strong motive to make her disappear?

I open yet another new document, as though starting from scratch could bring any semblance of order. Now, who could Charlie be seeing?

It's not a particularly long list until you consider what it is. Then it's almost too long to bear thinking about. Married men that Charlie knew and had ever expressed an interest in. Charlie was always getting crushes, but I never thought for a second that any of them had actually gone anywhere.

There are four possibilities by my count: two teachers, the netball coach and Charlie's neighbour that she's babysat for a couple of times.

Mr Danes is our headteacher and I don't think he's a likely candidate. He gave my mum an admin job after she quit hers when Rose went missing, so I actually know him fairly well and he's never seemed romantically interested in Charlie. Honestly, I've always thought that he had a crush on my mum, but she'd already gotten together with Coop before she and Mr Danes met. Still, I can't rule him out because Charlie's had a thing for him since we were eleven years old.

Mr Denham teaches French and half the girls in our year think that he's irresistible. I'll admit the accent is appealing, but I'm certainly not going ga-ga over him the way Charlie has been. He definitely makes the list.

Mr Cosford, or 'Coach Dan' as he prefers to be known, is another contender. He's all muscles and teeth. He never grew out of being a school jock and I honestly have no idea what Charlie sees in him, but I guess he does resemble Marcus Kain in fifteen years time.

The neighbour, Lance Pentuck is another tricky one.

He has kids. I'm not sure if any of the others do, but I've never heard of them if they have. Charlie *knows* Mr Pentuck's kids. She *looked after them*. Could she really have an affair with him after that?

So that's it. Four names. Four names of married men that Charlie has told me she likes. It's possible that she didn't tell me about someone of course, but that would have required pretty remarkable forethought on her part. She'd need to have suspected right away when she met him that something might actually happen with a guy, and that just seems unlikely. I'd put my money on one of these four.

Now the question is, how do I go about dissecting their lives?

# Chapter 9

It turns out that if you want to get to know someone really well, social media is not the way to go. Three hours of online stalking and all I have is superficial ephemera. Lance Pentuck has cute kids and likes rock-climbing. Mr Danes and Mr Denham have hardly any social media presence at all, probably because they're teachers, and Coach Dan is a little bit in love with himself.

None of this is useful.

After much digging I find that Mr Denham has an Instagram account. It isn't linked to his Facebook so it took me a while to figure it out, but in one post on his timeline someone mentions it and there's a link. I'm not allowed Instagram and neither is Charlie. Ironically, our mums discussed it and decided that posting videos online might put us at risk. Mr Denham however, seems to favour pictures. He has endless photos of food and a lot of pictures of him with his wife. I don't want to be unsupportive of Charlie but I have to admit, Mrs Denham is beautiful. I don't know if a man with a wife like that would sleep with a teenaged student, but maybe I'm being naïve.

Either way, there's nothing here that helps me. There's no helpful pictures posted the night of the party showing he was out of town, no alibi conveniently presented. I gaze at the picture of Mr Denham and his wife, celebrating their twelfth anniversary last month and I try to imagine him as a monster. The trouble is, I've been playing this game for years and everyone looks like monsters now.

Coach Dan feels like a much more promising possibility to me. He's posted a selfie on his very public, linked Instagram and Facebook pages every single night for over a year. This in itself I find utterly mind boggling, but the key fact is that he didn't post his usual example of self indulgence the night of the party. One night out of hundreds, and it just so happens to be the night Charlie goes missing? They're nearly all pictures of him in a gym and they're all posted around the nine-thirty to ten pm mark. He's given them inspirational captions as though he's some kind of role model and not a kids' sports coach. Would someone like him, clearly desperate for attention and validation, sleep with a student? I can believe they would.

Just the thought gives me a twinge of guilt. I don't even know Coach Dan since I've never taken part in any kind of sports or extra curricular activities like Charlie does. I've been keeping a low profile while Charlie has been actively living. Maybe I should have gone with her. Maybe if I'd been on the team too then nothing would have happened between Charlie and Dan. Or if something *had* happened, I'd at least know about it.

I stop, burying my face in my hands and rubbing my eyes with the heels of my palms.

I'm getting distracted. I need to stay focused but my

guilt keeps leading me off on tangents. I try to remind myself that I'm not responsible for what's happening. It's not my fault for not taking netball, it's not my fault for not taking Charlie's crushes seriously, it's not my fault for not seeing the threat in front of us, it's not my fault for leaving the party without her, it's not my fault that once again the girl closest to me has vanished and I'm left standing here.

It's a lot of reminders to have to go through. I'm not entirely sure they can all be true.

"Penny?"

My mum's voice is gentle but it brings my head up like a whip.

"Mum? Has something happened?" I ask quickly.

"No love, I just wanted to let you know that dinner's almost ready," she tells me.

My stomach heaves at the thought of food and mum must see it in my eyes.

"You need to eat, even if you don't want to. It won't help anything for you to be collapsing from hunger."

She's sensible and calm and I just don't understand it. My mother has been sent into a tailspin of panic and fear by trips to the supermarket. She's had weeks when she can barely walk down the street. Days and days that she's cried as Olly and I leave for school because fear is drowning out common sense. How can she suddenly be fine when Charlie is missing?! Our family trauma is playing out again right now in front of our eyes and she's talking to me about dinner.

"I need to focus," I snap.

I know it isn't fair to be angry at her. I should just be glad that she's doing well, not resenting it, but I can't help it. The fear that's been pooling inside me is shifting and bubbling into anger, spilling out.

"You'll focus better after you've eaten."

She's calm but she looks so sorry for me, so sad. My anger fizzles away as quickly as it appeared and I realise that I feel empty. Food would be good.

"I'll be down in a minute," I tell her limply, not sure whether I showed enough of my feelings to need to apologise.

"We'll be waiting."

I finish typing up Coach Dan's lack of selfie for Saturday and then I head downstairs. I half expected that I wouldn't be able to bring myself to eat, but I haven't had anything besides pop-tarts and cupcakes all day and the first bite of paella tastes like heaven.

"Penny, which is your favourite Pokemon?" Olly asks me seriously.

"You know my favourite," I remind him.

"You still like Pikachu?"

"I do."

"I would want a squirtle I think," he tells me pensively.

"I would want a jigglypuff," I say without really thinking.

"What?! But you like Pikachu best!" he cries indignantly, clearly feeling lied to.

"Pikachu is my favourite, but if I could only have one I think a jigglypuff would be it. Pikachu might be dangerous to keep in the house, with all our electricity and everything. But a jigglypuff..." I trail off.

"Which one is Jigglypuff again?" mum asks.

"The one that makes people fall asleep," Coop tells her.

She and I both blush. I want to tell her that I wasn't thinking of her and her endless prescriptions for sleeping pills, but she'd know I was lying. She and I both have our problems with sleep.

"A jigglypuff sounds nice," she agrees.

"A squirtle might make the house wet!" Olly cries, horrified and excited by the prospect.

Just like that, he's off. The rest of the meal is a lesson on Pokemon and a discussion on the various ways in which they might make daily life inconvenient. The more Olly talks, the more I laugh and the more a hard knot in my chest loosens. I hadn't even realised it was there but it feels amazing when it does slacken. I'm very aware of the breath moving in and out of my lungs. Everyone's voices sound a touch too loud and the world feels too vivid to be real, but God I wish I could stay here, stay like this. Maybe the police will find Charlie. Maybe she ran away and she's holed up somewhere, safe and sound. Maybe she'll be home soon and everything will go back to normal.

I keep repeating these words to myself, over and over. With every repetition I feel lighter. By the time I've cleared my plate and made my way upstairs, I'm sliding along the ceiling, bobbing along like a helium balloon.

Gravity comes back with six words. Six words from the same anonymous Facebook account, posted to the timeline just minutes ago.

'Maybe she got what she deserved.'

I need to focus.

The NoMatter Facebook profile is still completely blank. No photos, no posts, no nothing.

I scan back through the other comments and pictures that people have posted but nothing stands out, no gleaming revelations. There aren't any more pictures from the night of the party posted, just pictures of Charlie at various social gatherings and school events. The page is looking more and more like a memorial. The comments and posts are different though. They're all impassioned pleas to Charlie to come home or condemnations of her decision to run away. No one seems to even be considering the possibility that she didn't run off, that something happened to her. It's just me and NoMatter.

I fall asleep propped up in bed, my laptop open in front of me and when I wake it feels almost as though no time has passed. My eyes ache as though they've been glued to a screen the entire night and my back feels stiff and tender. I stand and stretch but I still feel cramped, hunched over, my limbs tethered together with thick chords of panic. I want to move. I want to run. I pull on my gym clothes and slip downstairs. The house is still quiet in this early, dawn peace. I go to the front porch and dig through the shoe bucket for my trainers. Thanks to mum's life-long "no shoes in the house" policy, the shoe bucket is huge and it takes me a while to find what I'm looking for. When I finally get outside it feels like surfacing from underwater. The cool air fills my lungs and I start moving. My short, uneven strides quickly lengthen to a more regular, even gait and soon the world is rushing past me. I've never run outside before, I've been a habitual treadmill runner since I was thirteen but I've never run in the streets like this, too afraid of who might be lurking. That fear seems insignificant now. It's already failed to keep us safe, so I just leave it behind.

I run until my legs ache and my shoes rub and my breath is heaving in and out of my lungs. I run until I can't keep going and then I drop down to a walk, tired but elated. I've run round the outer edge of our small town and I'm not sure where to go now. I didn't bring any money so I can't go and buy a drink, but I don't feel ready to go home yet. Instead I stroll in the direction of school, thinking that maybe I'll feel closer to Charlie that way, but once I reach the street I change my mind. I want to feel closer to Rose.

The Rose Owens Garden. It was built the year after she went missing. She disappeared during the summer holidays but she'd been about to start secondary school. She'd been 'preparing me' for weeks, telling me that she was going to be very grown up now and I would be at 'baby school' all on my own. I'd cried and cried until we made one another matching friendship bracelets and promised to wear them every day. As it turned out, she never actually got to go.

All the same, the school had donated a piece of land to become The Rose Owens Garden, a space to remember a lost little girl who would have been a student there. Charlie always said it was macabre, a memorial for a child who might still be alive, but I disagreed. I don't think that Rose is alive, and if she had been she would have loved that garden. The whole space is a maze of rose bushes- they're in every colour and size, bordering the pathways on both sides, leading to a few secluded benches, set back amongst the bushes. It feels private and magical and the Rose I remember would have been enchanted.

I make my way to one of the benches and collapse gratefully down onto it, rubbing my sore calves.

"Been for a jog?"

I whip round but then relax slightly. Mr Danes. He lives close by and he's the one who planted the garden. It makes sense that he's here.

Then I picture his name on my list of four and I tense again, fixing a smile to my face.

"Yep, just a quick run to clear my head," I tell him, my voice carefully calm.

Should I go? I like Mr Danes, but he is on my list. I probably shouldn't be here alone with him but, what better opportunity will I find to talk to him?

Charlie has been missing for so long I've lost count of the hours.

"How are you doing?" he asks me, his voice gentle.

"Not so good," I admit with a shrug.

"That's understandable."

“Charlie didn't run away,” I tell him firmly. I'm not sure if I'm looking for some kind of telling reaction or if I just want someone to believe me.

“People can do surprising things sometimes,” he points out gently.

I feel a stab of annoyance.

“People do surprising things. People do surprising things like hurting people. People do surprising things like making girls disappear.”

My voice is so harsh I hardly recognise it and Mr Danes flinches. He rises from his position, crouched by a rose bush with a small pair of shears, and he comes to join me.

“May I?” he gestures to the bench beside me and I shrug again so he sits down.

“You're right. You of all people know that sometimes awful things happen. I just don't want you to find this situation any more difficult than it needs to be. What happened to your sister... well, things like that don't happen every day. Charlie is a strong young woman and I have every hope that she's just fine."

I want so much to believe him but I'm too busy analysing every word he's saying. Are these the platitudes of a guilty man?

"You're not worried about her?" I ask him, watching his face carefully.

He sighs.

"I am immensely worried about her. Whatever situation she's in, I'd feel a lot better if she was home. I helped with the searches for your sister you know, but I never actually got to meet her. I've known Charlotte Hople since she was eleven years old! I very much hope that she's home soon."

He looks tired and sad and I feel a twinge of guilt for ever putting him on my list to begin with, but this isn't about feelings, it's about Charlie.

"We were at a party with the whole year group, celebrating the start of summer. You must feel the same way we do about the summer holidays I suppose, being a teacher. The first day of summer must be a big deal for you too," I suggest, trying to keep my voice even.

"I actually have quite a lot of work over the summer too. A headteacher's labours are never done!" he tells me in his soft, slightly theatrical voice.

I can't tell if he realised what I was angling towards and was intentionally evasive, or if he just answered my question innocently.

"Did you help with the search for Charlie?" I ask instead.

"No, I didn't actually."

I turn to face him quickly but he goes on,

"I would have of course, but I wasn't here."

"You weren't here? On Sunday?" I ask, not sure what to make of that.

"My wife, Olivia, and I were away for the weekend. Not quite a 'start of summer' celebration, since we were visiting her parents in Swindon, but still- I didn't hear about Charlotte until Monday morning and by then the searches had already stopped."

My heart clenches tight.

One day. The searches were started and stopped in one day.

I'd realised that they weren't going on any more, but I hadn't processed quite how brief they'd been. Just a token effort. A gesture to the haunting memory of Rose, when really no one saw a connection but me. I feel myself start to tremble as my body cools down too quickly from my previous exertions.

"Rose would have loved this place you know?" I tell Mr Danes through chattering lips.

"She would?" he asks, his voice brightening slightly.

"We used to play a game, like a contest, whenever we went out. I would get a point every time I saw a penny, and she would get a point every time she saw a rose. She almost always got more points than me, but we were never really keeping score. We loved that game. She would have thought that this garden was amazing."

"I wish I'd had the chance to meet her," he tells me.

"Me too," I agree, shaking more than ever. The heat of exercise has faded, leaving me chilled to the bone.

“Come on, let's get you home,” he tells me, giving me an anxious look.

I hesitate for a moment, but he wasn't here on Saturday night. He was away with his wife. I push myself up to standing and follow him through the garden, the heady scent of roses filling the morning air.

We walk in silence to Mr Danes' house. It's just a few doors down from the school but even that brief movement helps to warm me up.

“Where have you been?! I woke up and you were gone!” an acid tone hisses and I lean around Mr Danes and see his wife standing in the open doorway of their house, wrapped in a fluffy pink dressing-gown.

“I was just along at the school-” he begins but she cuts him off.

“At that garden again you mean,” she spits, rolling her eyes, but then they land on me and she freezes, her face flooding with the heat of shame.

“I was just going to give Penny here a lift home,” Mr Danes tells her, his voice tight.

I step back reflexively, not wanting anything to do with whatever argument they're engaged in.

“Oh, I'm sorry, I-” she falters and breaks off.

“I can walk,” I tell them quickly, suddenly just wanting to get away.

“No, no, don't be silly. It'll be quicker to get a lift. Sean, I'll see you when you get back. Sorry.”

I'm not sure if the apology was for my benefit or Mr Danes, but we shuffle over to the car together and both awkwardly wave goodbye to her as she stands, still in the doorway.

When we've turned the corner Mr Danes clears his throat.

“Sorry about that, we're just-”

He doesn't finish. He doesn't really need to.

“She doesn't like the garden?” I ask curiously.

“She doesn't like how much time I spend there. She'd rather I was at home,” he explains, his voice is level but his expression is grim.

“But you don't want to be at home,” I add quietly. I

hadn't meant to say it, but the crackle of anger and bitterness between Mr Danes and his wife had been so familiar. I remember that brittle, fearsome charge with perfect clarity from the weeks before my dad left.

"Sometimes, people's priorities change. It's a very difficult thing to deal with in a marriage," he tells me sadly.

I understand. It's exactly what happened to my parents. They'd been so happy before, sometimes turbulent, sometimes angry, but always a team. Then, in an instant everything changed - different priorities. Rose was gone. Dad decided that the most important thing was to find her, mum decided the most important thing was to protect me. Instant rift.

I don't respond to Mr Danes, I just rest my head against the window and let the world slip by for minute.

# Chapter 10

"Penny?! I didn't even realise you were gone!" mum cries, pulling me into a quick hug.

"Just went for a run," I mumble, slipping past her into the hall.

"Thanks Sean," she calls to Mr Danes as he pulls out of the driveway with just a brief wave, then she turns back to me, catching my arm before I can slip away.

I face her and her eyes study me, taking in every detail. My cheeks are red from running, my hair is escaping its ponytail and hanging around my face. Her gaze roves over the freckles, the dark eyes, the red hair.

She's not looking at me.

A quick shower and I'm back to work.

I let out a sigh of relief as I cross Mr Danes off the list. He and his wife may be having marital difficulties but I don't think Charlie is the cause of them. Even if she were, he was away Saturday night so there's no way he could have taken her.

One down, three to go.

"Penny!"

"I'm not hungry!" I call back without thinking.

I am actually, but I don't want to deal with mum right now. She's going to say something about me going out running this morning and I already feel as though I'm walking a tightrope over my own anger.

"Penny!" she calls again. There's a warning in her tone now that tells me it's in my best interest not to argue.

I pull my wet hair up into a bun and slowly make my way downstairs, dragging my feet as one headed to the gallows.

"Mum?" I call from the hallway.

“In here darling,” her voice answers from the lounge.

Darling? That's not quite what I was expecting.

I step into the lounge and stop dead in my tracks. DS Walters is sat on the sofa with a cup of tea and a polite smile.

“Has something happened?”

“Hello Penny, I just wanted to ask you a couple of questions,” she tells me in that infuriatingly calm voice.

With a sigh I settle myself into an armchair. Clearly this isn't going to be something big, if there had been any real progress she'd surely be getting straight to the point.

“A couple of questions?” I ask, doing my best not to show my complete lack of confidence in their investigation.

“Yes. Did you know that Charlie had been in contact with her father?”

Whatever I was expecting, it wasn't that. I sit forward in my seat, my heart in my throat.

“What?!”

"Am I to take it that you were unaware of the contact?" she asks me.

"Charlie found her dad?" I ask, nonplussed.

For as long as I've known her, Charlie's dad has been a difficult subject. When we were little she used to make up stories about him being an adventurer or a spy and coming to whisk her away with him. As we got older she developed a more cavalier attitude, all blunt jokes and witty one liners about being abandoned. I knew that she thought about him, she always had but -

"I didn't know, she never said," I mutter.

"Is that where you think she's gone? She's with her dad?" my mum asks quickly, her eyes wide and hopeful.

"It's a possibility we're exploring," DS Walters offers vaguely.

"What does that mean? Either she is or she isn't."

My voice is harsh and I clench my hands, trying to reign in this new unexpected temper of mine.

Mum gives me a warning look but DS Walters actually looks sympathetic.

"We called him. He confirmed that she got in touch, but he claims that he told her he wasn't interested in having any further contact. He apparently told her that he has no interest in having a relationship with her. It's possible that he's lying of course, so we're sending someone to check in person. Its also possible that she went to see him anyway."

My head is spinning and I miss the next question. I only realise that I've actually been asked something when mum reaches out and lays a hand on my arm.

"Penny?" she asks softly.

"Sorry?"

"Has Charlie mentioned Scotland at all?" DS Walters repeats.

"Scotland? Is that where he lives?" I ask.

"Has she mentioned it at all?"

"No she hasn't. But how would she get to Scotland? Has she been spending money on her debit card? Has she bought a train ticket or something?" I ask.

"There haven't been any charges on her card but

we've already ascertained that she has access to money from some source that no one knew about," DS Walters reminds me.

"She hasn't spent any money on her card at all? None?" I ask, watching her intently.

She just stares back at me.

"But you're not concerned?" I ask, incredulous.

"If Charlie is staying with someone then she may not need to spend any money. If someone collected her after the party-"

"Her dad who's in Scotland?" I cut in, a definite note of sarcasm in my voice.

"Or someone else-"

"This married man. Who didn't hurt her of course, she's just run off."

DS Walters looks tired and I wonder if she's been having these same arguments with Wendy.

"At this time, there's no reason to suspect that Charlie is in danger. She's seventeen years old, she was clearly keeping secrets and she argued with her boyfriend immediately before the last time she was seen. Statistically she is far more likely to have run away than –"

"Disappeared like Rose."

I cant help it, the words burst out of me before I can check them and once they're out there's no getting them back. I don't turn towards her but I see mum flinch, clutching the arm of the sofa for support.

"Penny, there's no reason to think that the two events are connected."

DS Walter's tone is definite and her face is serious but that doesn't mean that I'm convinced.

"I think you're wrong."

I leave mum to smooth things over with DS Walters and I go back up to my room without another word. Anger and fear are like ripples beneath my skin, chasing one another around my body making my limbs twitch. For all DS Walters tells me they're doing everything they can, I feel like they're sticking their heads in the sand

and refusing to see the truth that's right in front of them.

I grab my phone and fire off a message to Luke before I can change my mind or talk myself out of it. I don't precisely know what it is that I'm hoping he'll do, maybe I just want someone to be on my side. Plus, it might be a good idea to have backup for what I'm going to have to do next. I pace my room, hoping that the sound of my furious footsteps carries downstairs to the lounge. If I could stamp out a message of my dissatisfaction in Morse code I would do it.

To my relief, Luke replies to say that he'll come right round. The knowledge that I won't be alone is enough to turn my boiling anger down to a simmer. I manage to sit down at my desk and pull up some of my research and although my thoughts are fizzing too fast for me to catch them I'm still bent over my laptop when Luke bounds up the stairs and enters my room without knocking.

“Hard at work I see!” he notes jovially.

“Looking up how hard it is to learn Morse Code.”

“Well I'm sure that'll come in handy.”

“You never know what skills you might need,” I counter smoothly.

“So is that the plan for today then? Morse code lessons? We can probably find a Youtube video or something...”

“Nope, we're going to go and question married men who might have been sleeping with Charlie.”

Luke doesn't say anything and when I look up at him his expression is unreadable.

“What?” I ask.

“Charlie was sleeping with a married man?” he asks me.

“Possibly. I don't know for definite, but the police think she might have been.” I admit.

“And you want to go and talk to them?” he asks me slowly.

“Yes. Yes I do,” I reply, keeping my wording simple since he seems to be struggling with the concept.

“How do you even know who it might have been? If

you're not sure it was even happening?" he asks me.

"I know the married men that Charlie has crushes on," I explain with a shrug.

"Of course, because who *doesn't* have multiple crushes on grown men with wives," Luke remarks drily.

"Charlie's always liked 'older men'," I tell him with a shrug, my jaw tensed defensively.

"Then what was she doing with Marcus?" he asks.

I sigh,

"On *so* many levels, I don't know. I always thought that her crushes were just a game really, I never thought that she'd actually act on one. I don't have any idea what she saw in Marcus but it didn't really phase me that he was our age, you know? I thought he was a creep, but I still thought he was a more likely boyfriend than Mr Danes."

"Mr Danes?! " Luke cries, so obviously horrified that I can't help but laugh.

"Don't worry, Mr Danes has an alibi. Charlie has always had a crush on him though."

"You questioned him already?" he asks me, his eyes narrowing suddenly.

"Don't worry, I was subtle about it," I reassure him.

"You shouldn't have spoken to him alone," he insists.

"I ran into him by accident and didn't want to pass up the opportunity. Besides, you don't really think *Mr Danes* is dangerous do you? He has elbow patches on his jackets!" I say with a smile.

"If you didn't think it was possible he was involved then you wouldn't have talked to him! Don't act like I'm being paranoid here, you shouldn't be talking to anyone alone if there's the slightest chance that they could be a threat."

His eyes are dark and I know that he's remembering Marcus Kain's arm against my chest as he pushed me into the wall. If I'm honest, I've been thinking about it more than I'd like too.

"Well, I messaged you, didn't I? So I won't be alone," I say, shrugging with all the nonchalance I can muster.

I think for a moment that he's going to keep arguing, but then he shakes his head gently and his shoulders relax.

"Who are we talking to then?" he asks lightly.

"There are three names on my list now that Mr Danes has been cleared. Coach Dan, Mr Denham and Mr Pentuck. I still need to talk to Sarah H too," I remember. Being called down to the police station drove it out of my head, but Marcus did claim that Sarah H is who Charlie went to after their argument at the party.

"I recognise three of those," he tells me, raising one eyebrow in enquiry.

"Mr Pentuck lives a few doors from Charlie and she baby-sat for his kids a couple of times. I don't know him but Charlie raved about how good looking he was for *weeks*," I explain.

"Alright, so do we start with him? Since you know where he lives?"

"No, I actually want to start with Coach Dan," I tell him, biting my lip and looking back at my laptop screen.

“Why him?” he asks curiously.

“Well, he posts a picture of himself every evening after he finishes his workout. I guess it's part of his marketing for his services as a personal trainer. The thing is, he's posted a picture every day for months and months, but he didn't post one on Saturday. It's the only evening that he's skipped.”

I know it isn't anything concrete and I'm half waiting for Luke to dismiss it as meaningless, but he just nods to himself calmly.

“So you think that he might not have remembered to post a picture because something happened on Saturday that made him forget,” he adds.

“Something like abducting Charlie.”

“What time does he usually post his picture?” Luke asks me.

“Normally between nine and ten.”

“We know that Charlie was still at the party during that window,” he points out.

I bite my lip again, feeling the fragile skin snag on

my teeth.

"I know, but I'd still really like to know what made Saturday different from every other day for Dan Cosford."

It turns out that if you're a personal trainer and you run your business out of a home gym, it's actually not that hard to find your address. It's in town so we decide to go on foot rather than traipsing all the way back to Luke's house to borrow his dad's car again.

Dan Cosford lives in a small, pebble-dashed, end of terrace house on a street full of identical constructions, all clearly ex-council properties. A sign on the side gate tells us we've found the right place. It reads 'Get Dan and Dirty- Fitness Boot-camp' and as far as I'm concerned the police should be able to arrest him just for that. A sweat-drenched man opens the gate just as we reach it and puts out a hand to hold it open for us. I'm not sure that I'm actually ready to go inside but it's not like having my questions prepared in advance helped at all with Marcus, so I step through the gate and into an astro-turfed garden.

"Did you forget something Barry?" Dan calls, hearing our footsteps and leaning out of a charcoal grey cabin that takes up at least the bottom third of the garden. His smile falters when he sees me and Luke but he steps out to greet us and his tone is polite.

"I think I recognise you two, are you here to sign up as clients?" he asks.

"Um, maybe, could you tell us a bit about it?" I ask, fighting my instinct to drop down to a whisper.

"Of course! Always good to see young people interested in fitness!" Dan cries, ushering us up to the cabin.

When I first caught sight of it I felt a sort of pang, part suspicion and part hope, but of course Charlie isn't concealed inside. The cabin is fitted out with a full range of gym equipment, all gleaming and smelling faintly of bleach and disinfectant. I wonder if I might be able to find an excuse to search his house.

“I offer one on one sessions, small group boot-camps and larger groups throughout the summer, held on the field up the road,” he tells us, going on to talk us through some of the equipment and payment options.

“What did Charlie do?” I ask abruptly, not exactly adept at social finesse.

He falters, knocked off the regularly trod track of his elevator pitch.

“Charlie?” he asks, looking at me. I try to decide if his gaze is intense or just questioning- panicked or just confused.

“Charlie Hople, she told me she came here. What sort of class did she do?” I repeat.

It's a lie of course, Charlie never came here for Personal Training sessions as far as I know, but if she was here for any other reason, then maybe he'll jump at the excuse.

“Charlie Hople from the netball team,” he says flatly.

Am I imagining the unease in his voice?

“Yes, that Charlie Hople,” Luke chimes in, his voice even.

“She's missing isn't she? Ran away?” He asks me, a frown just slightly creasing his brow.

I don't know what to say. I want to tell him that Charlie would never run away, but I also don't want him to think that I suspect him of anything. If he starts to get defensive he might not talk to us at all.

“There was a search on Sunday, did you hear about it?” Luke asks in the slightly scandalised tone of a local gossip.

It's beautifully done and I can't resist casting an admiring look at him.

“Yeah, I heard, the school called me. I helped search the woods,” he tells us, a slightly defensive edge to his voice.

“It's crazy isn't it? Most people can't believe it, a second missing girl, a second round of search parties, in one small town,” I say, letting some sadness creep into my words.

Coach Dan looks definitely uncomfortable now but not necessarily defensive. I've found over the years that lots of people are uncomfortable around me because of Rose. They don't know what to say or do and it makes them feel ill-at-ease. Now though, I'm wondering if it's something more. I study Dan's face and in every twitch, every movement, I'm looking for guilt.

"Did you help search for Rose too?" I ask him.

"Your sister? No, I was away. I would have though, but I was out of town," he tells me, a muscle twitching in his jaw.

"But you helped look for Charlie," Luke repeats, casting a quick glance at me.

"Yeah, we trawled through the woods but there was nothing there. That was before the police realised she'd run away though," he explains, clearly wondering what on earth this awkward conversation is in aid of.

"You think she ran away?" I ask him.

"That's what the police said," he repeats, narrowing his eyes.

"Did she ever say anything to you to make you think that she might want to run away?" I ask him.

"No, but why would she? I'm just her netball coach," he states firmly.

"Well, yeah, but Charlie's always really liked you. She actually has a crush on you to be honest," I tell him, watching closely for a reaction.

I get one.

Dan steps towards me, his voice instantly raised to a shout,

"WHAT THE FUCK IS THAT SUPPOSED TO MEAN?! WHAT ARE YOU IMPLYING?!"

I flinch back and Luke steps between us.

Dan's face, flushed red, breaks into a sneer.

"I'm not going to *hit* her!" he shouts, turning away from us and running his hands through his hair in a self soothing gesture.

"Do you know what an accusation like that could do to me?!" he demands in a tight voice, looking between us.

"Charlie is *missing*!" I hiss back, my own anger rising

to meet his.

"Well it's nothing to do with *me*! Clearly I haven't run off with her, have I!"

"I don't think *anyone* ran off with her! I think she's in trouble!" I spit.

So much for not showing my hand.

Dan deflates somewhat at my words, his hands back in his thick chestnut mane.

"I have nothing to do with Charlie," he states clearly, "I am just her coach."

I want to believe him, I really do. Despite his anger and the fear still coursing through me, I want to believe that this man couldn't hurt my friend.

"Where were you on Saturday night?" I ask him, willing my voice not to shake.

He gives a harsh laugh.

"Saturday night?! I was at the hospital, with my pregnant wife. I'm sure there are surveillance videos, not that you could get hold of them. You're just a couple of bloody kids!"

He sounds like he can't quite believe he's having this conversation and I'm worried he's going to kick us out.

"What about someone else? Did you ever see anyone hanging around Charlie? Did you ever hear her talk about a guy? Someone older? Someone married?" I ask quickly.

"No I didn't! But I don't pay attention to teenaged girls!" he hisses, a muscle in his neck tensed.

"What about Mr Denham?" I ask, throwing caution to the winds.

I hear Luke half choke beside me but I don't take my eyes off of Coach Dan's face. To my surprise he puts his head back and laughs.

"Serves that loser right! Thinks he's fucking God's gift to women, with his fake accent and his bloody hair!"

"Did you ever see him with Charlie? Did she ever mention him?" I press.

"All the girls mention him!" he shrugs, bitterness crackling in the air around him.

"I need to talk to him," I tell him desperately. This

conversation has definitely moved out of my control and the urge to run is mounting every second.

Dan Cosford looks at me, a twisted smile on his face and I want more than anything to take a step back. I fight the urge, remaining rooted to the spot while he stares me down.

"I just so happen to have his address."

# Chapter 11

"What was that?!" Luke cries, half running along the street beside me.

I want to tell him very calmly that that was us questioning a suspect, but I'm shaking so much that I don't think I can form the words. When we reach a grass verge I let my legs give way and twist myself into a sitting position, resting my forehead on my knees.

As I determinedly slow my breathing, Luke is still ranting beside me.

"He was terrifying! I really thought he was going to attack us! He says he has an alibi though, but I guess we need to check it... but I mean, if his wife is pregnant he couldn't have been seeing Charlie, could he? If his wife is pregnant he- he-"

"He has a lot to lose."

The words taste bitter in my mouth. I want to believe that Charlie would never have a relationship with someone who was about to have a baby, but then again I want to believe she would never have a relationship with someone married. I can't be sure. I can't bet her life on it.

"But if he was at the hospital..." Luke reminds me.

"*If* he was at the hospital. He's right, it's not like we can check the surveillance footage."

"Do you think he would lie though? I mean, what if we found out? That would make him look guilty."

"Everybody lies. And to get rid of us? Yeah I think he would absolutely have lied. I don't know how to find out though, I doubt he'd take kindly to us knocking on the door and asking to speak to his wife," I muse.

"So we didn't find out anything," Luke comments grimly, flopping back onto the grass beside me.

"Sure we did. We found out that we can't cross Dan Cosford off the list yet and we got Mr Denham's address," I point out.

"You really want to keep questioning people?" Luke asks me, clearly reluctant.

"Charlie's still missing," I remind him.

"Yeah, but the police are looking for her, right? Surely they're going to question people like Coach Dan and Mr Denham?"

"I don't know. Clearly they haven't been to talk to him yet and he's her netball coach. Surely that's someone they should be speaking to? They think she went to find her dad in Scotland, but she's still not switched her phone on and she hasn't spent any money on her debit card. They're so sure that she ran away but she just wouldn't do it. She wouldn't do that to her mum and she wouldn't do it to me."

He doesn't respond but I can tell that he wants to. He's casting furtive glances at me and his cheeks are tinged pink.

"What? Go on, say it," I prompt him.

"Well, it's just, you guys didn't seem that close at the party. You've always been inseparable at school but... I don't know, things seemed different," he explains.

It isn't what I want to hear right now but he's not wrong.

"Things *have* been different. Charlie's seemed... uncomfortable around me recently. I think she might be outgrowing me, getting bored of being friends with me. But that doesn't mean that she would run away from her life when she knows how scared I would be. How scared her mum would be!"

My tone is fierce and I look up guiltily but Luke doesn't look angry at me, his eyes are bright.

"Ok, I was just thinking, Occam's Razor. The simplest explanation is usually the truth."

"Ironically, I've always thought that was a bit of an over-simplification," I comment.

"What is?"

"That definition of Occam's Razor. It's more like- the explanation that requires the fewest assumptions is usually the correct one."

"What's the difference?" he asks with interest.

"Well, obviously sometimes ridiculously complicated things are true. It might be the most simple option to decide that Charlie has just run off, particularly if it means that you don't have to worry too much or exert too much effort looking for her, but you have to make an awful lot of assumptions. You have to assume that Charlie decided to run off, because there's no proof of that. You have to assume that she had somewhere to go and didn't need any money to get there or that she had a secret stash of cash or another money source that no one knew about. You also have to assume that she's the sort of person who would stay missing even though she's seen exactly what a missing child does to the people who love them."

"That's a lot of assumptions."

"Exactly. Statistically, it may be more unlikely that Charlie was taken against her will, it may be the more complex theory, but at least mine is based on facts not assumptions."

"Alright, I'll trust you on that. You're her best friend

and I don't even really know her," he concedes.

"You don't really know her," I repeat quietly.

"Hm?"

"Luke, why are you here? Why are you helping me?" I ask quickly, getting the words out fast before I can change my mind.

"You messaged me, remember?" he points out.

His tone is light but he shifts slightly closer to me on the grass. I can't tell if it's on purpose but suddenly I'm very aware of his proximity. Of the bare flesh of his arm just centimetres from mine.

"You know what I mean, why did you come to mine in the first place?" I press, my face flooding with heat.

He moves slightly closer and now his hand is beside mine where it rests on the grass. We both look down at those hands with absolute focus and he edges his across to lace his fingers with mine. My breath catches in my throat and I turn quickly to look at him. He's obviously nervous but he tries for a small smile and then leans over, his lips brushing mine.

Luke is gentle, tentative, but his touch has set my skin on fire. I wouldn't be surprised to see actual smoke curling up from around our clasped hands. The kiss lasts just a few seconds but I feel as though I haven't breathed in minutes.

This is nothing like Alex Hall with his bold moves and his roving embrace.

“You're not hoping that I can get you a pro-football career are you?” I ask in a whisper.

Luke sits back in surprise.

“I'm sorry, what's that now?”

“Nothing, sorry... just- nothing,” I smile at him and try to recapture the moment but my words were a needle though our delicate bubble and the moment's gone.

“Are you a football coach or something?” Luke asks me, still confused.

I laugh, burying my face in my hands, unable to speak.

“I mean, I'm a rubbish player, I was always stuck in goal and never bloody saved anything! I hope that's not a deal-breaker."

I still don't think I could talk, so instead I take a handful of Luke's shirt in my free hand and pull him towards me, pressing my lips to his.

When we break apart we're both smiling and I feel the desperate need to rush home and call Charlie about this. Then a wave of guilt washes over me. Luke must read it in my eyes because he gently rests his forehead against mine for a moment before squeezing my hand and pulling me to my feet.

"So, what's next?"

Next is Mr Denham.

He lives fifteen minutes drive away so we walk back to Luke's and get the Landrover. He spends almost ten minutes in the house getting the keys while I wait outside in the driveway and when he comes out he looks irritated.

"Sorry about that, have you got the address up on Google maps?" he asks.

"What was that? Are you alright?" I ask him uncertainly.

"Yeah, I'm fine, mum just thinks we're mad," he tells me casually.

"You told them what we're doing?" I ask in surprise.

"Well, sort of. I told them we're trying to talk to people to see if anyone knows anything, but I left out the part about interrogating grown men about their potential extra-marital affairs."

"Good call."

"Your parents don't know what you're doing?" he asks me, his eyebrows raised.

"Mum would worry about me too much and Coop would worry about mum," I tell him simply, "and I haven't seen dad in almost a year. I don't even know where he is now."

"He moved after your parents' divorce?" he asks, his tone careful.

"Not right away, he stayed a few months searching the woods and following every flimsy lead he could find, looking for Rose. Eventually the search took him further and further away."

I can hear the bitterness in my voice, but really I understand. I've always felt more guilty about dad than anything, he's never given up and it's completely taken over his life.

I can feel Luke's eyes on me and I realise that this is the most we've really talked about what happened to Rose, all he's had is my conviction that Rose and Charlie's disappearances are related, with no context or details. The trouble is, that's all I have too.

I fix my gaze out the window and watch trees and houses flick by as we pass them.

"I had just turned eight, Rose was ten but she was going to be eleven soon. It was almost the end of the summer holidays and we'd spent almost every day out in the woods, playing and exploring and climbing trees. From what I remember it was just like every other day. She was teasing me, telling me that she was going to be too grown up to play with me because she was starting secondary school. I kept crying about it that summer until she made us matching friendship bracelets, purple for her and pink for me. I remember the knots kept coming undone and she eventually tied them to our shoelaces. I have this perfect image in my head of her hands tying the bracelets on. I was so jealous because I hadn't learned to do laces myself yet... I remember that I fell. I cut my knee."

My fingers trace the scar as I talk, my mind reaching for details that I've always handled gingerly, treating them with care.

"Rose ran towards home to get mum because it was really bleeding. I remember watching her disappear into the trees. I got so upset and angry when she didn't come back. I thought she'd forgotten about me. It felt like hours later that I walked home myself, blood running down my leg. Mum had been hanging out the washing in the garden, her hair was damp and she smelled like lavender. She looked up at me and smiled as I came through the door. Then everything changed."

That's all I remember. Everything else came later. Rose had never made it home that day. They searched the woods for any trace but there was nothing, no sign of her, she just vanished without leaving a single sign behind. It was a terror that had a fairytale quality to it when I was little, but as I grew older and educated myself on the awful things that happened to people, the meaning changed. 'Vanished' became 'taken'.

"I'm so sorry Penny," Luke tells me, his voice gentle.

"The police looked but there was nothing to go on. They were sure at first that I must have seen something, they questioned me for hours but the more they asked me the less I remembered. Eventually they called in a child psychologist to talk to me and she basically determined that they'd traumatised me completely and got them all reprimanded, suspended or fired. It was too late though, for years I didn't remember anything at all about that time. Slowly bits and pieces started to come back, just what I told you, but even that's uncertain. I can't trust my own memories now, after ten years and layers of trauma," I tell him.

"But you think the same person took Charlie?" he asks me.

"The thing is, she was out there in the woods with us almost every day that summer. Statistically, child abductions are carried out by someone who knows the victim. They've watched them, they've seen them playing. If someone was watching Rose that summer, Charlie was right there, almost every day too. It just doesn't feel like a coincidence that of the three of us who were out there in the woods, two are missing!"

Luke doesn't say anything but I don't blame him, what is there to say? I have no proof, I don't remember anything useful and the police are sure Charlie ran away. For all my theories, we're still on our own.

Mr Denham lives in a beautiful house overlooking a golf-course. The bricks are ornamented with climbing roses and I can hear the sound of a fountain somewhere out of sight. Mr Denham either married money or inherited it, because there's no way he could afford this place on a teacher's salary.

"Bloody hell!" Luke exclaims, looking up at the impressive structure.

"Exactly what I was thinking!"

I hesitate, my usual antipathy towards ringing doorbells still playing it's part.

"Are you having second thoughts?" Luke asks me.

I give him a determined look and press the doorbell before stepping back to stand beside him. After a few seconds I hear movement coming from inside the house and the door is answered by what seems to be a maid or a cleaner. She looks at us expectantly and I blush, wishing I had some innocuous excuse for being there.

"Is Mr Denham in?" Luke asks brightly.

"One minute," the woman tells us, pushing the door closed again and shuffling away.

We stand awkwardly on the step but a minute later the door opens again and Mr Denham stands before us with a look of polite enquiry on his face.

“I hope you two aren't looking for any extra French work! I'm afraid I'm done for the summer!” he tells us cheerfully.

I don't know why teachers do that. I wonder if they all learn awkward half-jokes as part of their teacher training course.

Luke and I chuckle politely but then I get to the point.

“No sir, we're actually hoping to talk to you about something,” I tell him, looking up at him expectantly.

He waits for me to elaborate but I don't, opting to just maintain eye contact and appear as unthreatening as possible.

“Um, of course, would you like to come in?” he asks, holding the door open.

And just like that, we've scaled the first hurdle.

It's an impressive house on the inside too. The floors are a slightly incongruous marble but everything is light and open, thanks to floor to ceiling windows across the back of the house. They've taken a period home and then sliced away everything except the front, replacing it all with modern architecture and industrial accents. I'm not a fan.

"Gosh, this place is amazing," Luke comments, looking around.

There was just the slightest hesitation in his words and I suspect that actually he feels much the same way about it as I do, but I can't be sure.

"So how can I help you two?"

"I want to ask you about Charlie," I announce, throwing caution to the winds.

"Charlie?" he responds, his expression blank.

"Charlie Hople."

"Your friend at school," he adds, looking for confirmation.

"That's the one. Do you know where she is?"

"No, I'm afraid I don't. Do you?" his tone is definitely more confused than alarmed and I'm not sure I'm navigating the conversation particularly well.

"Well no, no one does," I tell him, shaking my head

impatiently.

"Sorry? Is this some kind of riddle?"

"Charlie's missing," Luke tells him, unable to bare my purposeless babbling any more.

"Missing?" he asks quickly, his eyes widening in surprise.

He looks between us as though expecting one of us to suddenly shout "just kidding!" and explain that this whole senseless conversation has been a joke. When neither of us does so he beckons for us to follow him and leads us through to a seating area populated by impractically white furniture and decorated with pretentious modern art. My focus is captured by a statue that looks to me like a violently inclined watering can and I struggle to pull my eyes away from it. People may think that my interest in True Crime is weird, but personally I think that collecting modern art is a sign of an abnormal mind.

"Penny?"

With a jolt I realise that someone has addressed a

question to me and in my infinite wisdom I've allowed my attention to wander.

“Hm?” I ask, eyes wide with enquiry.

“I said, maybe you should tell me what's going on,” Mr Denham repeats, now watching me with mild concern as though worried I might be unhinged.

I breathe out slowly, trying to give myself time to think. It's not an unreasonable question but I do wish that it wasn't quite so open. If Mr Denham is involved then I don't want to tip my hand by telling him how much we know, or rather, how much we don't know. Then again, maybe I can learn something by watching his reactions.

“Charlie never made it to mine after the year-group party at Luke's on Saturday. No one has seen her since and no one knows what happened to her.”

I state the facts baldly and at first I think I've struck gold. The colour seems to drain from Mr Denham's face and I actually consider that he might be sick, but then he leaps to his feet and steps towards us, his manner frenzied and his French accent wavering in an out.

"Oh my God! Since Saturday?! Have the police been called?! What's happening?! Are there any leads?! They must talk to her parents! The family should always be suspected! What's happening?!" he demands desperately, unable to understand why we're just sitting here, doing nothing.

"The police were called Sunday morning, they searched the woods but-"

"Oh my God! The woods?! To think of someone lost, alone in the dark out there!" he cries, in agonies at the very thought.

Honestly, of all the reactions that I was expecting, this didn't even make the list. I have no idea how to respond to this display of blind panic.

"They didn't find anything in the woods though," Luke says, I think aiming for reassuring but coming out more like alarmed.

"Then where are they looking now?! What can I do?! How can I help?!"

He looks at us eagerly and I try to think of any way that I can tactfully broach my question.

“Did Charlie ever mention anything to you? Did she ever talk about anyone? A man maybe?” I ask hesitantly, feeling my face contort of its own accord into an expression of comical enquiry.

“Me?! Why would she tell me?! If only she had!” he wails, literally covering his eyes with one hand, like a fifties movie starlet.

Girls and teachers alike have always swooned over 'sensitive, sexy Mr Denham'. I wonder incredulously if this is what they mean or if this is just what his sensitive nature becomes when pushed to extremes by circumstance.

“Well, I know Charlie really likes you, she's always said you're one her very favourite teachers,” I tell him.

I quickly regret my words.

Mr Denham dissolves now into full body-shaking sobs. I make out the words 'favourite teacher' and 'never knew' but nothing else coherent. I look at Luke in dismay, not seeing any path to retrieving the interview or handling the flood of tears. To my immense relief, Mrs Denham relieves us of this duty by sweeping onto the scene, her arms outstretched at the ready.

"My Henry! Mon amour! What has happened?!" she cries in a deep, lilting voice, folding her husband in a passionate embrace.

He's utterly unequal to the task of answering her and she turns her beautiful grey eyes upon Luke and I, sat awkwardly on her pristine white sofa.

"One of his students is missing. Charlie Hople."

At my words her eyes widen in shock and sympathy and her husbands weeping redoubles.

"Ah non! Une petite!" she cries, clutching her husband tighter and stroking his hair tenderly.

"We must help! We will do whatever we can my love, there is always hope!" she declares firmly.

Her words have a calming effect on Mr Denham and he raises a tear stained face to look at her.

"You're right. We'll contact the police, the school,

the poor girl's family, we'll find a way to assist!" he agrees, rubbing his red, swollen eyes.

I decide that it's best we make our escape while we can and I hastily usher Luke towards the door.

"That sounds like a wonderful plan!" I tell them brightly once we've reached the safety of the hallway, "any help you can give would be much appreciated, I'm sure!" I add, hand already on the doorknob.

I keep a bright, fixed smile on my face until the door is firmly shut behind me and I at last feel as though I can breathe.

"This better not impact my French grade, I'm already doing terribly," Luke tells me, shaking his head sadly.

"Rubbish at French, rubbish at football, is there anything you're good at?" I ask him in concern.

"Anagrams. I'm fantastic at anagrams. I just *see the word*, you know?"

"I'm not going to lie, that's unlikely to come in handy," I tell him.

"Says the girl who was looking up Morse Code."

"Morse code is a valuable skill! What if I'm trapped somewhere and the only way to get a message out is Morse Code?!" I demand.

"How are you getting this message out? And why is it limited to Morse Code?" he queries interestedly.

"I'm not sure, smoke signals maybe?"

"So you're trapped somewhere with a fire?"

"Maybe I'll start a fire and use it for smoke signals," I suggest.

"So you're trapped, you set fire to your location, and you think that Morse Code smoke signals are going to save you? You're banking on someone seeing your smoke signals, realising what they are and understanding Morse Code. I think you'll find you're actually just in a race against time for the fire brigade to find you before you burn to death."

"Actually most people who die in fires die of smoke inhalation," I tell him.

"Yes, that's a totally normal thing to know."

“I have diverse interests,” I retort defensively.

“I'm learning that, yeah,” he agrees with a smile.

We both sober at the same time, replaying the conversation we just had with Mr Denham in our minds.

“I don't think he did it,” Luke tells me.

“Neither do I, but we don't *know*.”

“You think all that could have been an act? It was pretty over the top,” Luke notes.

“I don't think so. His wife didn't react like it was unusual, did she? If he'd been acting, surely it would have been out of character and she wouldn't have just taken it in her stride.”

“But how do we confirm it's definitely not him?” he asks.

“I don't know. Follow him around maybe? See if he leads us to Charlie? He couldn't have her stashed in the house, it's so open plan she'd probably be visible from every room. If he had her here I don't think he'd have let us in. Besides, his wife would have to be in on it.”

“Can we be sure she's not? It would explain why

she'd go along with his fake reaction to the news," he asks me curiously.

"Statistically it's unlikely. There are documented cases of couples working together in abductions and murders of course, but more often it's an individual working alone."

"Gosh, you're full of fun facts!" he gives me a playful nudge but then his face falls.

"Murder," he mutters.

"What?"

"You said abductions and murders."

"I didn't mean Charlie, I don't think Charlie's *dead*," I hasten to clarify.

"You mean Rose?" he asks me tentatively.

"There's been no trace of her for ten years, so- yes I think she's dead."

I leave it at that. I don't go on to say that really, deep down, I *hope* she's dead. He hasn't listened to the true crime podcasts that I have. He hasn't read the books. He wouldn't understand that there are worse things that could happen to a little girl.

# Chapter 12

I can't help but feel that we've been left in limbo. I seem to have so many questions in my head that I can't decide which one to try to answer. Do I keep questioning men that Charlie has a crush on? Do I try to contact her dad? It all feels a bit vague. I'm rooting around in the dark because that's where Charlie vanished. She stepped out of that party and disappeared into the dark of the night -

I'm an idiot.

I let myself get distracted by Detective Sergeant Walters and her theories when I should have been following the facts. Charlie argued with Marcus, everyone saw that so it's the last confirmed point on the timeline, but according to Marcus Charlie went from him to Sarah H. I was on my way to see her when I got the call to go to the police station and it drove the plan right out of my head! I need to get back on track and find out what Sarah H knows. Charlie might even have told her where she was planning to go next or who with.

Thanks to a couple of attempts on Charlie's part to coax the two of us into becoming friends, I know her address, so we head straight there.

"What if she's not home?" Luke asks as we reach the house.

"Then we'll just have to track her down. Sarah H is the sort of person to who likes to fill her time productively so we might end up tracking her down at any number of summer jobs," I admit with a sigh.

"Productivity?! Argh! In the summer?!"

Luke is at least half joking but I appreciate it all the same. Sarah H has a talent for making me feel like I'm a total failure for not accomplishing more, while simultaneously making me feel more reluctant than ever to even try.

I hold my breath after we knock on the door, almost

hoping that no one answers, but a moment later Sarah H is staring down at me with a haughty expression.

"Penny. Gosh. What a surprise," she comments drily.

"Sarah H! As I live and breathe!" Luke exclaims, drawing a small smile from me.

"Luke Burrows, hello," she adds with a sigh and a nod in his direction.

"Is there a reason for you two being here? I don't mean to be rude but I do need to leave for work soon."

"I'm here about Charlie," I tell her in a rush, "Marcus said she went to you after their fight at the party..."

She looks at me blankly and I'm just starting to think that Marcus was making the whole thing up when she gives an impatient jerk as though waiting for me to continue.

"And? So what?" she snaps.

"She did?! Well what did she say?! Where did she go?!" I demand.

"Not that it's any of your business, but I don't

know."

"You don't know? How can you not know? If she went to talk to you-"

"She did. She came to me, as her friend, but she was smashed! I could barely understand a word she said and she left while I was fetching her some water to try to sober her up a bit."

I feel my hopes ebbing away.

"You don't know anything at all?" Luke probes.

"She was sobbing and babbling but it was mostly just about Marcus and Claire and how no one likes her," Sarah replies, checking the time on her phone.

"She said no one likes her?" I ask, feeling a pang of hurt.

"She probably just meant Marcus," Luke tries to reassure me.

"Do you remember anything else?" I ask.

Sarah sighs but does appear to give it some thought.

"She definitely talked a lot about Marcus, and she said something about being ugly, and about people not needing her. It was typical sad drunk girl stuff really."

I wish more than ever that I hadn't left the party. I hate the thought of Charlie crying and feeling like no one needed her or wanted her around. *I* need her! *I* want her! If I had stayed, who knows how different things would be now.

"Why are you here Penny Cooper?" Sarah H asks, pulling me from my melancholy self reflections.

"What?"

"Why are you here playing Nancy Drew? The police are looking for Charlie, so what difference do you think a seventeen year old is going to make?"

Her question makes me feel small and stupid and I try not to wilt under her critical gaze.

"The police think Charlie ran away," Luke tells her, taking my hand in his.

"Maybe she did. It does happen."

"Not to Charlie. She wouldn't do that," I respond with conviction.

"Why? What's more likely, that the police are totally

wrong, or that you are?"

"You think Charlie ran away? You think it's a coincidence that she disappeared ten years after her friend disappeared in the same town?" I ask, incredulously.

"You think this is about your sister, Rose?!" she asks me, surprised but clearly sceptical.

"They knew each other! Do you know how rarely girls vanish into thin air?!" I demand.

"No, but I'm sure you do," Sarah retorts, rolling her eyes at me and my 'unusual interests'.

"The chances of the two events not being connected-"

"Are for the police to determine!"

Losing all patience with my theories, Sarah steps back into her house and closes the door behind her with a bang.

"Well that went well," Luke comments, still staring at the spot that Sarah recently occupied, now just a green door.

"About as well as I expected," I add with a shrug.

"She's not your biggest fan is she."

"Not even top ten. I'm not keen on her either to be fair. She's definitely my least favourite Sarah. Sarah G is much nicer! And Sarah S is funny!"

"She is the weakest of the bunch," he agrees cheerfully.

"Besides, it turns out that she has no helpful information and she's as blinkered as the police are about Charlie's case!"

"Penny, about that, I've been thinking..." he falters.

"What?"

"Well, I completely believe you that Charlie didn't run away. I believe you that she wouldn't do that, that someone took her. I believe that," he tells me, gripping my hand.

"But?" I ask, my heart stuttering in my chest. I need him to be on my side and I suspect that in another moment he won't be.

"Well, I just think you need to consider that it might

still have nothing to do with what happened to your sister."

There's a humming in my ears.

"It's just, she was ten years old. Charlie is almost eighteen and she looks nothing like your sister did. I thought that with abductions like this-"

"Preferential sex offenders," I cut in.

"What?"

"You're talking about preferential sex offenders. The sort of person who might snatch a little red headed girl from the woods and never give her back. You think that because Charlie isn't a little read headed girl it isn't the same person. The thing is, this isn't a TV show. You can't put up the pictures of the victims and say 'Oh my God! They could be sisters!' and find the next person to be targeted. You can't look at Rose and look at Charlie and figure out the killer's 'motivation'. You're thinking about it too *simply*. It isn't *simple*," I insist, my blood boiling and my vision growing a dark tinge around the edges.

"But maybe it *is* simple. Maybe you're so desperate

for it to be connected to Rose that you're not thinking clearly. Marcus Kain was her *boyfriend*! We know they had a fight, we know he has a temper. He pushed you up against a wall for fucks sake! I don't know why you're not even *considering* him!"

"Because he was eight years old when Rose went missing!"

"THIS MIGHT HAVE NOTHING TO DO WITH ROSE!"

We both sit back, breathing deeply, faces flushed. I'm itching to run again but I'm too far from home so I slump back in my seat like a petulant child.

"Drive me home," I bark, turning to face the window.

Without a word, Luke starts the car. We drive back to my house in silence and I slam the car door behind me when I get out. I don't even glance back at Luke and he only waits a moment before reversing back out of the driveway and leaving. Anger is still throbbing in my chest, pressing against the walls of my heart. I try to slow my breathing but it feels as though I'm not getting enough air and I feel panic starting to set in.

I can do this. I can do this. I can do this alone if I have to. I can do this.

I'm not *desperate* for it to be connected to Rose!

Rose was never found! I would be much happier if I could just think that Charlie ran away, that she was hiding out somewhere safe, but I know she's not! I know she's in trouble! I know with every fibre of my being that it was the same person who took Rose! And now there's no one in the whole world who believes me.

"Hello *Pen*dulum. You've been in and out a lot!" Coop remarks with a chuckle when he sees me in the hall.

He started the 'Pen puns' years ago but this is a new one. I try to smile but the curve of my lips makes me feel sick.

"No Luke today?" he asks, seeing my flushed face.

"He's gone," I say simply, slumping against the

closed front door.

"You're worried about Charlie?" Coop asks in his simple, straightforward way.

"I am," I choke out, gripping my hands into fists to keep from crying.

He comes towards me and I'm worried that he's going to hug me, utterly destroying my flimsy veneer of stability, but he stops short.

"I know that you don't think she ran away, but the police are trained for this Pen. They've been taught what to look for and what to do. They're looking for her and the best thing that you can do is trust them. I know you have good reason not to trust the police to find someone, but there's nothing more that you can do."

He's so kind, so gentle, and so wrong.

I don't want to argue with Coop and I know it wouldn't do any good if I did so I just slip past him and make for the solitude of my room. I've missed lunch but I can already smell the beginnings of dinner being prepared in the kitchen. Everything my mother makes has onions in it and the first sign of an impending meal has always been the smell of onions being sautéed. Olly is watching the Pikachu movie in the lounge and I can hear it from upstairs. Any minute now Coop will tell him to turn the volume down. It's all so normal and safe that I feel out of place. I am teeming with fear and anger. I'm so saturated with them that I feel utterly out of place in this normal, untarnished environment. I don't belong here.

Until I get to my room.

I open my door and I can't breathe. I'm petty and immature so my first reaction is a small stab of satisfaction at being prove right, but then terror washes over me and almost drops me to my knees.

*Do you think it's connected? Do you think it's connected? Do you think it's connected?*

It's not a question now, it's a taunt, repeating in my head, stuck in a loop. It's the beat of my heart and the thrum of my blood and the tick of the clock with each second that passes.

*Do you think it's connected? Do you think it's connected? Do you think it's connected?*

I step forward.

Lying on my pillow is a single, perfect, rose.

# Chapter 13

I tear down the stairs and run to the front door, flinging it open and casting my eyes up and down the street. It's a stupid thing to do but I can't fight the impulse any more than I can just stop breathing.

"Penny?"

I spin round, mum is standing it the doorway to the kitchen, spatula in hand and a questioning look on her face.

"Hi mum," I offer, trying to breathe evenly and mask my panic.

"You're not going out again are you?" she asks, her brow creasing.

"No, no I'm not, I just- has anyone come to the house today? Anyone for me?" I ask, painstakingly keeping my voice level.

"No poppet, sorry. Were you expecting someone?" she asks.

I know that she's thinking of Luke and I hate that I blush.

"Has anyone at all come to the house today? Has anyone come inside *at all*?" I ask, stressing the words. I've always been so careful not to give her any reason to worry, any reason to panic, but maybe now is the time that we should.

"No. What's going on?" her voice is perfectly steady and I feel a surge of anger.

"HOW ARE YOU OK?!" I roar.

Coop is instantly in the hall, ready to mediate or separate as required but my mum holds up a hand to him and comes towards me.

"Penny-" she starts but I cut her off.

"YOU'VE BEEN A MESS! FOR YEARS! HOW ARE YOU OK NOW?!"

I'm pulsing with anger but I'm also desperate for an

answer.

“YOU HAD A SCREAMING PANIC ATTACK WHEN I TOOK TOO LONG IN A STARBUCKS TOILET! I HAD TO LEAD YOU WEEPING TO THE CAR AND BEG THEM NOT TO CALL THE POLICE! CHARLIE IS *MISSING*, HOW ARE YOU JUST *FINE*?!”

She winces at my words but puts her arms around me and I crumple like wet tissue paper, clinging to her form. I sob into her shoulder until I feel light and foggy, insubstantial.

“It sounds awful,” she murmurs into my hair.

I pull back, looking into her eyes, needing to know.

“For ten years, I think I've been waiting for the other shoe to drop, waiting for the next disaster, terrified. Now it has... and you're still here.”

Her face is sad, guilt painted into the lines around her eyes. I wilt under the weight of her gaze. I can still feel a small kernel of rage and injustice, but mostly I feel loved.

She's relieved it's not her child this time.

She's relieved it's not me.

"Penny?" a small, wavering voice calls from the doorway of the lounge.

I look past mum to where Olly is gripping the doorframe, his eyes wide and fearful. I force my face into a smile and reach out a hand, beckoning him over to join our embrace. He dashes in and I hoist him into my arms so that our faces are all pressed together.

I don't tell mum about the rose.

I finish watching the movie with Olly and then we all have dinner. Mum made spaghetti bolognese, one of my favourites, but I just keep thinking about Charlie. I try to piece together my recollection of Saturday evening, try to stitch the fragments of recalled conversation together word by word. Was there anything unusual? If there was, I didn't see it at the time and I don't see it now.

After dinner we watch a film on Netflix, me, mum

and Olly all piled onto the sofa. Olly's feet pressed against my knee is the only thing that keeps my heart from beating out of my chest.

Someone was in the house.

How did they get in?

Someone knows that I'm asking questions.

Someone thinks that I'm a threat.

I wish that I could feel some sort of savage pride that they're worried, but honestly I have no idea who it is. I feel no closer to Charlie now than I did in those first, gut-wrenching moments on Sunday morning when I realised that she was gone.

Maybe this isn't a warning, maybe whoever took Charlie isn't worried about me at all, maybe it's just a game. Maybe they just want me to feel afraid. If that's the case then they've done a stellar job. I can barely breathe as everyone gets ready for bed after the film's over. I look from Coop to my mum to Olly and adrenalin courses through me.

This is my fault.

I have to keep them safe.

I double check all of the doors and windows. I make sure that the spare key isn't still outside even though I know it's not. I triple check the doors and windows.

I make a cup of tea and breathe in the steam, trying to settle my racing heartbeat.

"Penny, are you going to bed, love?" Mum asks when she sees me hovering on the landing.

"Yep, on my way now," I tell her with a smile.

"Alright, good night."

Now it's just me and I have no choice but to open my door and go into my room.

For a moment I let myself believe that I imagined it, that it won't be there when I step inside, but there it is. It's a deep, blood red, a perfect bloom with seven inches of stem. I gingerly lift it from the pillow and put it into one of my desk drawers, shutting it tight.

Out of sight, out of mind.

Yeah right.

I sit down at my desk, the rose humming in the drawer beside me and I boot up my laptop. I add everything I can think of, every detail of every conversation, but the words are like static on the page. There's too much information and none of it helps. I check my emails but there haven't been any new pictures sent through all day. I go back through the ones I already have, I look again for any sign of Charlie even though I've scoured them a dozen times. I have the feeling I'm missing something, like fingers trailing up my spine setting my hairs on end. The pictures trail off as the night went on. People stopped thinking about photos the more they drank I suppose. There are some girls who kept up a steady stream of photography throughout the night, but they didn't get any shots of Charlie, they aren't her crowd, they're more likely to hang around with Claire.

That's it. Marcus and Claire.

I check again, to make sure that I'm right, but I am. The last photo of Charlie is from eleven forty. After that she isn't in a single picture. And neither are Marcus and Claire.

This doesn't have to mean anything. Maybe they were still at the party and just not in any pictures. Maybe they left and it had nothing to do with Charlie. There's no way they could have been involved with Rose's disappearance and - temper or not - I don't think that they're involved with Charlie's now. But -

I can't help but remember what Luke said: that maybe I was overlooking the obvious.

I take a sip of my tea but it's grown cold. Time is slipping away from me and I'm no closer to bringing Charlie home. My eyes ache with tiredness but I still feel the fizz of fear throughout my body. I check the doors and windows again but everything is still locked up tight. Peering out into the darkened street it's easy to imagine that every shadow is someone crouched, watching. Eventually I have to give up my vigil and head back upstairs. I change into my pyjamas but then I slip quietly into Olly's room. He's a small lump, gently breathing under Pokemon sheets and I climb in beside him, feeling myself relax at last.

I've got him. I'll keep him safe.

I haven't shared a bed with Olly before and it's an experience that I won't be in a hurry to repeat. It turns out that my brother is not a peaceful sleeper. He doesn't so much toss and turn, as stretch, roll and cartwheel. He is however, delighted to find me in with him when he wakes up in the morning. He snuggles into me, a giggling mass of cuddles and warmth that almost makes up for the bruises that I'm sure are already developing.

Once I've disentangled myself from the mass of brother and bedding, I return to my own room while Olly goes in search of breakfast. I flop down on my desk chair, checking my reflection quickly for black eyes or possibly a broken nose. I appear to be miraculously unscathed, though I still feel sore and bruised all over. I switch on my laptop and look back over my notes in case I missed anything last night, but it's all just as useless and inconsequential in the morning light. There aren't any new emails with pictures either so I bring up Facebook, hoping there might be some new photos there. Instead I see another comment from NoMatter.

'She brought it on herself.'

The words send a chill through me. I'm not the only one who believes that something bad has happened to Charlie Hople, I'm just the only one who thinks that she didn't deserve it.

Is it NoMatter? Are they the one who has Charlie? Why else would they believe that she didn't run away when that's the narrative that everyone else in town has accepted?

I need to figure out where to go from here but I'm at a loss. I haven't talked to the last name on my list yet, Lance Pentuck. Should I see him today or should I cross him off the list altogether? After all, the rose was left in my room before I'd even met Lance.

If I had to make a guess now, based on everything I know so far, I would have to guess Coach Dan. He was so angry when we spoke to him and I only have his word for it that he was at the hospital on Saturday night. I don't trust him.

Making a snap decision, I pull on some shorts and a t-shirt and go downstairs. I move quietly and manage to get out of the house undetected and immediately break into a jog. My legs are still sore from my run to the rose garden and I move slowly. Still, I get there eventually, the 'Get Dan And Dirty' sign coming into view. No one is leaving as I arrive this time and I don't have the nerve to ring the doorbell, so I station myself across the street, perched on a low garden wall, and I wait. I have no idea what I'm waiting for - perhaps for Coach Dan to come outside and yell at me? His wife to leave the house so that I can waylay her?

The twitch of a curtain gives me my answer. I cross back over the street and, gritting my teeth, ring the doorbell of the house next door. It's opened in just seconds and a small, plump woman with silver grey curls is smiling up at me.

"Hello dear, are you looking for someone?"

How on earth am I supposed to answer that?

"I was just wondering about um- about your neighbours," I explain haltingly.

"The workout classes?" she asks me.

"Actually no, well- I mean, yes. Yes, him," I stammer incoherently.

She just gazes up at me, smile unwavering.

"I'm Deborah, but you can call me Deb," she tells me, miraculously undaunted by my inability to converse like a normal human being.

"I'm Penny. Penny Cooper," I tell her gratefully.

The reaction is immediate. Her eyes widen slightly, then narrow as she scrutinises me more closely. Then her whole face is transformed by pity but her eyes are bright with excitement. I know this reaction, I've seen it before. To some people, tragedies like my family's are like catnip.

"Penny Cooper! You poor lamb! Let me get you some tea!" she cries, all broken-hearted felicity.

"You know what, tea would be lovely!" I tell her with

a wide smile.

She matches me grin for grin, unable to believe her luck. Ordinarily I would be slinking away from this situation, but for once I plan to make the most of it. This woman thinks that I'm a mystery to be harvested, but I intend to be the one who walks away from this exchange with information.

She gets me set up at her small dining table, with a pot of tea and an entire lemon drizzle cake between us. I expect that I'll be presented with fresh slices until my well of interesting information runs dry.

"Penny Cooper, you poor thing," she remarks, shaking her head sadly.

I nod my agreement, lips pursed into a sad smile, projecting the brave young victim she clearly wants me to be.

"You look just like your sister, dear. Of course her picture was in all the papers at the time, and you look just like her!" she pronounces these words as though she's offering me some kind of compliment, as though no one could imagine a greater honour than to be the spitting image of their dead sibling.

"People used to think we were twins," I admit.

The words don't come easily. For years I've stubbornly refused to discuss Rose or the events of that day and now it's like a muscle that's atrophied. I've lost the knack of talking about her naturally.

"It was such a tragedy, the town's never seen anything like it!" she remarks, shaking her head again and setting her perfectly set curls bouncing.

"Until now. There were searches again on Sunday, for Charlie, Charlotte, Hople," I say quickly, leaping on the opening before she has a chance to seal it shut.

"I heard that a young girl ran away," Deb tells me a little reluctantly. Clearly she'd rather keep the focus on Rose.

"Charlie didn't run away," I say firmly.

"Are you sure?" she asks in surprise, "I'm *sure* I was told that-"

"Charlie's my best friend, she wouldn't run away.

The police are looking for her."

I know I'm making it sound as though the police suspect foul play, but I'm pretty sure that's the only way to make this topic salacious enough to hold Deb's interest.

"Well I never! You'd think a small town like this would be safe!" she cries, curls swishing in horror.

"Your neighbour is her netball coach," I say, trying to keep my voice level. I need to tread carefully here. I don't think I should outright accuse Dan of anything, I don't know if he and Deb are close.

"Her netball coach?!" Deb exclaims, as though this is prime gossip.

I can't tell if it really means something to her or if she's just mentally lining up Dan as a possible source of more information.

"Yes, she really likes him, she thinks he's great," I probe, watching her closely for a reaction. The trouble is, Deb is a caricature of normal interaction and she reacts to everything as though she's performing for the people in the back. At my words she widens her eyes and flings her hands up to her mouth theatrically, with a gasp that's practically a scream.

"Well I never!" she cries spectacularly unhelpfully.

"Is that surprising?" I ask desperately.

"Well! And her so young..." she comments in the tone of 'what is the world coming to.'

"Young?" I ask in increasing frustration.

She purses her lips to show that she's not sure whether she should explain, though of course she's desperate to. I adopt a plaintive, wide-eyed expression.

"Please, I'm just so worried about my friend," I implore.

"Well, you didn't hear it from me, but I don't trust that man. I know for a fact that his poor wife has caught him more than once! I hoped that the baby would be an end to all that, but some men are just rotten to the core!"

So, Dan Cosford cheated on his wife.

"Do you know who he was with? Who besides his wife I mean?" I ask quickly.

"Some young woman who teaches a Zumba class in St Neots. There have been others too mind."

A woman who teaches a Zumba class isn't likely to be Charlie's age.

"What about the others? Did you ever see them?" I ask, pulling out my phone and flicking through to a picture of Charlie. "What about her? Have you ever seen her here?"

"Is that your friend? She doesn't look familiar," she admits.

I deflate for a moment but then quickly regroup.

"What about Saturday?" I ask.

"Saturday?"

"Yes, Saturday night. Do you know where your neighbours were?" I elaborate.

"At the hospital!" she chirps immediately.

I wilt completely.

My best suspect has an alibi.

"Poor Tina was having contractions. I told her it was probably just Braxton Hicks but she was petrified. The baby isn't due for another six weeks. There for absolutely *hours*! I had to get a taxi home because I can't drive at night any more and I would have been too tired to even if my eyes were still what they used to be."

"You went with them?" I ask, surprised. She isn't who I would choose for moral support.

"Well someone had to drive Tina," she tells me.

"Dan doesn't drive?" I ask, struggling to follow the conversation.

"He does, but he wasn't here," she explains.

"But, you said they were both at the hospital Saturday night," I remind her, trying not to sound accusatory.

"Yes, in the night they were, but at first it was just Tina and I because he was working or some such nonsense. Dan arrived just after midnight and he stayed with her until morning. They both came back home at around seven."

"Just after midnight?! Do you know what time exactly?!"

"No later than quarter past, I would say," she tells me meditatively.

"And which hospital was this?"

# Chapter 14

My head is in a whirl. I feel as though I haven't had a straight-forward thought in days. Every notion leads to a question and then another and another.

Dan Cosford didn't arrive at the hospital until 00.15 and Charlie was last seen at 11.40. Would that be enough time? Thirty five minutes to make someone disappear? Maybe if he was already waiting outside the party for her at 11.40 and she left right then... but how long would it have taken him to get to the hospital? It depends where he took her after the party.

I keep looping back round to one question. Where do you hide a teenage girl?

There are a few abandoned houses around town, Dan's a local, he might know them, or he might have a place of his own like a storage container or something.

I don't loiter outside the Cosfords' house any more, I've already got what I came for. Coach Dan's alibi either holds up or it doesn't. I'll need to test out the timings to be sure and now that Luke and I aren't on speaking terms I don't have access to a car. Or a driver.

Lance Pentuck is up next. He's on my list so I still want to talk to him, even if I have to do it alone. I walk in the direction of Charlie's house. I can't remember Mr Pentuck's house number but I'll know it when I see it-Charlie points it out every time we pass by. It has a dark green door, potted plants out front and each time we see it Charlie announces that it's the house where the local DILF lives. I've always suspected that she does it just to make me cringe but now I'm not so sure.

When I reach Charlie's street I stop in my tracks. There are two police cars outside Charlie's house, one still has its lights flashing, sending ineffectual strobes across the house, almost invisible in the bright sun. Next thing I know, I'm running. I tear down the street, in the middle of the road because the pavement is too narrow with it's border of cars. I swerve onto Charlie's front path but I've picked up too much momentum to slow down all the way and I collide with the front door with a thud. I step back, massaging the shoulder that took the brunt of the impact, but a second later the door is opened and a uniformed officer is looking at me with definite hostility. I push past him as though I haven't noticed and burst into the lounge, looking around me wildly for answers.

Wendy is on the sofa, her face pale and tear-stained and I'm pretty sure that she's still in the same outfit she was wearing on Sunday morning. I feel a pang of guilt for not being here but, really, it isn't me that Wendy needs. She needs her daughter back.

My gaze moves to DS Walters, seated precariously on the edge of the Hoples' sagging armchair, her lips pursed at the sight of me. What is that expression? Annoyance? No. Guilt maybe?

"What's happened," I ask flatly.

Wendy half rises at the sight of me, but it's as though the physical exertion is too much. She sags back down, her arms still extended, reaching for me. I rush forwards, taking her hands in mine and settle next to her on the sofa.

"Penny would know," Wendy says to Walters, her voice small and hopeful.

"Know what?" I ask, looking from one to the other.

DS Walters sighs.

"Something has been found. In the woods. We need someone to confirm whether or not it belongs to Charlie."

I go cold. It's an odd sensation, as though someone has opened a hole in the top of my head and is pouring ice water into my body, filling me from the bottom up.

"What is it?" I ask, my voice barely a whisper.

"A shoe. A dog walker found it early this morning and brought it to the police station," she tells me, gesturing to one of the other officers to bring it over.

"A dog walker?" I ask, "But you searched the woods, there was a huge search on Sunday, are you saying they missed a *shoe*?!"

She flinches and I feel a savage satisfaction that I've wounded her, dented her professional veneer.

"Can you confirm whether this is one of the shoes that Charlie was wearing the night of the party?"

She hands me an object in a clear evidence bag and the world stills. I think at first that it's my mind's reaction to an overload of adrenalin, but then I realise that everyone really has stilled, watching me in silence, awaiting my proclamation.

I turn it over in my hands, slowly, carefully.

It's a wedge high-heel, tall and black, with three straps, two of which are unbuckled. One looks snapped. The insole is a pearlescent cream, clearly showing a smear of dark, reddish brown.

They read my answer in my desolate, panic-stricken face but DS Walters repeats it anyway.

"Penny, can you confirm whether or not this is one

of the shoes that Charlie Hople was wearing on the night of the party?"

I nod and then clear my throat, moistening my mouth and tongue that suddenly feel dry as the sahara.

"Yes," I croak, "This is hers."

The shoe is swiftly removed from my slack grip and whisked away.

"Was that blood?!" I ask quickly, looking after the vanished shoe in desperation. It feels foolish, but I wish they'd let me hold on to it for a little longer.

"We're having it tested," DS Walters tells me in her calm, efficient voice.

"But it was blood, wasn't it? Charlie's?" I ask frantically, feeling Wendy grip my arm.

"It does appear to be blood, we're having it tested for type and DNA but these things take time," she tells us.

"Time?!" I demand, my voice rising.

"Penny-"

"Charlie has been missing since SATURDAY

NIGHT!" I roar, Wendy flinching beside me.

"Pen-"

"I *told you*! I told you that Charlie would never run away! I told you that someone took her! I told you that she was in trouble! Her bloody shoe has been out there all this time and you didn't even find it?! You weren't even really looking were you! You were so sure that you knew what had happened, you were just going through the motions! You don't even *know* Charlie, but you were sure she'd run off!"

I scream the words at her, my whole body pulsing with a rage that I didn't even know I was capable of feeling. She looks steadily back at me, her expression inscrutable and in the face of that calm professionalism my anger ebbs away.

"What happens now?" I ask, chest still heaving.

"We are looking for Charlie, Penny, and we will keep looking for her," she tells me sincerely.

"You said someone was going to see her dad," I remember, throwing an awkward look in Wendy's direction.

"Yes, we did confirm his account. There's no sign that Charlie was ever there. It seems that he really did tell her that he doesn't want any contact with her," she tells me.

Oh God, poor Charlie. All those dreams and stories and it turns out that her blunt jokes about abandonment were closer to the mark.

"When did she call him?" I ask.

DS Walters checks the notes in her file before answering me.

"A little over a month ago," she says.

I let that sink in for a moment.

"That's around the time Charlie started acting different. That must be what she was keeping from me."

I thought that I would feel relieved to know what had been going on with her, and that it was nothing to do with me, but I just feel sad. Sad that Charlie's dad doesn't want to know her, sad that she didn't feel she could tell me, and sad that it had started to change things between us. Maybe if it hadn't she'd still be safe now.

"That's when she started to behave differently?" DS Walters asks.

"It's when she started seeming frustrated and... distant. It's when she started wanting to date Marcus Kain and go out all the time," I explain.

"Marcus Kain, this is the boyfriend from the party, yes? The one she had an argument with?" DS Walters asks.

I can practically see the cogs turning, a new narrative being written to fit the new evidence.

I want to tell her that Marcus had nothing to do with it, that he was too young to have hurt Rose, but the memory of Marcus' arm against my chest stops me. The memory of those pictures holds me back. So many pictures from the party and none of Marcus, Claire or Charlie after eleven forty.

"Yes, they argued," I say instead.

DS Walters narrows her eyes slightly and I almost

wish that I could be there when she questions him. I doubt he'd get away with pushing her against a wall.

The officers leave en masse, a small army in matching uniforms, off to put the fear of God into a teenage boy. Once they're gone the house is so quiet that the air feels thick, like cotton wadding. Wendy is still in her position on the sofa, like she's afraid to move. I'm afraid too. I'm afraid that if I stay in this house any longer I'll be trapped in the same fear, caught in it, frozen in place like Wendy.

I go to the door, desperate to be outside. I look back at Wendy, guilty that I'm leaving her alone now when she so clearly needs someone, but she isn't looking at me, her eyes are wide and vacant, her thoughts far away. I slip outside, closing the door softly behind me.

It feels strange, like leaving the cinema in the middle of the day. It seems like it should be dark outside. After everything that just happened, Charlie's bloody shoe and Wendy's stricken face, it feels as though hours should have passed, not minutes. I walk back to the pavement and turn right, following the street along a few houses to a dark green door bordered by potted plants. A woman is outside with a watering can, tending to a lavender in a terracotta pot but she looks up when I stop walking.

"Have you just come from Wendy's?" she asks me, looking back at the retreating police cars.

Her kind face is crumpled with worry.

I nod, not trusting myself to speak.

"Is she alright?" she asks me, seeing my pale face.

"They found a shoe," I mutter, my voice small and breathy, my eyes instantly brimming with tears.

"Oh God," she whispers, her hand going to her mouth.

"She's on her own, Wendy is I mean," I tell her quickly, my voice raspy and foreign.

"Oh, no problem," she tells me instantly, all gentle efficiency.

She sets down the watering can, dusts her hands against her jeans and pushes her front door open.

“Lance! I'm going to Wendy's!” she calls into the house.

A second later a man with a baby on his hip appears, a look of enquiry on his face.

“What was that, love?” he asks his wife.

“Wendy needs someone, I'm going to pop round there,” she tells him quickly before kissing both him and the baby and hurrying away.

“Everything alright?” Lance asks me, seeing that I'm still standing, rooted to the spot.

“They found a shoe,” I repeat, suddenly aware that tears are streaming down my face.

“Oh God, do you want some water or something?” he asks me, looking after his wife like he wishes that she'd come back.

I hesitate for a moment but the baby in his arms persuades me. No one murders someone in front of their own baby, surely. Well... there's been some debate about Gary Ridgeway but he always denied it. Not because he was a stellar parent, just that the presence on the scene of an infant introduced too many variables.

"Yes, please," I mumble and follow him inside.

It's a small house and absolutely packed with life. The stark contrast to the one I just left makes me feel incredibly grateful that Mrs Pentuck has gone to sit with Wendy. Maybe she can carry some of this life and energy with her, enough to keep Wendy going. Lance sits me at a small table and places the baby in a high-chair beside me. I can see two more children playing in the garden, the french doors from the kitchen wide open so the sounds of their laughter fill the house. Lance was clearly in the middle of something in the kitchen and there appears to be batter of some kind spattered around the surfaces and walls.

He presents me with a plastic beaker of water and then scatters some cheerios over the tray of the high-chair for the baby to amuse itself with. He watches the kids in the garden playing for a moment and then, once he's reassured that they're happy and occupied he turns his attention to me.

"Are you alright?" he asks gently.

I nod and have another sip of water.

"You said they found a shoe," he prompts, looking quickly at the baby as though worried it might hear something inappropriate for its tender age.

"In the woods," I confirm, watching him.

He sighs and looks utterly sad.

"Maybe that'll help. Maybe it'll point them in the right direction," he suggests, like someone clamouring for a silver lining in a very dark sky.

"She babysat for you," I say, not sure how else to bring up their connection.

"She did, just a couple of times before Mia here was born. Lizzie's been on maternity leave since then so we haven't really had a night out in a while," he tells me, blushing and grimacing good naturedly.

I nod vaguely, my mind moving very slowly.

"She's very nice though, Charlie, the kids loved her," he tells me, his eyes back on the two little ones running around in the back-garden.

I don't know why I'm here. Lance Pentuck is still standing by the french doors, keeping a distance of a couple of metres between us like he doesn't know how to interact with people my age. He's not looking at me like the sister and best friend of two of his victims, he's barely looking at me at all, he's watching his kids play, making sure they're safe.

Mum always drummed into me that anyone could be a threat. You never knew what someone's intentions were, any stranger passing in the street could be a monster. I've listened to enough true crime to know that in some ways she's right, but I'm not passing Lance Pentuck in the street, I'm sitting in his kitchen next to his baby, talking to him from across the room.

I don't think he's a monster.

I stand up to go and smile faintly at Lance's obvious relief.

"Thank you for the water," I tell him.

"No problem. I'm sure she's- I hope she's..."

He doesn't finish the sentence and I'm glad of it. I

feel hollowed out and I think that an insubstantial platitude might crack my outer shell.

I walk home in a thick fog. The police finally believe that Charlie's in trouble and I feel more alone than ever. I wish I could call Luke. Maybe I should.

The trouble is, I remember the kiss. I remember the electricity of it, the perfect, singing charge, but I also remember the way his face looked when he said that this all had nothing to do with Rose. I remember the way his voice sounded, raised in anger. I want to unpick the memories, separate and smooth them out, but I'm too tired. I really like Luke but I still feel angry with him. The feelings are all jumbled up and it's too much to face right now. I need to find Charlie.

Still, there is a small lingering doubt that Luke was right. The police are definitely turning their attentions towards Marcus Kain. Perhaps I am missing something here.

Assuming that she hasn't moved, I actually know where Claire Netherhall lives. We were partnered together on a history project a couple of years ago. It was excruciating. Apparently, being quiet and not having many friends should mean that I've signed some sort of contract agreeing to be a perfect student and get top grades. Claire was outraged at my mediocrity, but I've never done particularly well with History, I can't remember all the names and dates.

Her house is on the far side of town, but Upper Chalfont isn't a big place. I set off on foot and take the time to let my hair down and tie it up in a fresh bun. I wish it seemed less important, but I have a vague feeling that if I don't at least look presentable I won't even get past the door.

I've spent a decade avoiding people like Claire Netherhall. The sort of people who look at what you're wearing, who you're talking to, how you behave and then tell you that you're wrong. You are living incorrectly. It takes a monstrous effort for me to ring the doorbell on the tiny, boxy little house and as I wait, beads of sweat break out on the back of my neck. Back in the school project days, Claire's mother reminded me of every single pageant mum on every reality TV show from Toddlers And Tiaras to Crowned. She somehow managed to present the image of damsel-in-distress and heinous-vulture all at the same time. I'm relieved when it's Claire that answers the door, though she doesn't look particularly pleased to see me...

"What do you want?" she demands, crossing her arms over her chest and looking down at me like dirt on her shoe.

"I want to talk to you," I reply, forcing my voice not to drop to a whisper.

"About what?" she asks me, making no move to invite me in.

"About the party last Saturday. About Charlie," I tell her.

She rolls her eyes and flips her cascade of golden hair over her shoulder.

"I'm pretty sure we've done this already. I don't know anything about your skank friend," she declares.

"They found her shoe in the woods this morning. The police think that something bad happened to her," I explain.

"That's not my problem," she replies, a slight smile lifting the corners of her perfectly painted lips.

I feel my anger stretch and flex its claws. There must be something of it in my eyes because Claire definitely reacts. She almost looks impressed.

"Fine, whatever, you can come in," she tells me carelessly, leading the way indoors.

The house is just as I remember. It's a temporary shell with the absolute minimum of money expended on it since its owners have plans for bigger and better things. There aren't any pictures on the walls, no knick-knacks or personalisation at all, since at any day Claire's mother might meet a nice billionaire and move them both into his mansion. It hasn't happened yet but not for lack of trying.

Claire flounces into the lounge and flops down into a characterless beige chair.

“So something 'bad' has happened now, has it?” she says with a smirk.

“Yes. It has,” I tell her definitely, but again she just rolls her eyes.

“Charlie Hople is just desperate for attention, as usual,” she snaps.

I glower at her but I don't have a good response. Charlie does like attention. It's not how Claire's making it sound, but Charlie has felt overlooked and sometimes I think she is louder than needed, to compensate. More than once Charlie has described herself as the Ron Weasley to my Harry Potter. It always made me feel that she was reading the books wrong, but still- the meaning was clear. Charlie knows that losing Rose devastated my life, but it also made me a celebrity overnight. Even now, ten years later people still fix their eyes on me everywhere I go. Charlie and I enter a room and people don't even see that she's there. She gets shunted into the background. We both hate it. We would swap if we could, I would happily trade all my notoriety for her invisibility. School is different. Teachers are careful with me, they make allowances, but kids are cruel and insensitive. I'm as quiet as possible at school, while Charlie is bright and bubbly. According to Claire, too bright.

"She's in trouble Claire," I mutter.

"Well if she is, it's nothing to do with me," she announces calmly, examining her perfect nails.

"You saw her at the party, you and Marcus-"

"Charlie had no *business* being with Marcus!"

"They were seeing each other! They'd been making out all evening!" I bark at her, not sure why I'm defending a relationship that I hated with every fibre of my being.

"Marcus is just too nice for his own good, he doesn't know how to say no to people sometimes," she explains to me.

I can't help it. I snort.

"Marcus is a really nice guy!" she insists venomously.

"Yeah, right up until you say something he doesn't

like and he slams you into a wall," I comment darkly.

"What? Marcus wouldn't do that," she counters, shaking her head firmly.

"He has a temper Claire," I tell her seriously.

"He's just passionate! He's the sort of person who protects the people he cares about!" she insists.

I can't imagine Marcus caring about anyone but himself but I don't think that saying that would win me any points with my current company.

"Charlie was last seen at eleven forty that night. There's no pictures of you and Marcus after that. Where did you go?" I ask instead.

"I told you, we were together all night," she tells me triumphantly.

"Where were you? Where did you go?" I press.

"I'm telling you, we were together the whole time, neither of us could have hurt your friend," she explains as though she's talking to a very simple child. I make a mental note to send her some articles on couples who kill together. The same articles I discounted in the case of Mr Denham and his wife. Yes, I'm a hypocrite.

“Were you still at the party? Still at Luke's house?” I probe.

“No, we left. We came back here,” she tells me.

“Both of you?! What about your mum?” I ask on impulse.

“She doesn't mind, she likes Marcus, his father is in finance,” she says as though this explains everything. Maybe it does.

“You were both here?” I ask again, a headache starting behind my eyes.

“Yes, I just told you that,” she snipes impatiently.

So Marcus tried to get Charlie to sleep with him and when she refused he moved right on to Claire.

“Marcus and I are *together* now,” she tells me proudly.

“Since the party?” I ask, my annoyance clear in my voice.

“Marcus and I are a much better couple, we make sense! Him and Charlie didn't! She's not even pretty!

Marcus has liked me for *years*."

"Why have you only just got together now then?" I ask, allowing myself to be petty.

Claire's face pinches in annoyance.

"He was too young to settle in a committed relationship. But this tragedy has brought us together," she proclaims, very seriously.

"Did he tell you that? Or did you tell him? Besides, I thought you said that nothing has happened to Charlie. She just ran off, right? So how is it a *tragedy*?"

I can see I've worn out my welcome. I wrack my brains quickly, trying to think of anything I still want to ask.

"Claire, what time did you and Marcus leave the party?" I ask before she can kick me out.

"We left at about twelve but Charlie had already gone. I told you, it was nothing to do with us," she explains, clearly bored at repeating herself over and over.

"Wait, how do you know she'd already left?" I ask.

"Because I *saw*! She left a few minutes before us,

when she realised that she couldn't claw Marcus back into her grip."

"You saw her leave?! What time?! Do you know where she went? Did she leave with anyone?!" I ask quickly, leaning forward in my seat, my hands gripping my knees.

"Yes I saw her leave, she was going to yours," she tells me, looking at me like she thinks I'm an idiot.

"What?"

"When we saw her go to the gate Marcus made a joke about her not walking through the woods, you know, because of your sister, and then she said that she'd already called someone to drive her, someone who *actually cared* about her," Claire explains, rolling her eyes again. I wonder if they get tired.

"You saw her go and she told you that someone was picking her up? That they would drive her to mine?" I demand.

"Yes!" Claire snaps.

"Claire why the hell didn't you tell anyone this?!

Why didn't you tell the police?! This whole time they thought she ran away!" I cry, rising to my feet and taking a step towards her.

She flinches back in her chair as though she thinks I'm going to attack her and for a moment I want to. I want to jump at her and hit her and scratch her and scream at her until she cares that Charlie is missing.

"Maybe she *did* run away, *I* don't know!" she claims defensively.

"You heard her say that she'd called someone to drive her to mine! What, you think they just got lost?!" I demand hotly.

"Maybe she changed her mind! Maybe they picked her up and she decided to run off with them!" Claire counters.

I bury my face in my hands and try desperately to resist the urge to slap her.

"It's a five minute drive Claire! That's a lot to happen in five minutes!" I hiss.

"Well - I – don't - know! It's nothing to do with

me!" she insists again.

"What time was it?" I press.

"I told you, not long before us."

"What time exactly?"

"Urgh!" she exclaims impatiently, pulling out her phone and scrolling through her pictures.

"There, it was 11.51 and we left at about twelve," she tells me.

I snatch the phone from her hand and stare intently at the screen. There she is, in the background of a selfie of Claire and Marcus kissing, Charlie walking out the garden gate.

"You knew you had this?!" I demand.

"YOU PSYCHO! GIVE ME BACK MY PHONE!" she roars, lunging for it.

I hold it behind me, out of her reach.

"You knew I was looking for pictures of Charlie from that night!" I shout at her.

"This is nothing to do with me!" she shrieks.

"No?! I thought that this was the *trauma* that

brought you and Marcus together?!" I remind her.

"You're a bitch!" she spits at me, "I am so glad that Alex came to his senses and ditched you!"

Clearly she thinks that she's insulting me but I unexpectedly break out laughing, my head all the way back, like I've never heard anything so funny.

Alex Hall. He seems a world away now. I can't remember what I ever even thought I liked about him.

"Alex Hall is a self-serving creep. Just like Marcus. Just like you."

I hold my arm out, keeping her at a distance while she silently fumes at me, and I send the photo to myself along with any others from that night. When I'm done I throw her phone down onto the chair behind her and stride to the front door. Claire's voice follows me as I go.

"Your skank friend brought this on herself psycho!"

I slam the font door behind me, my body ablaze with anger. If Claire had talked to the police, if she'd told them what she'd heard, how much time would have been saved? If they hadn't had to wait for someone to stumble across a broken and bloodied shoe in the woods, maybe they would have already found Charlie by now.

I run home, wishing I could keep going, keep pounding the pavement, my steps falling in line with my heartbeat and gradually slowing it down from its hummingbird pace. I want to knock on doors and search houses. I want my friend back, but Charlie's face is watching me pass from every lamppost and fence. The flyers with her picture are still up from that initial search on the Sunday but the corners are curling, the paper crinkling and the colours bleeding out at the edges. Charlie's blurring out of existence. I need to work smart.

When I get home I go straight up to my room. I don't want to have to explain to anyone about Charlie's shoe and Wendy's terrified face. I sit down at my computer and I type up everything I learned from the police and from Claire. I feel a small spark of elation at being able to update my timeline but the stretch of time after 11.51 on Saturday night is so long now that I can barely think about it.

How long has Charlie been missing for now?

I add Claire's pictures to the folder on my desktop and then start to go through them. I search each and every one for any sign of Charlie. I suspect that Claire was intentionally staying close to Marcus so Charlie is in the background of quite a few. After Marcus and Charlie emerge from the utility room, there's a dramatic shift. Charlie and Marcus are no longer locked in an embrace and Claire is much closer to Marcus. Then comes the fateful kiss followed by a staggering number of pictures of Claire and Marcus, snapped by an artfully pouting Claire, her arm outstretched to capture as much of their forms as possible. Objectively I can recognise that Claire is attractive. She has perfect, straight golden hair, a perfectly made-up face and a fantastic figure. I've often seen her and her mother at the gym, their matching dyed hair tied up in identical ponytails, working themselves to exhaustion to stay perfectly trim and toned. Still, the contrast between her pout and Charlie's wide smile doesn't do her any favours in my eyes. She makes a much better match for the self-absorbed, shallow Marcus Kain though.

When I get to the picture of Charlie at the garden gate I stop, staring at it, absorbing every detail. Only a sliver of her face is visible but it's clear that she's crying. She looks drunk too, as though her grip on the gate is keeping her upright.

Who would she call? In that state, who would she trust to drive her to mine? It couldn't be someone at the party if she called them to pick her up. I scan through the other photos quickly but it looks as though all of our close friends are still there, playing beer pong or slouched around the fire. She couldn't have called any of them, it must have been someone else. If she was seeing someone, if she was having an affair with a married man, I suppose it must have been him. But then, what happened? Why did she never make it to mine? She was upset, did she start to make a scene? Threaten to tell his wife? Why did he suddenly need to make her disappear?

Or, was she lying? Had she not called anyone?

Maybe she set off on foot for mine, drunk and weeping, and someone who had been watching her took advantage of her vulnerability.

I need to talk to DS Walters, I need to know whether Charlie called someone just before 11.51.

I print off the picture of Charlie leaving and a full copy of my notes and put it all in my bag. After the hours I spent at the police station after Rose disappeared, I'd promised myself I'd never go there again but now it'll be twice in as many days.

I go up to the front desk, manned by a uniformed officer safely ensconced behind a sheet of perspex. I hover awkwardly until he looks up from the papers in front of him.

"Can I help you?"

"My name is Penny Cooper, I need to see DS Walters," I tell him.

"She's very busy at the moment but I can-"

"It's really important," I insist.

"I'll see if she's available, if you want to take a seat,"

he offers, gesturing at the row of plastic seats bolted to the wall behind me.

"Thank you," I tell him, staying where I am.

He calls back and looks faintly surprised by whatever it is that he's told.

"She'll be right out," he tells me, looking at me curiously. He's young. Too young to have been working when Rose went missing.

DS Walters appears through a doorway and, smiling, motions for me to follow her. She leads me to a small office with a desk, over full but meticulously arranged. She sits down behind it and nods towards the empty chair across from her.

"How can I help you Penny?" she asks me calmly.

"I found out what time exactly Charlie left the party, but I need to know whether she called anyone," I explain in a rush.

"I'm sorry?"

"Charlie's phone records. You have them, don't you. Can you tell me if she called someone between eleven thirty and eleven fifty?" I ask, trying to keep my thoughts clear.

"Penny, you must know that I can't tell you that. It's part of an ongoing investigation," she tells me.

"But it's important! She called someone to drive her to mine!" I explain.

"Penny, walk me though what you're talking about."

I take a deep breath before starting again.

"At the party, Charlie was with Marcus, but then he kissed Claire. Charlie was upset, she decided to leave. She told Marcus and Claire that she'd called someone who cares about her to drive her to mine. Now, I know she might have been lying, just saying it because she was upset, but if she was telling the truth then that has to be the guy! I've been trying to figure out who she might have been seeing, but if she made that call then we can just check who the number belongs to!" I tell her excitedly. I've handed her the photo and pulled out my notes as I've been talking and she's sifting through them, her eyebrows raised.

"Penny, do you mean to tell me that you've been questioning people that you think may have abducted your friend?!"

Her tone of horror sets my insides writhing.

"You weren't looking for her," I mutter in a small, stubborn voice.

"Penny, we have been looking for Charlie Hople since she was reported missing! I know that you don't think that the situation has been handled well, and I can admit that we may have been premature in assuming that she ran away, but we *have been looking*. We scoured every inch of those woods and we've spoken to people close to your friend. We've searched her social media, her emails, her phone records. We are looking for Charlie. You should not be putting yourself in danger trying to do our jobs for us!"

I don't say anything, I just stare down at the desk, my face flushed.

"What made you suspect these men?" She asks me after going back through my notes.

"Charlie likes them, she has crushes..." I tell her.

"We have actually spoken to a number of these people already," she admits.

"Dan Cosford?! He was really angry when I asked him about Charlie and he said that he was at the hospital all night but he didn't get there until after twelve!"

"Penny, I can't confirm who we've spoken to," she reports firmly.

"What about the call then? Did she make one?" I ask hopefully.

DS Walters looks at me blankly and at first I'm sure she isn't going to answer, but then-

"There was a call made. Just after eleven forty. It was to a burner phone, the number can't be traced. Wendy doesn't know anyone using that phone number, but do you think that you could have a look at it? See if it's a number that you know?"

"Yes! Of course!"

She opens a manilla folder in front of her and sorts

through the pages until she finds what she's looking for, a report of Charlie's calls for the past month. She slides it towards me, pointing out a highlighted number right at the end. I pull out my phone and start to type it in but nothing comes up. Unwilling to give in I manually check through my contacts. Now that it includes most of the people in our year at school it takes me a couple of minutes but there's nothing there. I don't have the number.

"No, nothing," I admit.

I go to hand the call sheet back to DS Walters, but as I do I notice that there are other highlighted entries. Just a couple, the same number, calls lasting between five and ten minutes.

"Was she talking to them before a month ago?" I ask.

DS Walters just looks at me.

"Ongoing investigation, right," I mumble.

"Indeed."

"Can you find who a Facebook account belongs to?"

I ask suddenly.

"A Facebook account?"

"I started a page, looking for Charlie, asking if anyone knows anything. There's one person who left a couple of comments that seem different from the others. Everyone else on there assumes that Charlie ran away but this one person doesn't. They said that she got what she deserved," I tell her.

"The account named NoMatter?" she asks, one eyebrow raised.

"You've been on the Facebook page?" I ask, surprised.

"Of course. I have someone trying to identify the individual behind the NoMatter account, but I feel I should point out that there's no reason to suppose that they actually know anything or that they're involved. Unfortunately the internet brings out the worst in some people. This may just be someone looking to make trouble or trying to get a reaction out of you."

She's wrong. I know she's wrong.

"What about Rose?" I ask.

"Sorry?"

"Who were the suspects when Rose disappeared? How many of them are still local? Two girls from the same town, they must live here, right?" I query.

"Penny we talked about this before. There's no reason to think that the same person took both of them. We-"

"Do you know that for sure? Can you really say for definite that it's a coincidence? Charlie and Rose *knew* each other. We all played together all the the time! What are the odds?! Maybe if you told me who the suspects were, I'd be able to tell you if any of them knew Charlie. I could tell you if any of them have been hanging around," I plead.

"Has anyone been hanging around?" she asks me, her even tone starting to grate on me.

"I didn't think so..." I admit.

"Well then-"

"But I didn't think that Charlie had contacted her

dad. I didn't think that she was involved with anyone but Marcus. Apparently there are lots of things that I didn't know," I tell her, my breath catching in my throat.

"Penny, if there's something that you'd like to tell me about your sister's disappearance, if there's something that you remember, then we can absolutely do that. However, I'm afraid I can't give you the name of past or present suspects in an ongoing investigation. I can assure you that, as unlikely as it is that the two events are connected, we will revisit any and all suspects from Rose's case."

"But you won't tell me who they are," I repeat dejectedly.

"You can't get involved in this Penny," she tells me, finally putting some feeling into her voice.

"But I *am* involved! This is the second time in my life that I've gone home without someone that I loved! The second time I've literally *lost* someone!"

"Penny, this isn't your fault,"

"Maybe not, but I still want to fix it."

# Chapter 15

DS Walters sends me away with a sympathetic smile and zero new information. I shouldn't be surprised really, with all the true crime podcasts I've listened to a theme has definitely emerged: the police are human. Occasionally corrupt, sometimes blinkered, often lazy, but always human and therefore flawed. I'm not on the police's side, so why would they be on mine?

I write down the mystery phone number while I can still remember it and then before I can change my mind I hit dial. The call connects but it just rings out without even going to a generic voicemail. I think again about calling Luke, but I can't face another argument. I don't want to see that look of pity and frustration when I say that Rose's killer is behind all this. Still, I wish that I could call him, I need someone on my side.

I stop in my tracks.

I'm an idiot. I know exactly who I should call. I know someone who's totally invested in finding out what happened to Rose, someone who's investigated every possible connection to my sister for the past ten years. Someone who knows her case inside and out and might be able to help me track down Charlie. I can't believe I didn't think of it before.

I pull out my phone and dial, relieved when it connects. I haven't used this number in months and part of me was afraid it would be out of service, but after it rings out, an achingly familiar voice sounds.

"This is Shane Owens, I can't answer the phone right now but please leave a message and I'll get back to you as soon as I can."

"Dad? It's Penny. I need your help, something's happened. Charlie's missing. Please come back to Upper Chalfont as soon as you can. I need to find her and I think it might be the same person, the one who took

Rose."

When I hang up I clutch my phone like a life line, willing it to ring. Now that the idea has occurred to me, it's taken hold. I feel completely certain that my dad will be able to help me, I just hope he's close enough to get here in time.

I stagger home, feeling drained and feverish. Each second that my phone doesn't ring seems to last an age. By the time I walk through the front door, years have passed.

"Penny! Are you alright sweetheart?! Wendy called us," mum tells me, wrapping me in her arms. I breathe in the scent of her and try to feel comforted but I'm just exhausted. She gazes at me anxiously until I realise that she's waiting for a response. I don't have one for her so I just shake my head and half shrug, knowing that if I try to speak I won't be able to keep from crying.

"Come on, you have a lie down," she insists, leading me upstairs.

She helps me navigate my way out of my shorts and

t-shirt and into some pyjamas. I climb into bed and she tucks me in, stroking my hair back from my face and pulling the covers up to my chin. I don't even know what time it is, but within seconds I'm asleep.

At least, I think I'm asleep. I might be running. Or that might be Rose. I might be the one crying on the ground. My knee stings and I'm worried the blood will drip onto my shoes and spoil my friendship bracelet. Rose would be cross if it did and she might not make me a new one. I don't want to go to school without her, I'm jealous that she's growing up and leaving me behind.

But then she isn't.

I half remember that Rose isn't growing up at all, but I'll still have to go to school alone, and my knee still stings, and Rose isn't back yet. I'm all alone in the woods and the trees are reaching down their limbs to snatch me up and I wish Charlie was here, she'd hold my hand while I wait for Rose. Why isn't she here?

I snap awake like someone flipped a switch inside my head.

I'm clammy with sweat, the droplets drying in the air since I've kicked my duvet aside at some point. The sheet is a tangled mass beneath me so I must have been thrashing about in my sleep.

It's been a long time since I've had that nightmare about the woods, I'd let myself think that I'd outgrown it but here I am, panting on the edge of my bed, scared to look out my bedroom window because I know that the woods are right there, pressing up against the house. I stagger to the bathroom and switch the light on, feeling the slight ease of my panic when everything is thrown into sharp relief. The toilet, the sink, the shower, everything is just the same as always. That's the worst thing about nightmares, the lingering fear that stays with you when you wake, making you throw suspicious glances at anything and everything. I splash cold water onto my face and look at my reflection in the mirror. I look tired. It's barely 4am and still dark out, there's nothing I can do yet so I head back to bed. The trouble is my sheet. It's wet through with sweat and I know my spare set is in my laundry basket, waiting for me to get around to washing them after an incident involving my bedding and an entire cup of tea last week. I drape the sheet over my radiator and wrap my duvet around myself before creeping from my room. I tread carefully across the landing and down to Olly's room. He's there, safe, sound asleep. He's also spread out like a starfish and I don't think I can handle sharing a bed with him again. I quietly shut his door and pause. There is one other option.

I open the door opposite mine and slip inside. It's been a while but I still know this room like the back of my hand. There's the pink wicker chair in the corner with clothes still draped over it. There's the white table and vanity that I was so jealous of I thought I might burst. The single bed in the middle of the room, that never got upgraded to a double like mine because it was the perfect size for a girl of ten.

I lie down on the bed, on top of the covers with my own duvet draped over me. It smells musty and stale but

I breathe it in, trying to detect any trace of my sister's lingering scent. I can't find it. There's nothing left.

I wake feeling lost. I have to blink a few times to remember where on earth I am, but then the floral print of Rose's bedding comes in to focus and I remember. I sit up with a sigh, I can't afford to start having nightmares again, I don't have time for this right now; Charlie needs me. I push myself up to standing and carefully tread across the room and slip out of the door. I don't want mum to know I slept in there, she wouldn't like it. At first she encouraged me to go into Rose's room as much as I wanted, but she would always hover in the doorway, watching to make sure nothing was moved or changed. I stopped going in.

I go back to my own room, closing the door behind me. It's seven am now so I quickly change and brush my teeth before heading straight downstairs for something to eat. My dad still hasn't called me back or even messaged me and in the light of a new day I don't feel surprised. If anything, I feel embarrassed for even trying.

I shrug the thought off as I push open the door to the lounge.

“Morning Olly Wally!”

I lean over the back of the sofa and wrap him in a hug, but he wriggles free.

“Are you doing pop-tarts?!” he asks me with life-or-death urgency.

“I am if you want some, strawberry or chocolate?” I respond with a grin.

“Chocolate please!” he cries happily, slumping back into his seat to continue watching Pokemon, safe in the knowledge that an obscene amount of sugar will shortly be en-route.

I find Coop in the kitchen, reading the paper with a grim expression. I slide a couple of pop-tarts into the toaster and then join him at the counter, shifting another paper towards me. It looks like we have a few.

“What's with all the-” I begin, but then I stop, the words catching in my throat.

The front page is half taken up with a picture of Charlie's smiling face. The headline reads, 'Missing Teen Feared Dead'. My vision swims, I feel bile searing my throat and I almost gag.

"I went out and got these when I saw the local paper this morning," Coop explains, gesturing to the sea of papers before him. It looks as though every one has mentioned Charlie, if not given her the headline story. The police may not believe that there's a connection to Rose but the papers certainly seem to. The local paper has opted for 'another missing girl' and a small picture of Rose is included beside that of Charlie. She looks strange in black and white, almost timeless. The fiery red of her hair coloured over in dark grey, her smile fixed, frozen in the camera flash - she looks so young. Placed next to Charlie, Rose looks so much a child.

I sift through the other papers. Rose's face appears again and again, sometimes in black and white but mostly in colour from the bigger, more established publications. My hands are moving faster and faster, my eyes running from page to page until suddenly-

My face.

There I am, staring up at myself from the page, smiling.

I recognise that photo but I have no idea how they got hold of it, I suppose Wendy must have given it to them but I can't believe she'd do it without warning me, without asking if it was alright. The photo is from that summer, the last summer with Rose. I'm standing in the middle with one arm around each of them. We're all looking into the camera, our smiles wide and our cheeks flushed. We'd been running through the woods all day playing pirates and we were tired and tattered but happy. My dad was the one who'd taken the photo and I can still remember his smile as he snapped it. He printed off copies for each of us and I still have mine, up on my wall. Charlie has hers too, I check it every time I go round there, but she's never taken it down. I skim through the story, my lungs slowly hardening into cold lead.

'Lightening strikes twice in a small town where a

second girl has mysteriously vanished a decade after her childhood friend disappeared without a trace.'

Lightening strikes twice.

I look back at the picture. The three of us look so happy, so alive, so free. How can I be the only one left?

"Penny?"

Olly's voice is small and hesitant.

"The pop-tarts are burning."

He's right. Without me to watch over them the pastries have burned, the sugar blackened and the edges turned to charcoal. The sickly scent has filled the room and I didn't even notice. I dash back to the toaster, pressing the button far too late and gingerly pulling them onto a plate with the very tips of my fingers.

"Sorry Olly, I'll do you some more," I assure him quickly, grabbing another pack from the box and starting again.

To my relief, Coop steps forward to take over pop-tart duty and I can run upstairs. Closing my bedroom door behind me I switch on my laptop and start typing.

More news articles. Even true crime blogs seem to have started picking up the story. Now that Charlie's bloody shoe has been found, foul play is suspected and suddenly everyone is taking notice. There are theories spinning out from the mundane to the ridiculous on the online forums and lots of people are asking why the police haven't been taking the case seriously until now. In some ways it's nice to see so many people agreeing with me that there's an obvious connection to Rose, but I could do without their certainty that a serial killer is hunting in my town. The more I read, the more it becomes clear that pretty much no one believes Charlie is still alive. She's been missing for days, not hours and the general consensus is to give up hope. I respond to a few threads, suggesting that she might be being held alive still, but there are too many for me to address them all. In defeat I navigate away from the message sites and over to Facebook. The page I made for Charlie has blown up, there are suddenly hundreds of thousands of followers and countless messages and posts have been left. I could spend all day going through them and I probably wouldn't catch up. I want to see if there have been any more posts from NoMatter but a quick scan through doesn't give me anything. I need to scroll right back to the start and look at each one to be sure I don't miss anything, but new posts are popping up all the time and I keep getting distracted. Phillip Green, who I don't think I've ever heard of, is sure that Rose and Charlie were both taken by someone local. He says that the odds of someone just passing through town, twice, are infinitesimal. Cathy Marks thinks that they were both trafficked. She thinks that there's an abduction ring operating in town and that Rose and Charlie were both sold into slavery. Niquita Shahn thinks it must have been someone who knew all of us personally. She thinks that I should be under police protection if I'm not already. She thinks that I might be the next target, the next girl to disappear. Colin Wenworthy thinks it was me. My eyes falter as they run over his words, not wanting to take them in. He thinks that I killed Rose. He thinks that I killed Charlie. He agrees with Niquita that I should be with the police, he thinks that they should lock me up where I can't hurt anyone else. He says the disparity in Rose and Charlies' ages is the biggest clue. I'm not a preferential killer, I'm a psycho who kills girls who're close to me.

I think I might be sick.

Colin's theory is actually one of the most popular. The number of people who've given it a thumbs up makes my head spin. Can people really believe that I'm capable of hurting anyone? Let alone someone I love?

Niquita Shah is coming in second. More and more people have piled on, adding their own thoughts and ideas, fleshing out the framework she's provided. A local killer. A monster lurking in the suburbs, pretending to be normal while secretly selecting his targets. This is what I've been thinking too, this is who I've been searching for, but seeing it written out like this makes it look ridiculous, sensational. Call me contrary but the more excited strangers who agree, the less likely it seems to me. I feel as though the steady ground beneath my feet, the absolute certainty that I had felt, has turned to sand and is sliding out from under me.

"I brought you a pop-tart."

I spin around, my eyes wide. I hadn't even heard the door open but Olly is there, holding a plate with two chocolate pastries positioned on top. He places it on the desk when I don't move forward to take it from him.

"Are you alright Penny?" he asks me, looking up at me with big, anxious eyes.

I'm spared from answering by the doorbell. I dash down the stairs and along the hall to the door, pulling it open.

"Penny!" a wide smile greets me and I'm eight years old.

"Dad?"

Somehow, he looks exactly the same. I think it's the smile. On our yearly visits around my birthday, he always looks tired and sad and distracted, but today he's smiling and it makes him look just like the dad I remember from when I was little.

"Sweetheart!" he cries, pulling me into his arms. He smells of leather and mint and I nestle into his embrace gratefully.

"Dad, you came," I murmur into his shoulder.

"Of course I did, sweetheart! I set off as soon as I got your call! I would have been here sooner but I was off in Newcastle and it was a long drive!" he tells me a little ruefully.

He drove here from Newcastle?! I feel tears pricking my eyes and I blink them back hard but it's no use, a second later they're sliding down my cheeks and dripping from my chin. My dad smiles at the sight of them and wipes them away with a thumb.

"You thought I wouldn't come?" he asks me astutely and I feel colour rise in my cheeks.

"I wasn't sure," I admit.

"That's my fault," he tells me, the smile dropping from his face, "I haven't been here enough."

I don't disagree so I just shrug and offer him a faint half smile.

“I'm sorry Penny, I haven't been the best- I should have... I'm here now.”

His tone is serious and I can see the sincerity in his eyes, setting off a new wave of tears. He pulls me back into his arms and I just breathe him in, happy to believe for a moment that he can make everything better.

# Chapter 16

"Alright, tell me everything you know."

We're sat in the library, newspapers spread out around us on a table for six that we've shamelessly taken over.

I let out a slow breath.

"It's not much," I admit.

He watches me expectantly so I try to figure out where to start.

"Well, it's like it says in all these," I tell him, gesturing to the papers, "we went to a party on Saturday night. I left before Charlie but the plan was for her to sleep over at ours, at mine. Even when I left, that was still the plan; I gave her a key but she never arrived. When I woke up in the morning I realised she wasn't there and I called everyone I could but no one knew where she was. Coop took me to Wendy's in case Charlie had just gone home instead but she hadn't."

He's watching me with such intensity that it sets my blood fizzing inside my veins. He's giving me the kind of focus I haven't seen from him in years.

"I know that she had a fight with her boyfriend because she wouldn't sleep with him. I know her phone is off or broken because messages aren't reaching it. They send, but her phone doesn't receive them. I know she hasn't spent any money since she went missing but I know that she got money from somewhere the police haven't been able to trace. She was talking to someone that she didn't tell me about. She was keeping secrets. I don't really know anything else."

Dad's still staring at me and I know that he's absorbed every word I've said. The thought makes me slightly giddy and bolsters my nerve enough that I keep going.

"I know it might sound crazy, but I'm sure it's

connected to Rose!" I tell him in a rush.

"Of course it is," he agrees without hesitation.

My heart stutters then swells.

"You agree with me?" I ask him, almost convinced that I must have misheard.

"Of course! I told the police again and again that they needed to keep looking for Rose. I knew that it was only a matter of time before another girl went missing, but they wouldn't listen to me. If they're allowed to just get away with it, then why wouldn't they do it again?! The police thought that I was just desperate, hysterical. They told me that they'd done *everything they could*."

His tone is dripping with disgust and and I feel a surge of relief. It's not just me, the police told my dad the exact same things that they told me- I was too emotional, they were doing their best.

I nod sympathetically and he presses on.

"If the police were really doing everything they could then there wouldn't be so many children disappearing! If you knew *half* the things I've seen,

Penny! There are huge networks of people, gangs and businesses and middle men, all working to take kids and shuffle them around the country. They trade in drugs and girls and stolen goods, I've been working my way in for years now! I'm sure that someone knows something, I just have to get close to the right person and everything will come out. They must have a contact locally but I haven't been able to find out who it is," he admits, his eyes wild.

"You think she was trafficked?! Charlie too?!" I ask quickly.

"It's just one possibility, I admit, but it's one that I think is likely. The fact that there was never a single trace found, that there were no witnesses, it just seems to me that it was a professional operation. If I can get far enough into the network, maybe I could find her and get her out."

"Rose?" I ask in a small voice.

"Of course!" he confirms, his eyes wide and dark.

He still believes she's alive. I've known it on some

level but it still feels like a punch to the gut. Mum and I have moved on with our lives, accepting in our own minds that Rose is dead and has been for a long time, but dad has never given up. He's been searching for ten years. I feel a twist in my stomach, somewhere between jealousy and shame.

"And you think they took Charlie too? Why?" I ask, not brave enough to keep the conversation in situ.

"There's always a market for young girls, Penny. Always."

"So you think it was a coincidence? The fact that Charlie knew Rose, that they were both close as kids and were both taken?" I ask, trying to wrap my head around what he's saying.

"Possibly. Or possibly someone liked the connection, thought it more exciting to take another girl with a connection to the first," he suggests, "It takes a certain kind of monster to be involved in something like this, even from a business angle."

"Online a lot of people are suggesting that Charlie

was taken because of her connection to Rose... it's what I've been thinking," I admit, "What if she was taken because she reminded the killer of Rose? Like a trophy?" I ask, feeling a pang as he flinches at the word 'killer'.

"It's possible. It's definitely possible. All the more reason for us to finally find out what happened to your sister. If we find Rose, we find Charlie."

I want to pause the conversation there because surely he has that backwards. If we find what happened to Charlie, we find what happened to Rose. Charlie has been missing a matter of days. It's terrifying but it's nothing compared to Rose, missing for a decade. Charlie's abduction is fresh - there should be fresh clues, possible sightings, actual evidence. More than that, there's a good chance that Charlie is still alive! I hope. Surely our priority should be finding her, following her trail.

I try to suggest this but dad brushes my words away.

"The police are on that. They may be useless but at least they can look up phone records, check CCTV, that sort of thing. We need to go deeper. We both agree that there's a connection between now and ten years ago, but we need to make sure that it's actually being investigated."

"How?" I ask.

Like he said, we can't access phone records or CCTV. We can't get into Charlie's emails or watch her bank account.

"I need you to tell me everything. Everything you can think of," he tells me seriously.

"Everything about what?"

"About Rose."

My stomach sinks.

"What do you mean?" I ask, my voice so low it's almost a whisper.

My thoughts flash to Colin Wenworthy and his oh so popular theory. Does my dad suspect that I was involved?!

"The police buggered it up at the time sweetheart, I know that. It's not your fault that you couldn't tell them anything, they terrified you. I should never have let them speak to you, but I didn't know any better back then. If I had it to do over..." He trails off, running his hands through his hair.

He doesn't think I'm responsible, he thinks that he is. He blames himself for my failed memory. Hating myself, I give a small sigh of relief and his head snaps up.

"But you must have seen *something*! There must be memories locked away that you can retrieve! I told your mum that we should take you to a therapist, a hypnotist, anyone we could, whatever it took, but she wouldn't hear of it. You and Rose were together *all the time*! If anyone would have seen something, it's you."

He sounds so sure and I wish that I had something to offer him, to vindicate his belief in me.

"I still don't remember. I don't think I saw anything, dad. I remember Rose going-" I start but he cuts me off.

"Start at the beginning, start first thing that morning," he tells me.

I take a deep breath. I have to try.

"I remember that it was a Saturday. I remember you and mum were both home at breakfast and Rose wanted you to take us out somewhere... swimming I think." I dredge up the memories with a monolithic effort. All the insignificant details, laid bare.

"You said you couldn't take us, you had to work. Mum couldn't either, she had too much to do. It was the last weekend before school and she wanted to get Rose's new uniform sorted. I was so jealous that she was going to be wearing a blazer. Mum was going to sew on the school logo patch for her. Rose was teasing me about it and I got upset. Mum made her say sorry and then we decided to go and play in the woods. We'd done the same thing almost every day but I was still excited. I remember being glad we couldn't go swimming, I didn't like the chlorine smell or the way the sound bounced off the tiled walls. I always wanted to leave before Rose did and she called me a baby. I was happier in the woods... but I fell. We were playing pirates again and I was running behind Rose, chasing her, when I tripped on a root. She was moving so fast... she was so far ahead that I was sure she wouldn't hear me crying, but she did. She came back and she looked at my knee. It was a bad cut and it was bleeding a lot. She didn't call me a baby for crying and I was glad, but she looked worried at my leg and that made me feel scared. She told me not to worry, that she would go and get mum. I didn't want her to leave me, but I was scared to move my leg because it hurt so much so I stayed where I was, on the ground, and she left. She didn't go on the path, she walked straight into the woods in the direction of home. After a moment I couldn't see her any more..."

Tears wash down my face, hushing my voice. I open my eyes, look at dad and I see that he's crying too. Drops are spilling from his blue eyes unchecked and there's such anguish in his face that I look down, not wanting to intrude. Are we really so separate that I can't share this moment with him? This mutual tragedy?

"What happened then?" he croaks.

"Nothing happened then. There wasn't a sound, just

birds and leaves in the breeze. I don't remember hearing a single person, or seeing a dog walker, or anything. I remember just sitting there, waiting for Rose to come back for me. It felt like hours and hours but I don't know how long it was. I don't remember why I eventually decided to walk home alone, but I did. It hurt a lot and I was moving slowly, crying and feeling cross. I thought that Rose had forgotten about me, or that she was playing a trick on me. It wasn't until I got back home-

Mum was hanging out washing on the line. Sheets and towels and Rose's new uniform. She smiled when she saw me, then she saw my knee and rushed over. She took me in to the back porch and started to clean the cut and then she asked me where Rose was. I didn't know what to say. I don't think I said anything at all. She asked again and I remember her voice getting louder and I was scared that she was angry at me. I didn't know what had happened but I knew enough to feel scared," I tell him, my voice hoarse with the effort of holding back my sobs.

"And then she called the police," he adds in, his own

voice wavering.

"I suppose so," I agree.

"You suppose so?"

"I don't remember. I know she must have, because I remember police coming, but that's where everything really falls apart. It took years to remember up to that point, but I haven't remembered anything new in ages. I know that I went to the police station, I remember being alone in a room that felt cold. I remember going somewhere else too, maybe with nurses?"

"The hospital. We had to take you in to get your knee looked at. It was a deep cut and you had to have three stitches," he tells me, leaning forward, willing me to remember.

The hospital? How could I not remember? How could I not remember getting stitches?

I shrug and shake my head slightly and dad seems to get smaller before my eyes.

"I remember you being there, but it was dark outside," I tell him.

"Your mother called but I missed it, I was in a conference and had my phone on silent. When I got her message I rushed home but it was practically evening and you were already at the police station. From there we went to the hospital, then back to the station. They said they wanted to talk to your mum and me, get more information on anyone who might have taken Rose, we didn't even realise that they were talking to you too in another room. When we got you back you were pale and shaking and you couldn't remember anything about the whole day," he tells me.

I've heard the basics of this story before of course, but I've never really wondered exactly what happened. What did they ask me? What did they say that traumatised me so much that I blocked out the whole day completely? What if there's still something locked away that could help us now- help Charlie?

"Do you know why I was so frightened?" I ask.

"Not exactly, the officers talking to you said they just went over the days events with you, asking if you had seen anything, if anyone had been hanging around. They asked if anything else had happened that summer, but they claimed it was all just standard questions," he tells me, shaking his head slightly.

"Do you believe them?"

"Maybe. You were only eight years old and your sister had gone missing. I think being sat in an interrogation room with two police officers asking you questions all by yourself could be pretty traumatic anyway. They should have got a specialist in! A child psychologist or something! If they'd handled it properly, who knows what we could have found out?!" he exclaims, his frustration mounting.

I try not to wince but I can't help it. He does blame me. Maybe not directly, but he definitely thinks that if I had remembered I could have helped. I've been thinking the same thing for years but it still burns to hear it.

"So what do we do now?" I ask.

"Now we figure out who's responsible."

He says it with such conviction that I feel bubbles

rising in my chest. I can't tell if they're hope or fear but I suppose at this point they're almost the same thing.

"We need to figure out who took Charlie," I state with a nod.

"We need to figure out who took Rose," he corrects me, "I'm glad the media picked up on the connection, it means that eventually the police are going to have to treat the two cases as related and start looking for Rose again. For years they've done *nothing*!"

"What should they have been doing?" I ask curiously. Without any physical evidence to go off, a cold case doesn't have a lot of avenues of investigation open.

"They should have been doing what *I've* been doing! They should have been digging into the lives of everyone who knew Rose. They should have been investigating every one of her teachers, every adult who spent time with her. They should have been looking at everyone whose house bordered the woods. They should have been investigating every group in the country that has the ability to make a young girl disappear. You know, there are websites where people can bid on human beings - buy and sell them like property. I've never found Rose on any of the sites I've been able to find but I know there are others out there. Someone knows what happened to her! Someone took her from us!"

His eyes are shining with tears but his tone is fierce. He's looking older again now. The fluorescent lights of the library are throwing the lines of his face into sharp relief. There are grooves between his eyes and across his forehead. He looks sad and weathered, though the lack of freckles on his skin implies that he hasn't actually been exposed to the elements much. I wonder what it's like to intentionally build your life in the darkness, around the very worst of humanity.

"Where do we start?" I ask, my voice small.

"We start with that summer. We start with anyone that you remember hanging around, anyone watching you girls, anyone who spoke to you."

It makes sense. If someone took Charlie because of her connection to Rose, then that summer is the key. It must be someone who saw them together, who saw them playing.

"Rose vanished so completely, I don't think it could have been a crime of opportunity, or at least not entirely. Someone must have been watching, waiting for an opening. You girls were in those woods every day, someone could have been waiting for their chance."

A chill goes through me but I push it down. I need to focus. Who spoke to us that summer? Who knew Rose? Who knew we would be in the woods?

"It was ten years ago..." I say, running my hands over my face and sighing.

"Look, here, take a look at these names. Do any of them ring a bell? Is there anything that strikes you about any of them? Are they familiar at all?" he asks, pushing a sheet of paper towards me. It's double sided, there are dozens of names here. Some are familiar but many aren't.

"Who are they all?" I ask, scanning through the list.

"These are all the people who lived close by, had the opportunity or knew Rose in some way."

No wonder it's so long.

I take a pencil and start putting stars besides names that I recognise. Mostly they're just vague acquaintances, people that I know from around town, but that doesn't mean that they didn't do it. When I reach one name in particular I stop.

“Dan Cosford?” I ask sharply, looking up at my dad.

“Yeah, he lived right on the edge of the woods. I think he's moved now but still lives in town. At the time Rose went missing he lived a couple of streets from us, his house was right on the edge of the trees like ours. He helped with the search too, that's not uncommon. Lots of offenders try to involve themselves in the investigation.”

“He helped with the search?” I ask, not sure why those words are crawling up my spine on pincered feet.

Dad pulls out a folder and flips through it.

“Yep, he definitely helped with the search. I managed to get a copy of the sign-in sheet a few years ago,”

"He helped search for Charlie too," I say slowly, replaying my conversation with Dan Cosford in my mind. I'm sure there's something important that I need to remember. I wish I'd thought to bring my notes with me.

"He did? Does he know her?" dad asks.

"Yeah, he's the netball coach at school," I tell him.

"He works with kids? With young girls?"

The question turns my stomach.

The more we talk the more I realise that my dad is a different person than the one I used to know. He's seen things and done things that the dad of my early childhood probably couldn't have imagined, but to give him credit he really knows his stuff. I can tell that he's trying to be careful about what he tells me but every time he gets carried away he lets details slip of a life full of vice and horror. Not only that, but he's oddly twitchy. I keep thinking about what he told me about networks of drugs and crime but I'm too scared to ask what I really want to know. Our relationship feels too fragile.

"So you've been investigating? You've been talking to people?" he asks me eagerly.

"Yeah, I know it probably sounds crazy but the police thought she'd run away and *someone* needed to be really looking for her," I explain.

"It doesn't sound crazy at all!" he tells me, "It's exactly what I've been doing all these years!" he smiles at me with such evident pride that I feel like my throat is closing up and I have to resist the impulse to break the tension with a bad joke.

"When the police suggested that she was seeing someone, a married man, I started to think about who it could be-" I start.

"A married man? Why do they think that?"

"Well, Charlie had been given some money that they can't trace, and there are calls to a number that they can't trace either. So they think there must have been some kind of illicit relationship taking place and Charlie made a comment to me about sleeping with a married man. I thought at the time that she was kidding, but with the rest..."

Dad seems to mull this over, thinking through the possible implications, his brow furrowed.

"And there are men that you suspect? Men who may have seemed inappropriate with her?" he asks.

"Not so much that- they're men that Charlie has crushes on. I've never seen any of them act inappropriately with her, but I've never seen *any* man like that. Luke thinks it was Charlie's boyfriend Marcus, but he's too young to have been involved in what happened to Rose," I explain.

"Luke?"

I feel myself blush and try desperately to act cool and unconcerned.

"Yeah, Luke. Luke Burrows. He's a friend, he was helping me to investigate."

"Are you crazy?! You mustn't talk to him!"

I don't know what I was expecting, maybe some touching daddy-daughter moment from a nineties sitcom, but certainly not this.

"What? Why? You don't – do you know him?" I ask quickly.

"It was his house wasn't it?! The party! The Burrows family has lived in town for years! They lived here when Rose went missing, they have a farm! You could completely vanish a body on a farm! Richard Burrows!" he's almost shouting now and the librarian is starting to give us some less than friendly and approving looks. He pushes his list back towards me and stabs his finger at a name on one of the later pages. Richard Burrows.

"But, he wasn't even there the night of the party, he and his wife were out, that's part of the reason Marcus had the party there to begin with."

"So they say! But where was he? Do you know that? Because he was apparently home alone the day Rose went missing!"

I don't ask how he knows, he's spent ten years looking into the names on his list, if he says it I'm sure it's true. I think about Luke's face when he came out to the car to join me after talking to his parents. He said they thought we were crazy to be looking for Charlie ourselves. What exactly had they said to him? Could Richard have been trying to call him off without giving himself away?

"Maybe I could talk to Luke, ask where they were," I suggest, but I'm relieved when dad shakes his head.

"Too risky for now. We don't want to be too obvious and tip Richard off if he is involved, just don't talk to Luke. Don't trust anyone."

Great. That makes two parents trying to stunt my social development.

# Chapter 17

Dad calmed down when I agreed to stay away from Luke, but we could both tell that we'd worn out our welcome at the library so we gathered up our things and headed out in search of sustenance. I noted that dad looked even worse in the harsh light of a gloriously sunny day, but the weight that he'd lifted from my shoulders was incredible. Suddenly I wasn't alone. He accepted without question that Charlie was in trouble and that it was connected to Rose. He agreed with me that the police were crazy to think that it might be two unrelated incidents. Even better, he understood the world outside Upper Chalfont in a way that I had no clue about. True Crime podcasts were one thing, but my dad had the kind of real world experience I've been avoiding for years.

"Do you want to get a coffee?" he asks, squinting slightly in the sun.

"Sure!" I agree brightly, ignoring the fact that I don't drink coffee because it tastes absolutely disgusting.

We dip into the cafe on the Highstreet and dad sends me to the counter to order the drinks while he finds a table and goes through his notes. I order two Americano's, reasoning that since all coffee is gross the simplest option will be to just get the same as him. I feel embarrassingly grown up, placing an order for something other than hot chocolate, but the effect is slightly ruined by the waitress calling me Sweetie-pie and asking after my mum. That's the trouble with small towns, everywhere you look there's people who know you.

"Mum's fine thanks," I tell Trish with a smile.

"And I see your dad's back, did he come back to help with the searches in the woods at the weekend? Charlie Hople, that's your friend isn't it?" she asks me, nodding towards the table in the corner where dad has settled himself.

"Actually he only just got here today," I tell her.

Her eyes widen in surprise and I can't help but wince slightly. I should have called dad sooner. I should have phoned him the second I realised Charlie was missing, but I didn't even think of him, and look how much time I'd wasted because of it!

It's with a dampened mood that I carry the two coffees over to sit down beside my dad. He's pouring through pages of information but he looks up as I sit down and he gratefully takes a gulp of his drink and sighs with appreciation.

"Right, we need to figure out a plan of action," he tells me confidently, rekindling a little of my positivity.

First things first; I go through his list in more detail. Dan Cosford is the only name on there that matches my list of four married men. Dad has some information on him already, he has some previous employment details, his old address and some general bits and pieces. It looks as though Dan has been in trouble before, but never enough to secure him a criminal record. A source in the police told dad that Dan had been in multiple fights, but no one had ever pressed charges so it never went further than verbal warnings. Safe to say he has a temper though.

I take out my phone and navigate to Dan's social media page, showing it to dad. He scrolls immediately to the oldest posts but it doesn't go back ten years. I fill him in on Dan's supposed infidelity and I can tell that he's impressed. It's a warm bubble in my chest, pushing aside a little of my fear.

"What we really need to do it get into his house and have a look around," dad suggests.

"What?"

"He might have evidence hidden somewhere. If we can find a time he's going to be out..." he mutters, returning his attention to Dan's latest Instagram posts and searching for anything useful.

"We can't just break into his house!" I exclaim in a scandalised whisper.

Dad's expression hardens but I don't relent.

"It's illegal!"

"It's being committed. I thought you wanted to find out what happened to your friend, what happened to your sister," he retorts flatly.

"I do!" I hiss.

"Just not enough," he replies with a disappointed shrug.

"But we don't even know if there's anything there!" I remind him.

"How are we supposed to know if we don't look?"

"It might not be him!"

He just shrugs, his eyes sad, disappointment in every line of his face.

I can feel tears pricking my eyes and I turn my attention quickly back to the list. There are pages and pages of names, some familiar, some not. I can't imagine how he managed to put this together but I'm glad we have a starting point at least.

"Dad, Coop's on here," I say suddenly, brought up

short by the sight of it.

“I know. Didn't you never wonder if it was a little too convenient? The way he swooped right in the second I left?”

“But-” I don't know what to say.

Of course it's occurred to me that he appeared on the scene pretty quickly after mum and dad broke up, but I've always been relieved about it. The brief window between husbands wasn't a good time for my mother and she wasn't exactly a sparkling example of parenting. Clothes went unwashed, school went unattended and more often than not, I went unfed. Mum was a weeping, shaking wraith and I was too scared to go near her. I hid in my room wishing that I could turn the clock back to the beginning of summer when life had been normal, happy and safe. I've often felt grateful that it had only been a brief interlude of chaos before Coop had brought us back to the real world. I resisted the insinuation that his intentions had been anything other than good with every fibre of my being.

"No, Coop would never have hurt Rose, he didn't even really know her," I say, shaking my head vigorously.

"He knew your mum though, he knew her from work. He'd been to the house, we'd socialised, he was a familiar face. He knew the whole family through your mum, and... I wondered at the time if maybe she'd been seeing someone else..."

My world shifts.

"What?!" I demand sharply but he just ignores me, he's glaring down at Coop's name deep in thought.

"He was local too! He lived in the next town! And he wouldn't tell me where he was the day she disappeared! He refused point blank to answer any of my questions! That's why he and your mum decided that they don't want me around you, they didn't like the questions I was asking!"

I'm still shaking my head.

"There's no way. There's no way Coop was involved. I *know* him," I insist.

I can see that dad still wants to argue the point but I

don't let him.

"Dan Cosford is much more likely. He helped in the searches, he knows Charlie from netball and he has a temper. She even has a crush on him! Charlie doesn't *like* Coop!"

"We need to search his house then," dad states.

I feel like I backed myself into agreeing but I still don't want to. Dad sees me chewing my lip uncertainly and suddenly his eyes flash.

"You're not committed to this are you?! You say that you want to help but you don't!" he bursts out.

I physically recoil in my seat, stung and scared.

"I *do* want to help!" I plead with him.

"Then why won't you?!" he demands, staring me down.

"It's illegal! We can't break the law!" I hiss at him, keeping my voice low and glancing around me nervously. The queen of acting casual - I am not.

"I suppose there's a line then. At least we know how far you're willing to go."

He sounds so disappointed in me and I'm feeling so many things at once that I can't even pin one down to inspect it.

I take a breath but before I can figure out what I'm going to say he leaves. He just stands up and walks out with all his stuff, leaving me sitting there with my cold coffee and a sick feeling in the pit of my stomach.

I stand up to leave, fighting the urge to cry. I feel more hopeless than ever and I wish I could un-do about half the conversation that just happened. I hastily wipe my eyes before starting for the door but then I stop and turn my back, pretending to check my phone. Claire and her mother have just walked in and if there's one person I don't want to find me sobbing in a cafe, it's Claire Netherhall.

“Black coffee only darling! And make sure it's ice cold, that speeds up your metabolism and you've been looking a little chunky lately.” Ms Netherhall's voice cuts through the general chatter from the surrounding tables and I can't help but glance over at them. They're decked out in their perfect, skin-tight gym clothes, duffel bags over their shoulders and blonde hair in matching high ponytails.

"Did you do your extra cardio yesterday darling? No? *No matter*, you can do double today. You need to stay motivated if you want Marcus to stay interested."

Claire mumbles something incoherent back.

"I understand that darling, but it's all important! The devil's in the details! Did you pack a salad for lunch? No? *No matter*, we'll buy one from here. I don't want you tempted to buy something fattening just because you get hungry later."

Ms Netherhall's voice is still clear as a bell, piercing through the ambient sound and carrying clear across the cafe. My eyes however, are fixed on Claire. Her mother's words, her condescending catch phrase, it can't be a coincidence, can it? Almost as though she feels my eyes on her, Claire turns to face me, her gaze fierce, offering an unspoken challenge. I think back over the comments from NoMatter on the Facebook page I made for

Charlie. If angry, bitter Claire left them, does that mean that she's actually involved? I want to call dad but I know he'd dismiss it. I want to call Luke but dad's warning rings in my ears. Instead I run home and I go straight up to my room and note down every word of it in my folder of notes. Almost as an afterthought I record my argument with dad too.

There. Fantastic. The whole thing immortalised in a word document.

I don't know which part is worst, dad's suspicions about Coop or his obvious disgust of me.

I now have pages and pages of unrelated details and records of conversations, all diligently noted down in case it turns out to be relevant. I start at the beginning and commence reading through. My timeline is still distressingly sparse but my talks with other people have borne some fruit. From Claire I found out that Charlie called for a lift and said that it was someone who cared about her. From Sarah H I found that Charlie felt that at least *someone* needed her. I'd ruled out Mr Danes and provisionally ruled out Mr Pentuck unless he's the worlds best actor. Mr Denham is still more of an unknown, and Dan Cosford is still very much on my list of potential suspects, but at least there are general themes and patterns emerging.

Dan Cosford.

I read back through the notes again, something is bothering me but I'm just not seeing what it is. I compare them to my new notes, skimming over the sections in which I'm a total disappointment as a daughter.

Oh my God.

He lied.

I pull out my phone and dial my dad, my fingers shaking so much that they're slipping over my phone screen.

"Dad?! I'm so sorry, you're right! We need to look around Dan Cosford's house! He lied to me! I just went back through my notes and he told me to my face that he was away when Rose went missing and wasn't in town for the searches. Why would he lie about that?!"

# Chapter 18

So, what does one wear to go breaking and entering? In the absence of a trench coat and fedora, I go for all black, hoping that its a cliché for a reason. The look of obvious amusement on dad's face causes me to have some second thoughts but it's already too late to go back and change so I guess I'll just have to make the best of it. It was hard enough getting out the house once, twice would likely be too much to hope for. I decided that it was best to carefully avoid mum and Coop since I had no idea what I would say to them. I've never had much cause to lie to them in the past so, with so little practice, it's unlikely that I'd make a skilled dissembler. If only Charlie and I had made use of those fake IDs, I'd have had some experience sneaking around and misleading. As it is, I had to spend an inordinate amount of time in the bathroom and then shout my goodbyes as I closed the front door behind myself, leaving no opportunity for opposition. They've called my mobile a couple of times and they're going to be livid by the time I get home, but honestly, what on earth was I supposed to say?

"Hi mum, dad doesn't trust your new husband, I'm suddenly full of doubts and now I'm off to break into someone's house in case he's a homicidal maniac!" somehow I don't think it would have gone down well.

"So what's the plan?" I ask, not for the first time.

"They're going to be out, it says on his latest Instagram post that they're going to dinner with friends. We'll wait until they're definitely gone, find a way in and then look around."

"And what exactly are we looking for?" I ask nervously.

"Anything suspicious. Anything that ties him to Rose."

"Or Charlie," I remind him.

“Of course, or Charlie. Any young girl for that matter.”

“You think he might have hurt other girls?” I ask quickly.

“I don't know,” he admits, but his expression is grim.

My heart is pounding in my chest but it actually feels great to be doing something proactive. This is the first time that it seems as though I may actually be getting closer to my friend. No more sorting through my notes and scanning through pictures, now I'm actually *doing* something.

We park my dad's beaten up old car a couple of streets away, safe from the prying eyes of considerate neighbours, and we approach on foot from the opposite direction of Deb's house. There's a privacy hedge between the two properties and so long as we stay close to the wall we shouldn't be visible even if she's stationed in her post beside the window. At first we try to move naturally, as though we're simply strolling to the house for some perfectly normal pre-arranged appointment.

We ring the doorbell and then wait, listening closely for any sound at all from within. Their driveway is empty and we can't hear a single thing from inside so we proceed a little more rapidly to the side gate. It's a simple latch near the top that can be reached over the top of the gate, presumably in case a PT client arrives and needs to get in before Dan's available. Luckily there aren't any other locks and we're able to slip in easily. Dan really should be more concerned about home security. Saying that, his exercise cabin is locked up tight and the back door is similarly secured. We've made it as far as the garden but now we're stuck, unable to investigate more than the state of Dan's potted plants. While I start looking around hopefully for a back door key, perhaps concealed under some kind of obnoxious garden ornament, dad starts trying to find another way in.

"Here!" he whispers excitedly.

I spin round and see that he's found a window unlocked. I'm surprised that anyone would be so careless with a ground-floor window until I see that it's rigged to only open a short way.

"Do you think we can force it?" I ask, hurrying over to join him.

He tests it gingerly but there's no give. I step round him, eyeing it thoughtfully.

"I think I can fit."

"Are you sure?"

"Not completely, but it's worth a try, isn't it?"

He boosts me up and in, and although it's a very tight squeeze in places, I just about make it. I'm immensely glad of my ninja-getup as without it I would certainly have lost at least a few layers of skin to the manoeuvre. The window leads in to the kitchen and I have to slide some knick-knacks out the way to facilitate my entry and then crawl myself forward, off the counter and onto the floor with my arms alone, dragging the rest of my body behind me through the window and then into an undignified heap on the floor.

"Open the back door! Let me in!" dad hisses at me.

I pull myself up to standing, wincing slightly as I

stretch my arms and legs, and then go to the back door. The trouble is, there's no key in it.

Who on earth takes the back door key out of the lock?! Surely everyone just leaves it in place, rather than carrying it around with them?! If I'd had lingering doubts as to Dan Cosford's being a sociopath, surely this obvious deviation from the norm would have put them to rest.

Not that I have doubts.

"There's no key!" I stage whisper towards the window while I search around for where it might be kept.

"Look in the drawers!" he suggests helpfully.

"I've looked in the drawers! There's no key!" I hiss.

"There must be!"

"And yet, there isn't," I tell him firmly. "Do you want me to let you in the front door?"

He looks conflicted and buries his face in his hands in frustration for a moment, but then he pulls himself together.

"No, we can't risk anyone seeing us come into the house. If he has evidence and we don't find it today, he might destroy it. You look around and then meet me back here," he instructs me.

With a deep breath I move further into the house. It feels unbelievably strange to be walking around someone's home without their knowledge. In some ways I suppose it's quite empowering, but mostly I just feel terrified. I keep expecting that at any moment Dan Cosford is going to step through the door and ask me what on earth I'm doing. Or possibly murder me.

The house is quite plain. The walls all painted in the imaginatively named shades of white that people seem to go nuts for- Angel's Kiss, Whisper of Moonlight, First Snow, etc. The carpets are all unremarkable beige, but one thing I will say, it is incredibly clean! My mum would be inviting round everyone we know if our house was ever this spotless, just to make the most of it. Thankfully, with Olly around that's definitely never going to happen.

The few pictures that adorn the walls are mostly of Dan. Dan holding his Personal Training qualification certificate, Dan beside a flashy orange car that I'm pretty sure doesn't belong to him, and other photographic expressions of self-indulgence. Tina seems to be much more shy, she's only in the wedding pictures and there are only two of those on display, though one is an A2 canvas of the two of them smiling at the camera. I can't tell whether it's down to my swiftly developing bias, but I think it looks fake. The pose is awkward and the smiles are forced. The new Mrs Cosford looks timid, not the glowing bride that one might expect. There aren't any ornaments on the surfaces, not even a vase of faux flowers. It must make it easier to dust but it also makes it look a bit like a hotel room - impersonal and cold. There's no personality at all in the downstairs, let alone mementos of horrific crimes, so I venture upstairs hoping for something more substantial on the first floor. There's a bathroom, tiled in blue and white, with a medicine cabinet brimming with painkillers. I guess there's a price to pay for daily weight training. Despite extensive rummaging, I don't find anything of particular note. I go to the first bedroom, another white and beige space. I'm sure I read somewhere that they use a lot of beige in insane asylums because it has a muting, dehumanising effect. That might be complete rubbish of course, but it's the sort of thing that sounds plausible. I'm not sure how it would be relevant here, but I'm adding it to the points against Dan Cosford anyway. A small tally to reassure myself that despite the illegality, I'm doing the right thing.

There aren't any pictures on the walls in here and the bedspread is the same neutral beige as the carpet so I suspect that it's a guest room. I move further in anyway and drop down to the floor to check under the bed.

Interesting. There's an earring on the floor. It's a simple stud and I don't recognise it as being Charlie's...

It may be nothing, a woman does live here after all, it could easily belong to Dan's wife. Still, in such a clean and orderly house it looks utterly out of place discarded on the floor beside the bed. I look around but I can't find the matching piece. I check under the pillows and duvet but no luck.

Now I have a dilemma, do I leave it where it is or take it with me? If it turns out to be valuable evidence, I want it to be safe, but if I remove it from the house, how can I prove it came from here? For that matter, if I remove it from the house what on earth would I do with it? I can't exactly take it to the police and ask them to test it for DNA without telling them where it came from.

Logical thought to the rescue, my decision is made. I pull out my phone and take a couple of pictures of the earring, one close up and one in it's surroundings to give a bit of context. Then, congratulating myself once again for my ninja garb, I pull my sleeve over my hand and move the earring back, behind the leg of the bed to make it harder for anyone else to find and dispose of.

Confident that I've found all there is to find under the bed, I move on to the wardrobe. Again, I'm taken by surprise. The wardrobe is practically full and it appears to be all Dan's wife, Tina's, things. There are clothes on the rail, shoes on a rack and even pictures blue-tacked to the inside of the door. It reminds me a little of the way some of the girls personalise their school lockers. There are pictures of Tina Cosford with an older couple who look like her parents, or standing with her arms around another woman who looks so similar to her that they must be sisters. She looks so relaxed and happy, smiling with her whole body. I think again of the wedding photo.

I don't think it's just my bias, I'm sure this isn't a happy house.

I feel faintly sick searching through Tina's precious possessions, it feels like a terrible intrusion to dig through her life uninvited, and I don't find anything significant anyway.

I give myself a shake as I close the door carefully behind me and move on to the last bedroom. This is clearly Dan's space. The walls are painted grey and there's a large framed picture of a sports car on the wall above the bed. The dressing table has only men's products on it and the wardrobe contains only his clothes. I have no qualms whatsoever about searching the room from top to bottom. Under the bed reside boxes of memorabilia from Dan's earlier life. There's old school books and awards from children's sporting events, all adorned with his name. Clearly Dan Cosford is someone who believes in trophies. I feel the anticipation mounting the longer I search, the room seems to paint such a clear picture of the kind of man that Dan is that at this point I can easily imagine him being our culprit. I don't want to jump to conclusions, but I'm pretty sure he's a psychopathic killer.

I drop down to my knees before the wardrobe, rifling through the boxes stacked on the floor. There are books on nutrition, odd socks and other general life-debris. This isn't where he would keep a prized reminder of past crimes. I reach further back, sliding another box towards me. It looks similar to the others, but it was placed against the wall, out of easy reach and concealed by the boxes in front. I note the absence of dust and feel a tremor of excitement as I lift off the lid.

The urge to vomit is almost overwhelming.

Inside the box is a collection of women's underwear. There's lace and satin and more demure cotton and jersey, in a range of colours and styles. And sizes.

These belong to different women, I'm sure of it. The knowledge turns my stomach, not that it wouldn't be incredibly creepy for Dan Cosford to have a box of his wife's pants, but these are clearly from other women entirely.

I pull my sleeve down over my hand again and force myself to rummage through them, looking for anything that I recognise as belonging to Charlie or Rose. There doesn't seem to be anything in a child's size, but before I can examine them all my phone vibrates. I check the screen quickly and my heart drops to my knees.

They're back.

I put the lid back on the box and I go to stuff it back in place but I'm too late.

"Be quick Tina, I want to get back! And grab my watch too while you're up there, would you?!" I hear Dan call from the hallway downstairs.

I look round and a second later there she is, standing in the doorway, frozen.

She's the woman from the pictures in the wardrobe, but she isn't. She's paler, smaller, drained of colour and life except for the swell of her belly.

Her face is white with terror and for a moment I'm sure she's going to scream. I try desperately to formulate a plan, but as her eyes flick towards the door I realise that it isn't me she's afraid of.

"You have to run!" she hisses. The words are barely audible but the desperation in her voice cuts through me. I want more than anything to tell her to come with me, but what's my plan here? I'm dressed all in black, breaking into her house and searching through her stuff. I'm not a knight in shining armour, I'm...

Well, I actually have no idea what I am right now.

I shove the box to the back of the wardrobe and

stumble to my feet.

"TINA?!"

If possible she pales even further and I'm worried she might collapse. At the sound of a creak on the stairs I'm worried I might too.

Desperately trying to pull myself together I step quickly behind the bedroom door and press a finger to my lips. Tina opens the door a little wider, closing me into a small space between the door, the wardrobe and the wall, blocked from sight. I hear her steps on the carpet and Dan still coming up the stairs.

"Got it! Shall I wear the blue one?" I hear her voice, small and breathy. I wonder if she always sounds so nervous and fearful but Dan doesn't seem to detect anything unusual in it.

There's the faint click of a watch clasp before Dan responds.

"I suppose the blue will have to do since you've ruined the one you're wearing. I do expect you to be more careful than this Tina."

His voice is calm and level but it sends a shiver of fear through me.

"I know, I'm sorry, I was just feeling a bit shaky," she mutters.

"That excuse won't work forever. Once my baby is here you'll need to get your act together."

I can hear the mumbling of a reply but I can't make out the words. I'm straining to listen, alert for any indication that he might hurt her, but a moment later I can her him moving away, back down the stairs.

The door moves and I think I might faint but it's just Tina, her white face strained.

"What are you doing in my house?!" she hisses, her eyes wide.

"I-" I attempt a reply but I falter, not knowing how to explain.

"My friend is missing," I breathe the words, watching her face for a reaction.

She doesn't look surprised but then I doubt there'd be room for any other expression than fear.

"You need to run," she tells me again, "out the back door."

I move immediately, desperate to be out of that house.

"Wait! The key!" I whisper, turning back in the doorway.

With a look of comprehension she goes to the dressing table and carefully removes a single key from one of the drawers. She can't help the look of apprehension as she hands it over, she can't take her eyes off it.

"I'll leave it under the tea towel!" I tell her as I clasp it in my hand and go to the stairs, my heart racing. I move quickly and quietly, keeping to the outside edges of the steps where the support is always better. I place my weight on the banister as much as possible, willing my steps not to make a sound. In a few terrifying seconds, I've cleared the stairs and I'm in the hallway. The sound of the television tells me that Dan is in the lounge, amusing himself while he waits for his wife to change her dress. I pass the half open doorway in a single graceful bound and dash for the kitchen. Everything looks just as I left it, unnaturally clean and organised. I push the key into the lock and turn the handle as quietly as I can. My every instinct is screaming at me to run, to flee, to move as fast as I can and consequences be damned, but I force myself to go slow, turning the handle and keeping it in my grip as I gently push the door open.

"Penny!"

I turn and see dad, crouched down by the back gate, a look of panic on his face.

"Let's go!" he tells me.

"One minute!" I hiss back.

I carefully pull the key out of the back door, lock it and then shuffle forward to the still partially open window. I risk a peek up over the windowsill and find the tea-towel I'd clambered past earlier. I reach in and tuck the key beneath it, just out of sight. It would have to do.

Heart still pounding, I crawl over to dad, joining him in a crouch by the gate. With a brief nod to me he stands and quickly unlatches it and we slip though. Now we just have to move inconspicuously along the privacy hedge and then step onto the pavement as though we're not doing anything in the least bit suspect.

As we attempt this manoeuvre, all I can think is that we're lucky no one's outside to see us. By the time we get back to dad's car I'm drenched in sweat and shaking from the adrenalin. I collapse into the passenger seat and start taking deep, rather shaky, breaths.

"Penny, what happened?!" dad asks urgently.

I look at him, his eyes wide and his gaze fixed on me intensely.

"I found something."

# Chapter 19

It's getting late in the day and I'm feeling hungry and hopeless by the time DS Walters appears and leads us back to an interview room. I'm not sure that she'd even be speaking to us if dad hadn't made a scene out in reception, but either way we're here now - not that it's doing much good.

"We don't have probable cause to search Dan Cosford's home," she repeats for what feels like the thousandth time. Upon first hearing those words I'd felt a vague thrill, as though I was part of a crime drama from TV, but the novelty has most definitely worn off.

"But we're *telling* you there's something to find!" dad roars back, banging his hand down on the table.

I flinch and DS Walters throws me a fleeting

sympathetic look. I glare back. I can see her point, but I still think that she's being wilfully obstinate. While she's worrying about following the rules, I'm just trying to get my friend back alive.

"There's a box of underwear in his wardrobe!" dad tells her again.

"So you claim, but you're not telling me how you know that Mr Owens. What's more, I suspect that if you did tell me, I still wouldn't be able to use the information without potentially endangering my investigation. Now, I know that you suspected Mr Cosford's involvement in your daughter's disappearance -"

"Did you suspect him too? Have you looked into him?" I ask quickly, leaning forward to reinsert myself into the conversation.

"Penny. As I have already told you, I can't discuss suspects in yours sister's case with you."

Her tone is flat and I can feel dad unravelling beside me. Her calm demeanour is fanning the flames of his rage and I have to fight the urge to slide my chair away.

"WHY AREN'T YOU LOOKING FOR MY CHILD?! HOW CAN YOU STILL DO NOTHING WHEN ANOTHER GIRL HAS GONE MISSING?!"

The sound is like a concussion blast, washing over me and leaving me trembling. I can't help but be a little impressed at DS Walters managing to keep her cool in the face of such raw emotion.

"THERE WAS A BLOODY SHOE IN THE WOODS! AND WHAT ARE YOU DOING ABOUT IT?!"

She just stares back at him, waiting for him to quiet so that she can respond.

"We are searching for Charlie Hople Mr Owens. I wasn't working here when your daughter went missing but I am familiar with the case and I can assure you that if there is a connection we will find it."

"Have you managed to trace the number she was talking to? Is there anything else in the emails?" I ask quickly, slotting my questions in while I see the chance.

"The mobile number is a burner phone. It's untraceable, most likely purchased illegally. We are still combing through Charlie's emails and social media accounts and we are conducting interviews with anyone that we think may be able to help us."

Her voice is steady and sure but it still sounds like a company line to me, the sort of thing that you tell loved ones just to keep them quiet.

"Just, search his house," dad tries again, his voice low and tired now.

"To be clear Mr Owens, do you have any reason to believe that Charlie Hople may be inside that house?"

He doesn't speak. If there's one thing we're sure of, it's that Charlie *isn't* in Dan Cosford's home, but every time I think about that box in the wardrobe I feel a wave of terror. If Dan took Charlie, is there any chance at all that she's alive? They haven't found a body, but then they never found Rose's.

I push the thought down with a couple of slow, deep breaths.

The circuitous nature of the conversation is making me dizzy. I lapse back into silence and try my best not to think at all.

"I think it's time that Penny went home."

DS Walters' words catch me by surprise but I'm immensely grateful for them. I want more than anything to go home. I don't even know what time it is now and I feel drained, emptied out.

"Penny doesn't have to go," my dad says defiantly.

"She's clearly exhausted, I think it would be a good idea if we called her mother to collect her," DS Walters tells him, finally letting a little emotion drip into her voice.

He's still reluctant and part of me wants to demand to stay, to be here to support him, but in truth I'm glad that an adult is stepping in and whisking me away. It's only a few minutes before a uniformed officer knocks on the door to let us know that my ride home is here.

"Penny has a right to stay if she wants to, she has a right to hear the truth about her sister's case!" dad states, making a final stab at keeping me there. I allow myself to feel a small thrill at being wanted, but I still rise to leave.

"We're not attempting to conceal the truth Mr Owens," DS Walters tells him somewhat wearily.

"Everyone has something to hide!" he exclaims.

"You know who thinks like that? People with something to hide."

On that sunny note I head for the door. I don't say another word, I traverse the corridors like a zombie, following the uniformed officer with shuffling, shambling steps. I'm expecting mum but it's Coop waiting for me in reception. I'm too tired for doubts and uncertainty, instead I step into his arms and he folds me in a warm hug. He hurries me out to the car and drives me home without asking me a single question. I'm so glad that I could cry, I know I'm going to have to explain myself to mum and I don't think I could face going over and over everything. Even when we get back to the house, he doesn't say a word to me. He ushers me through to the kitchen, keeping mum at a nervous periphery with shushing noises and placating hands. Not until I'm sat down at the breakfast bar with a plate of macaroni cheese in front of me does he even let her into the room. I hear a snippet of kids TV from the lounge before she quietly closes the door and comes forward.

"I called dad," I tell her before she can ask me what's going on.

"I realised that darling, but why?"

"To help look for Charlie. He's been looking for Rose for ten years, if there's a connection then who better to help find her?"

Coop and mum exchange a look, clearly unconvinced that the two cases are related but not wanting to argue the point.

"What happened today then?" mum asks gently.

I take another bite of food before answering. Macaroni cheese is one of the world's most perfect comfort foods. Pasta in general is pretty phenomenal but add cheese sauce to it and I'm not sure there's anything better.

"Dad and I found someone who we think could be responsible," I say eventually.

"What?! Who?!" mum asks quickly, her usually olive face now as pale as mine.

"Dan Cosford."

I can see that the name doesn't mean anything to either of them. It's a bit of an anticlimax.

"Dan Cosford? Who- I mean-I don't-" she trails off.

"He's Charlie's netball coach. He helped with the search too," I tell them.

"Lots of people know Charlie, and lots of people helped with the search," Coop points out gently.

"Yes, but the police think Charlie was seeing a married man and Charlie has a crush on Dan Cosford. We know he has a temper and his wife is clearly terrified of him. Plus, he was in town when Rose went missing. He lived right on the edge of the woods. Dad already had his name down on a list! He told me he was out of town when Rose went missing, that he didn't get back until after the searches, but his name was on the sign-in sheet! He was there! He lied!"

Coop still looks uncertain but I can see my words acting on mum like a spell, she's moving closer, her eyes wide and feverish.

"Why? Why would he lie about that?" she asks me almost frantically.

"Exactly! We're sure he's involved somehow but the police won't listen, they still think this all has nothing to do with Rose!"

"Why won't they listen?! They should be talking to him! Surely they should question him!" mum cries, looking from me to Coop with a sort of desperation.

"If they have reason to talk to this man then I'm sure they will, they're the police" Coop tells her soothingly.

She nods slightly, in a vague, absent-minded way, but then her eyes refocus and she gives herself a slight shake.

"Of course. Yes, of course they will."

"But they won't! They don't believe us!" I declare,

not wanting her to slip back into acceptance of the status quo.

"Why don't they believe you Penny?" Coop asks.

Damn him and his reasonable questions.

"They say that there's no evidence. There's nothing to say that Dan's involved,"

Mum looks calmer by the second. She's resuming her detachment with practised efficiency. I want to shake her. I want to tell her that I broke into Dan's house and tell her what I found.

"I'm sure the police are doing everything they can Penny."

Her words are hollow and insubstantial. A single breath could blow them away.

I retreat to my room, not trusting myself to continue the conversation without losing my patience. I'm worn down to almost nothing and I just want to get to bed. Mum has laundered my sheets and changed them for me while I was out and I feel so grateful I could weep. It's been a long day.

I change into pyjamas, brush my teeth and crawl under the duvet, sinking into the warmth and safety like it's my own little cocoon. I wonder vaguely who'll I be when I wake up.

As it turns out, I wake as someone with answers. My unconscious mind must have been busily scratching away at the situation while I slept and I wake at precisely seven am, roused not by my alarm but by an epiphany- actually two epiphanies.

One - I know how the rose was left in my house without my mum knowing about it. She didn't have to let someone in to leave it, they had a key- the key I gave to Charlie before I left the party. I know it's not much, but it at least reinforces my conviction that whoever has Charlie was also responsible for what happened to Rose. I know that the police will shrug it off and carry on, but to me it feels like another piece clicking into place.

Two (and this is a big one)- I know who genieturns95@gmail.com is.

That mystery email account that Charlie had emailed copies of her homework assignments to. It seemed totally inconsequential, just a tiny mystery eclipsed by all the rest, until I realised who that account belongs to.

It's Charlie's.

Genie Turns and Glenda Harrow, the names on mine and Charlie's fake IDs. For some reason it seems that Charlie decided to imbue her overage persona with its own email account. She'd sent across copies of her homework so that she'd have a backup if anything happened to her laptop. I email myself documents all the time, I've already sent myself a dozen versions of all the notes I've made on Charlie's disappearance. Every time I update one of the documents, I send it to myself just to be safe - I can't believe it took me this long to work out that Charlie had been doing the same thing!

Now that I know, I need to get into that email account. I need to know who else Charlie was talking to and what she was saying. If she set up a secret second email account without telling anyone, there must be a reason. For a fraction of a second I consider going to DS Walters, but she's already demonstrated pretty clearly what she thinks of mine and dad's investigation. No, I need to find a way of getting into that account myself.

It's early but there's no help for it, I grab my phone and dial Wendy's land-line. She answers almost immediately and I can't help but wince at the implications.

"Hello?!"

Her voice sounds small and fragile.

"Wendy? It's Penny," I tell her hesitantly.

"Oh, Penny, love. How are you? I – uh -"

"I'm- I'm alright Wendy, how are you? Have the police said anything?" I can't help but ask.

"No, no. They're searching, they're running down leads, they'll keep me updated. They haven't really told me anything at all."

I recognise the weary frustration in her voice. It's a sensation that's been clinging to my skin for days now.

"Everyone is looking," I tell her, wanting to give her hope but knowing how irresponsible that might be. Charlie's been missing a long time now.

"Is Charlie's laptop there?" I ask quickly, eager to get to the point.

"Her laptop? No love, sorry, the police took it."

Of course. I should have guessed that but the news still hits me like a punch to the gut.

"Oh! Of course! Never mind, that's fine. I'm sure it's-" I trail off, my voice unnaturally high and strained.

"Sorry," Wendy says again, her voice breaking.

"It's fine Wendy, it's not important. I just wanted to look at her pictures," I improvise.

This was a mistake. Wendy breaks down into hoarse sobs and I just hang there, not knowing what to say or do.

"I'm sorry Wendy," I offer feebly.

"Oh, love- it's not your fault. I'm sorry- I just-"

"I know."

"Maybe, maybe you could come round soon love,

just to say hello. It would be lovely to see you," she tells me, her voice trembling so much that I can barely make out the words.

"Of course Wendy, soon."

Charlie's laptop would have had her email passwords cached. It's the only reason I'm still able to access my own account, my laptop has the details saved, otherwise I'd have to try to remember what on earth I'd set the password as years ago, or reset the bloody thing. Without Charlie's laptop I'm going to have to guess her password myself.

Now, I may be rubbish at Facebook, but I'm not a total caveman and I realise almost immediately that I need to relocate to have any chance of this working. I don't know how many tries Charlie's account will give me before it locks me out, but I'm pretty sure that I need to be connected to her home Wifi either way. Connecting from a different IP address always generates an alert to the account holder to confirm that the login attempt is legitimate. I'm guessing this would be a text message to her mobile phone, which is of course as missing as she is.

I can hear Olly in the lounge already and the clattering of crockery in the kitchen tells me that either Coop or mum is up and about too. I don't want to waste time on a family debate now that I feel I'm on the cusp of a breakthrough so I get dressed quickly and quietly and slip from the house unnoticed.

As I walk I hold an internal debate about ringing the doorbell and going in, but if I'm being totally honest with myself I know I'm not going to. I can't face seeing Wendy right now and I can already picture the look on her face when she finds out about Charlie having a secret email account. Besides, until I find out who Charlie was talking to and what she was saying I think it's best that Wendy stays in the dark.

When I get there I loop round to approach the house without having to pass the street-side window and then I duck down and run at a crouch to sit with my back against the wall below Charlie's bedroom. I pull my laptop from my bag and open up a web-browser. I opted for my laptop since I've used it here countless times before and it's set to automatically connect to their Wifi. I navigate to Gmail, type in genieturns95@gmail.com and then I freeze. I have no idea where to start. After a full minute of staring blankly at the screen I try 'password' but it doesn't work. I try '12345678' but that's a no-go too. I try 'MarcusKain' with only the slightest of shudders and I have fairly mixed feelings when it's unsuccessful. On a whim I give 'Scotland' a go and pay for my hubris with a warning that I have three tries remaining before I'll be locked out of the account.

My heart is racing and I have to take a few slow deep breaths. I know Charlie. She may have secrets but I know her day to day better than anyone. She's fun and bubbly and chaotic. She plays netball, she hates science classes, she loves to dance. She hates marmite but loves peanut butter. And she's terrible at remembering passwords. She's used the same one for the school intranet since we started there at age eleven. She's used the same passcode for her phone since she got her first ever ancient pink Nokia 'for emergencies'. Charlie's password for her normal email account is peanutbuttermonster. I type it in and when that little spinning circle appears I feel like I might cry.

I'm in.

The first thing I notice is the homework assignments that Charlie sent herself- they make up the main body of the inbox. When I scroll a little further back however, I see an email from an account named searcher83@gmail.com I open it with shaky fingers and my breath catches when I read it. It says, 'I'm always here, 07813972995." Its the phone number that Charlie had been talking to. That's why there aren't any more emails, whoever searcher83 is, Charlie had swapped to phone conversations with them. 83... I wonder what year Dan Cosford was born.

I scroll back to the next to last email from searcher83 but it's just as short, it reads- 'that must be difficult, but I need to know.'

Need to know what? I scroll to another but the theme is similar and there's no name, no personal details and they just seem to be asking Charlie to tell them something. To agree to go away with them maybe?

I go to the Sent folder instead. This is more like it. The very first email Charlie sent searcher83 is interesting. Annoyingly she doesn't use names, she apologises for getting in touch, she says she found the email address on a forum online and wants to talk to him. She chats a bit, talking about school and her mum and then she sort of hints that she knows something searcher83 might be interested in.

Reading it through now I'm almost aching with curiosity, I can only imagine how searcher83 felt.

The tone is strange, it definitely sounds like she's writing to someone that she knows, but possibly like she's not sure they'll want to hear from her.

I want to go through them all in more detail. I need to read every email in order and piece together the narrative. I start forwarding them to myself, in order of when they were sent. First hers and then his. Within a couple of minutes they're all duplicated in my own inbox and I stuff my laptop back in my bag and head off home. My thoughts are racing ahead of me, trying to put together some sort of story to make sense of everything. What was Charlie hinting at? Was she saying that she knew something about searcher83? Something connected to Rose? If she knew that searcher83 had been involved in my sister's disappearance then surely she wouldn't have been emailing back and forth and talking on the phone, surely she would have gone to the police! But what could Charlie have possibly known anyway? Maybe it is Dan Cosford. Maybe she was in his house and found the same thing I did. Maybe she found something she recognised as belonging to Rose.

I pick up my pace and get home at a sprint, flying up the stairs to my room. I fire off a quick message to dad telling him I got into the email account and asking him to come and pick me up. I log back into my laptop and start printing all of the emails out, making sure to arrange them in order, like a conversation. I've just started reading back through the first one again, noting for the first time that Charlie sent it right around the time her dad told her he didn't want anything to do with her. For some reason the timing makes me go cold. Charlie doesn't always have the best judgement when she's upset.

“Penny?” I whip round but it's just mum in the doorway to my room, watching me nervously.

“Mum?” I respond shortly, wanting to get back to my task.

“Penny, where have you been?”

“What?”

“You left the house without saying anything again. Were you with your dad?”

“No, I wasn't. He's picking me up soon though,” I tell her, frustration bubbling through my words.

“Penny, I don't think that's a good idea. I don't think you should be spending time with him right now.”

"What?!" I ask, surprised.

"He's not a very stable person."

I can't help it. A bitter laugh escapes me before I can reign it in.

Mum raises a hand in a gesture of acknowledgement and nods, closing her eyes.

"I know, I know. But your dad is different. He's been changed ever since Rose, he never forgave himself. He could never stop looking."

"If we all hadn't just *stopped looking* then maybe Charlie would be here now! Maybe she'd be safe!"

"Penny, people are looking for Charlie. The police are looking. You and your dad shouldn't be getting involved. There's going to be a vigil for Charlie this evening on the school field. You should come along to that, Wendy should see that everyone is pulling together," she tells me.

"A vigil?! What good is a vigil going to do Charlie?! What good is community spirit and positive thoughts?! Well-wishes aren't going to bring her home!"

The printer has finally finished it's juddering recreation of all the emails and I grab the wad of papers and stuff them into my bag before pushing past my mother and heading downstairs.

"Penny? Your mum's right, you should stay here. It's not a good idea for you to be around your father."

Coop's voice stops me in my tracks. I've been avoiding looking at him since dad told me about his suspicions but now I spin round and stare at him.

"Of course you think that! You wouldn't help my dad before, why would you now?!" I demand.

"What do you mean?" he asks me uneasily.

"Why wouldn't you answer my dad's questions?! Why wouldn't you tell him where you were when Rose went missing?! What do you have to hide?!"

"Penny! You have no right to talk to Coop like that!" mum cries, scandalised.

Before I can respond, my phone buzzes in my pocket and a quick glance tells me that dad is outside. I hitch my bag further onto my shoulder and stride for the door, slamming it behind me.

I climb into the passenger seat and let out a short yell of frustration.

"What is it? Have you read the emails?" dad asks quickly.

"No, I haven't had the chance but I have them all here, don't worry," I tell him, trying to calm myself down.

"What's wrong then, what happened?" he asks, studying my flushed face.

"Mum and Coop don't want us looking for Charlie. They don't want me around you at all!"

Dad sighs like he's not surprised and runs a hand through his auburn hair.

"Well I'm sure they'll change their tune eventually. We're getting close now, I can feel it," he tells me with conviction.

"Really? You think we're making progress?"

"Definitely! It's going to be a long day Penny sweetheart, I brought you a coffee, you'll need your energy! Americano, right?"

He holds out the drink and I feel a glow. It doesn't matter that I don't like coffee, my dad remembered my order from the cafe. I take a big gulp and he smiles at me before pulling away.

"So, talk to me about this email account," he prompts me as he drives.

"It was something DS Walters asked me about," I explain. "They went through Charlie's emails and there was nothing suspicious at all. They were able to verify all the addresses she contacted except one, genieturns95. I didn't recognise it at the time but it didn't really seem important anyway because Charlie only ever sent them copies of her homework. Suddenly though, last night it clicked and when I woke up this morning I knew that the account belonged to Charlie. Genie Turns is the name on her fake ID. She must have set up a fake email account with the same name. I was able to figure out her password and I had a quick look. She's been talking to someone and hinting that she knows something important."

As I talk I take occasional sips of my coffee and do my best not to wince at the appalling taste. When I've drained the cup I slot it into the cupholder beside me and pull the printed emails from my bag. I start at the beginning again, with that tantalising hint about Charlie knowing something interesting. Searcher83 responds by saying that it's nice to hear from her and he'd be interested to know whatever she might be able to tell him. There's a bit of back and forth then, just general chatting about Charlie's life, how she feels about not having any money, how hard she finds science class, etc. They clearly both knew what they were talking about, but they don't reference it again in the next few emails and I still have no clue what it was about. What did Charlie know?! About what?! It isn't until the fourth email that Charlie's words take my breath away. Searcher83 tries to bring the conversation back around to Charlie's mystery information, and she responds by asking her correspondent - 'What do *you* think happened to Rose?'

I excitedly read the section aloud to dad but it doesn't make sense. This should be the break we need. This is a verified link between Charlie's disappearance and Rose, but my thoughts are confused and jumbled, I can't grasp hold of them.

This means that Charlie is missing because she knows something about what happened to Rose! But - If Charlie is talking to the person who took Rose, if that's what they're discussing, then why on earth is she asking them what they think happened?

More than that, Charlie can't possibly know what happened to Rose, she wasn't even *there* that day!

I was starting to think that Charlie was blackmailing Rose's killer, holding some piece of information over them, but the tone is wrong. Charlie keeps talking about her day at school and her life in general. Is this some kind of game? She keeps talking about 'what she knows' without ever giving any details. But no-

She asked what they think happened to Rose.

Charlie doesn't think she's talking to the killer- she's talking to someone else- someone else who cares about what happened to Rose-

I try to put the thoughts into words but they're slipping away. The papers slide from my grip and I think that I hear someone saying sorry before everything goes dark.

# Chapter 20

It's dark.

It takes a while for that thought to even form in my mind with any clarity. It takes an age for me to work out whether I have my eyes closed. I do. But when I open them, it's still dark. There is a small lamp some distance away but its dim light just serves to throw the shadows into greater relief. The edges of the room are completely concealed so I decide to start closer at hand.

I'm not tied up. I'm lying on what seems to be an air mattress. It shifts beneath me with an undignified bounce when I move. The floor is bare wood, caked in grime. Wherever I am, it's not a building that's seen regular use in some time. I try to keep still since I don't know where dad is.

Oh God! Dad!

I can't wrap my already uncomfortably pounding head around it right now, so I try to push the thoughts and speculation aside and deal only with the reality in front of me.

I'm in some kind of abandoned building. It's dark so hours must have passed already. Whatever was in that coffee has left me feeling weak and sick. I *knew* coffee was evil!

I listen closely but I can't hear a sound. There's no movement, nothing to indicate that anyone else is here. I cautiously push myself to a sitting position and look around me. It's a house, or at least it used to be. Now it looks more like a wreck. The room is smaller than I'd imagined from my vantage point on the floor, the walls are bare brick and flaking plaster with the odour of mildew thick in the air. The lamp is a measly, battery powered contraption stood on what remains of a fitted kitchen island. Along with a small border of cabinets in the same corner of the room, it comprises the only furniture. I get shakily to my feet, my legs not entirely sure that they're accepting orders from my brain at this moment in time. I shuffle slowly, bracing myself against the sway and tip of the earth beneath me. I reach the kitchen island after what feels like an epic journey. Empty water bottles and food packets tell me that dad has been staying here for some time. Evidence of his obsession is spread out on the counter around the lamp, there are pages of notes, surveillance photos of Dan Cosford amongst other people, and countless other documents that I almost wish I had time to peruse. But I don't have time. I need to find Charlie.

I've just started towards the two internal doors when a sound outside halts me. It's the crunch of footsteps and it's enough to make my heart stop. What do I do?! Run back to the mattress and pretend to be asleep? Race forward and try to find Charlie?

My moment of indecision costs me the opportunity to choose. I'm still stood in the middle of the room like a lemon when dad walks in. I absolutely blame whatever he drugged me with.

"Penny! You're alright! I'm so glad!"

"Yes, I'm feeling an abundance of paternal care right now, thanks," I snap back, my voice hoarse.

"I brought you some water!" he tells me, hurrying forward with a carrier bag clasped in his hand.

I back swiftly away and he places the bag on the counter before backing up a few steps, his eyes bright.

I want to reject his offering out of hand but my mouth feels like it's been attacked with sandpaper and then filled with wallpaper paste. I check the bag and find a couple of bottles of water. I check the seal on one before opening it and drinking deeply. The cold hitting my stomach almost makes me heave but I fight the impulse back, wrapping my arm protectively around myself to keep the nausea at bay.

"Where's Charlie?"

"Penny, you have to understand-"

"Where is she?"

He looks trapped between frustration and fear but

I'm not in any mood to hear his explanations. There is no valid reason for what he's done.

"Is she alive?" I ask, my voice low.

"Of course! I would never- Of course! I've kept her safe!" he tells me pleadingly.

I'm desperate to believe him and his eyes flick towards one of the doors.

"Did you kill Rose?" I ask, dreading the answer.

"NO!" he roars, making me flinch back, lights popping behind my eyes.

"I'M DOING THIS FOR HER!"

A wave of relief almost knocks me off my feet and I have to clutch the counter to keep myself from falling.

"CHARLIE KNEW SOMETHING! SHE SAW A CAR!" he bellows, advancing swiftly towards me. I shrink down, making myself as small as possible, crouched on the floor. At the sight of me cowering he stops and shakes himself, his eyes wide and wounded.

"I'm not going to- I wouldn't-"

He backs away again, rubbing his arms with

trembling hands.

Drugs. I should have realised before but I didn't want to.

"Charlie didn't see anything dad, she wasn't there the day Rose went missing," I tell him as I slowly unfold back to a standing position.

"She was! She found me on an online forum and she messaged me! She told me she saw something and she never told anyone!"

"But she couldn't have. She wasn't there. Charlie was just lonely and hurt. She found her father and he told her he didn't want anything to do with her..." I try to explain, willing him to understand.

"No! No, she knows something! She saw a car! She told me! At first she didn't want to, she said she was scared... but then after that party she called me for a lift. We'd been speaking for a while. Emails at first and then talking on the phone but she wouldn't tell me what she knew. I kept thinking that if I could just get her to trust me... and she did! She knew I was staying close by and so she called. I said I'd come and get her..."

So much for him driving all night from Newcastle. I feel like a fool.

"What happened?" I barely even breathe the words.

"She'd been drinking. I brought her here, to talk, but she still wouldn't tell me what she saw! She was hysterical! She kept screaming that I just wanted to talk about Rose! *Of course I did!* I needed to know what she saw! But she was being so loud, I was worried someone would hear so I gave her something to make her sleep."

His eyes are desperate and it's clear that he really believes he has a chance of making me understand.

"But why didn't you let her go?! Why didn't you take her home?!"

"I was going to! The next day when she woke up she told me what she'd seen, she told me about the car, but then she was reported missing! I saw in town that there were people searching the woods again! I knew that sooner or later it would be connected to Rose and they might reopen the investigation!"

I feel a pang of self-loathing when I remember Trish in the cafe looking so surprised when I told her that dad hadn't been back in town for the searches in the woods. I'm an idiot.

"So you just kept her here? A prisoner, this whole time?"

"She's safe here!"

"What about the shoe? They found her shoe in the woods, with blood on it."

His whole face contorts with shame and I feel a stab of fear that he might be lying, that he killed my friend and nothing more than her body is concealed in this house.

"I needed the police to realise that she wasn't a run-away. They needed to think she'd been abducted so that they'd connect it to Rose!" he tells me impatiently, pacing slightly with a mania that frightens me.

I know there's no sense pointing out that Charlie *was* abducted. His eyes are wide and frantic, begging me to agree with him. I run my hands through my bedraggled hair and something on the counter catches my eye. I slide it out and stare at it. It's the picture of me, Charlie and Rose.

"You gave this to the newspapers?" I ask him, reeling from yet another emotional blow.

"They needed to make the connection! Otherwise the police wouldn't re-open Rose's case!"

"Do you know what you did to me?! Do you know what people are saying about me online?!" I shout and then immediately regret it.

Raising my voice has made my head swim and my vision darkens around the edges. The ground seems to heave beneath me and I drop painfully to my knees. Dad rushes forward, catching me in his arms before I collapse. Even now I want to sink into his embrace.

"Where's Charlie?" I murmur.

"You have to see sweetheart! You have to see it was worth it!"

"Worth what? Where is Charlie?" but I can barely get the words out because everything's going black again.

Hope. Just a tiny spark, the merest speck in the darkness, but in him it caught alight. It's a flame, a roaring fire that's burned everything else away.

His eyes are bright and his hands burn against the skin of my arms.

"I just want to find my daughter!" he cries desperately.

I'm right here.

But he can't hear me.

It's so hot, I think I can feel the lick of flames against my skin. It's bubbling, blistering, burning. I could dance my own smoke signals but I never did learn Morse Code. I open my eyes and I'm relieved to find myself in darkness. There's no fire. Sweat is running over my skin though. Whatever he drugged me with, it feels awful!

I shuffle up against the nearest wall and slide myself up it to an approximately seated position. As the dizziness recedes I see that I'm in a small room with the same bare floors and walls as previously. I assume it's in the same house as it's almost identical except for a couple of key differences. This room lacks the small kitchenette in the corner, and it contains Charlie.

I half rush, half topple towards her and I crawl the last few steps on my bruised knees, clutching her whole form in my arms. Something's wrong.

She's cold. Colder than anyone I've ever felt before. Colder than any living person has any business being.

I lay her back on her half deflated air bed and push her matted blonde curls off of her face. She's white as a sheet and her lips are tinged with blue. I try desperately to see if she's breathing, my own breath stopped in my chest until I can be sure, but I can't see anything. No movement, no gentle rise and fall. I press my ear to her chest, holding her close, and listen.

There!

It's slow, but it's beating. She's alive!

I scrabble in my pockets for my phone but unsurprisingly it's not there. I hurry to the door and bang against it, calling frantically for my dad, but he doesn't come. There's not a single sound. I don't know how long I was unconscious this time but he must have left again. I turn back to Charlie, limp and pale and impossibly still. She can't wait. We have to get out of here. I try to clear my head and think my way out of this. I wish Luke was here, with my brain so compromised a little brawn would really help right now. Or maybe just some moral support.

Alright, what do I need to do? What are the problems in front of me and how do I solve them?

First problem- Charlie. She still looks like she's not breathing. I tip her head back a little and breathe into her mouth. It might not be the right thing to do, but it's all I can think of. First aid courses haven't covered this situation. It might be wishful thinking, but I'm almost sure I can see her chest moving now.

Right, next up is the locked door. I examine the keyhole and the crack between the door and the door-frame. I can see two obstructions. It looks as though the latch is engaged with a key and there's also a bolt further up. I push it firmly and feel the two points of resistance. I try kicking the door but it only serves to reassure me that the wood and hinges are both in excellent condition, and to leave me swaying alarmingly on my feet.

Alright, move on from the door, we'll come back to that if we need to. Instead I survey the room at large. Aside from Charlie on her feeble air mattress, there's a pile of broken plywood furniture against one wall and a rickety wooden chair. The chair could potentially be used as a weapon but not while carrying Charlie. I go though the furniture mound but its all rotten plywood that practically breaks apart in my hands. The windows are boarded up but it doesn't look like dad did it, the wood is old and splintered. It must have been the previous owners or maybe the council trying to deter vandals and squatters. Not very successfully.

I manage to prise off one of the planks of wood quite easily but the next causes me much more trouble. I have to wrench with all of my weight to get it free and the exertion makes me sick, heaving my guts out in the corner of the room, my palms grazing on the rough floor with every retch.

How long will he be gone? How long do I have?

I stumble back to the window and admire my handiwork. There's enough space now for us to climb through, if Charlie was in any fit state to climb. I try to raise the window but it's stuck tight and closer observation shows that it was painted shut at some point. The paint is cracked and flaking now, but the window is still holding fast. I try some of the pieces of plywood but none of them are able to hold their own against the glass. Finally admitting surrender, I slam my hand against the surface in a practised hammer-strike and the glass shatters, causing me nothing more than a long, deep gash almost the full length of my forearm and some smaller, shallow cuts over my hand and wrist. Perfect. I'm in shorts and a t-shirt and Charlie is still dressed in her party clothes but with a large hoodie over the top. I think about using it to stem the bleeding but the icy chill of her skin stops me. I can see to my arm once I've got us both out of here. Now that the glass is broken, even the flimsy plywood is able to knock out the remaining shards and leave a clear space. It's not perfect, but for my plan to work it doesn't need to be. Well, technically I have two plans. Neither of them is great, but they're all I can come up with in a pinch, and this situation is a pinch if ever there was one. I'm not sure which plan I'll be going for, fate has to decide that for me. In preparation of Plan A, I duck down, concealing myself behind the pile of furniture debris and I wait, concealed in the shadows and hidden from the view of the doorway. I remain fixed in place, only peering out occasionally to check that I can see Charlie's chest rising and falling in the thin shaft of moonlight from the freshly exposed window. I'm just starting to think that I may have to resort to Plan B when I hear the front door open and close. There's some general shuffling and banging, the standard sounds of someone moving around the house and then I hear the bolt slide across and the key turning in the lock.

"Penny?" His voice is quiet, tentative, not sure of the

reception he can expect. He takes one step further into the room and freezes, his eyes on the smashed window. He runs forward, sticking his head out of the opening and looking around, calling my name. When he can't see any sign of me outside he roars in frustration and sprints back across the room and out the door, ricochetting off the wall in the hallway and tearing through to the main room and out the front door. I only wait a single beat and then I'm up, haring across to Charlie and lifting her halfway into my arms before stopping.

My heart racing, I lower her back down and dash though to the next room. With one sweep, I pull all the papers from the kitchen island towards me in a chaotic jumble and shove them into the convenient carrier bag, discarding the water bottle on the floor. I tie the bag shut, slip my undamaged arm through the loops of handles and race back for Charlie. I pause for another moment and I can hear dad's shouts coming in through the window as he frantically searches for me, though I like to think they're getting further away. I hoist her up, praying that I haven't wasted crucial time, and I half drag, half carry her out with me. The view from the front door is not encouraging. There are no street-lights, no light from the windows of other houses, no sign of life at all. I do the only thing I can think of and I drag Charlie in the opposite direction from dad. When in doubt, move away from the imminent threat of harm.

I make for the trees on the other side of the road and do my best to disappear into them.

More woods, bloody typical.

Charlie is a dead weight, pinned to my side by my grip on her waist and her arm held secure over my shoulders. I make my way forward as quickly as I can, but both of our feet are constantly catching on roots and I'm stumbling over uneven ground that I can't even see. I fall more than once but each time I hoist Charlie back up and continue on, the world spinning sickeningly around us.

I can hear shouting- is it him? I try to move away from it, stumbling in the dark but my head is spinning and I can't tell where it's coming from. I move further on, not sure how much distance I'm travelling, until I reach a fallen tree, blocking my path but providing me with an opportunity. I drop Charlie to the ground as carefully as I can and bury my precious carrier bag in the mulch under the fallen oak. Or possibly birch, or beech, or any other type of tree. It's dark and I can't really be sure. Then I hoist Charlie back up, trying to shift as much of her weight onto my shoulder as I can and I carry on. I'm not sure if my vision is darkening or if it's just the densely packed trees, but my legs are getting harder and harder to move. It seems like there are shouting voices on every side, I don't know which way to go. I see a light glinting and I try to head for it but it keeps blinking in and out.

Or maybe that's me.

Penny,

A coin,

Spinning in the air,

mid flight.

Heads or tails.

Tails or heads.

# Chapter 21

It turned out that I was heading towards the light.

The vigil for Charlie on the school sports field was just the other side of the woods, almost half a kilometre from the abandoned house. I can't believe now that I carried her that far, it felt like less.

By all accounts, we made quite an entrance. I staggered into their midst, dragging Charlie's seemingly lifeless form with me, and promptly lost consciousness.

Even though the darkness of my mind, I could hear Wendy's screams.

I dimly recall coming to, briefly, as I was loaded into an ambulance, but the calm assurances of the paramedics were enough to make me sink back into oblivion, the dark sliding up around me like cool water.

When I woke again the ambulance was moving. The sirens wailed, ricocheting rudely inside my skull. Sergeant Walters was seated beside me and her face was actually showing some kind of emotion, though I couldn't for the life of me say what it was. A paramedic was tightly wrapping my arm and I felt vaguely surprised that it didn't hurt more. I looked around absently for Charlie but there was no sign of her.

“She's in another ambulance ahead of us,” Sergeant Walters told me gently.

She gazed at me enquiringly and I tried to swallow.

I kept the details to a minimum.

I told her who, I told her where.

Everything else could wait.

They caught up to dad in Milton Keynes early the next morning. He was trying to buy a used car when a SWAT team dropped from the ceiling on zipwires. That's how I imagine it anyway. In reality it was probably mundane and a bit pathetic. I expect he begged them to understand.

Charlie pulled through. They kept her in the hospital for three weeks but she was awake after a day and straining at the leash of their restrictions. When she wasn't being questioned by police or examined by doctors, we roamed the hospital corridors dodging the occasional reporter and not talking about what had happened. Luke visited too. He was there beside mum and Coop when I first woke up and he stayed until the nurses threatened to call security. Apparently they take visiting hours very seriously when it comes to minors who've been the victims of violent crimes. Everyone has their pet cause I suppose.

We visited Charlie every day after I was discharged and I even slept there when they let me, on a fold out cot beside Charlie's bed. We'd giggle and laugh into the night and pretend in the morning that we hadn't been woken by nightmares.

It was the last day before Charlie was due to be sent

home that she finally broached the topic I'd been waiting for.

"I'm really sorry," Charlie mumbled, her cheeks flushed.

"For what?" I asked lightly.

I wanted to tell her that she had nothing to be sorry for, but I suspected that this conversation was a result of her mandatory counselling sessions and I wanted to be supportive.

"For messaging your dad behind your back."

"Yeah, admittedly that was... not great."

"I felt awful about it! I just wanted... I don't really know what I wanted," she finished with glistening, downcast eyes.

"You wanted to prove to yourself that your dad was an idiot not to want you," I suggested, having already given it some thought.

"He is by the way. An idiot." I added when she didn't respond.

"Well I'm sorry my dad's an idiot,"she replied with a

grin.

"Well I'm sorry my dad's a psycho who abducted you," I replied cheerfully.

"I'm sorry I lied to you," she said, turning to face me and taking my heavily bandaged hand in hers.

"It's fine-"

"No, I mean, I'm sorry I've been lying to you for ten years."

She stopped talking and I just stared at her, not sure what to say.

"It was true, what I told your dad. The day Rose disappeared, I was supposed to be home because I was in trouble with mum. She'd left me with Nan but I sneaked out. I walked to your house to see you but there was a car in the drive that I didn't recognise. I was scared I'd be in trouble if anyone saw I was there when I was meant to be home, so I just ran back. I don't even know if it was important, I just... I should have told someone. I should have told you."

My mind raced.

Was it important?

It could be....

Mum's account has always stayed the same and she never said that there was someone at the house that day, so why would there be a car in the drive?

Does it even matter? Rose disappeared in the woods...

Right?

## Acknowledgements

Acknowledgements might just be the hardest part of the book to write.

The people in my life are so utterly wonderful, that words don't really do them justice.

Andrew, my amazing husband, thank you for giving me the courage to start writing and the support to keep going. Thank you for being my partner and my soul mate, there's no one else I would want to share my days with.

Mum. What can I say? Thank you for everything. Thank you for raising me and loving me and caring for me.

Thank you for proof reading and editing and giving encouragement.

Adam, thank you for sharing your writing with me and letting me share mine with you.

Dad, thank you for your help and encouragement with the cover design, and all the rest of my art. Its wonderful sharing that with you.

I love you all.

BV - #0009 - 260325 - C0 - 203/127/25 - PB - 9781739571801 - Matt Lamination